FATELESS

Imre Kertész was born in 1929 in Budapest. As a youth, he was imprisoned first in Auschwitz and later in Buchenwald. He worked as a journalist and playwright before publishing *Fateless*, his first novel, in 1975. He was awarded the Nobel Prize for Literature in 2002.

Tim Wilkinson was born in 1947. He is the translator into English of many works on Hungary's history and culture, and the prose of several of its contemporary writers, in addition to Imre Kertész.

IMRE KERTÉSZ

Fateless

TRANSLATED FROM THE HUNGARIAN BY
Tim Wilkinson

VINTAGE BOOKS
London

Published by Vintage 2006

4 6 8 10 9 7 5

First published with the title *Sorstalanság* by
Szépirodalmi Könyvkiadó, Budapest in 1975

First published in Great Britain by
The Harvill Press, 2005

Vintage
Random House, 20 Vauxhall Bridge Road,
London SW1V 2SA

www.vintage-books.co.uk

Addresses for companies within The Random House Group
Limited can be found at: www.randomhouse.co.uk/offices.htm

The Random House Group Limited Reg. No. 954009

A CIP catalogue record for this book
is available from the British Library

ISBN 9780099502524

The Random House Group Limited makes every effort to ensure
that the papers used in its books are made from trees that have
been legally sourced from well-managed and credibly certified
forests. Our paper procurement policy can be found at:
www.randomhouse.co.uk/paper.htm

Printed in the UK by CPI Bookmarque, Croydon, CR0 4TD

FATELESS

ONE

I didn't go to school today. Or rather, I did go, but only to ask my class teacher's permission to take the day off. I also handed him the letter in which, referring to "family reasons," my father requested that I be excused. He asked what the "family reason" might be. I told him my father had been called up for labor service; after that he didn't raise a further peep against it.

I didn't head home but to our shop. Father had said they would wait for me there. He added that I should hurry as well because he might need me. In actual fact, that was partly why he had asked me to be let off school. Or else so that "he might have me there on his last day before being separated from home," since he said that too, though admittedly some other time. He said it to my mother, as I recall, when he phoned her this morning. Today is a Thursday, as it

3

happens, and on Thursdays and Sundays my afternoons, strictly speaking, belong to my mother. Still, Father informed her: "I can't let you have young Gyuri today," and then went on to give that as the reason. Though maybe it wasn't like that after all. I was rather sleepy this morning on account of last night's air-raid warning, so perhaps I don't remember it clearly. I am quite sure, though, that he said it—if not to Mother, then to someone else.

I too spoke a few words to Mother, though I no longer remember what. I think she may have been annoyed with me because I was obliged to be a little short with her, what with Father being there: after all, today it is his wishes I have to consider. When I was about to set off from the house, even my stepmother had a few private words with me in the hall, just between the two of us. She said she hoped that, on what was such a sad day for us, "she could count on my behaving appropriately." I had no clue what I could say to that, so I said nothing. She may have misinterpreted my silence, however, because she went straight on to say something along the lines that she had no wish to offend my sensibilities with those words of advice, which, she was well aware, were quite unnecessary. She had no doubt that with me being a big boy, now in my fifteenth year, I was quite capable of grasping for myself the gravity of the blow that had been inflicted on us, as she put it. I nodded. I could see she was content to leave it at that. She even moved a hand in my direction, and I half feared that she might perhaps be wanting to hug me. She didn't do so in the end, just let out a deep sigh, with a long, tremulous release of breath. I noticed her eyes moistening as well. It was awkward. After that, I was allowed to go.

I covered the stretch between school and our shop on foot. It was a clear, balmy morning, considering it was still just early spring. I was about to unbutton myself but then had second thoughts: it was possible that, light as the head breeze was, my coat lapel might flap back and cover up my yellow star, which would not have been in conformity with the regulations. There were by now a few things I had to be more on my guard against. Our cellar timber store is nearby, on a side street. A steep stairway leads down into the gloom. I found my father and stepmother in the office, a glass cage lit up like an aquarium, right at the foot of the steps. Also with them was Mr. Sütő, whom I have known from the time he entered our employment as a bookkeeper and as manager of the other, outdoor lumberyard that he has in fact already purchased from us since then. At least that's what they say, because Mr. Sütő, given that he is completely aboveboard regarding his race, does not wear a yellow star, so the whole thing is actually just a kind of business dodge, as I understand it, enabling him to look after our property there, and then again so we don't have to do entirely without an income in the meanwhile.

That had a bit to do with why I greeted him differently from the way I used to do, for after all he has, in a sense, risen to a higher status than us; my father and stepmother too were clearly more deferential toward him. Though he, for his part, sticks all the more stubbornly to addressing my father as "boss" and my stepmother as "my dear lady," as if nothing had happened, never failing to plant a kiss on her hand while he is at it. He welcomed me as well in his old, jocular tone, oblivious to my yellow star. After that, I stood

5

where I was, by the door, while they picked up where they had left off on my arrival. As I saw it, I must have interrupted them right in the middle of some discussion. I did not understand at first what they were talking about. I even closed my eyes for a second because they were still a bit dazzled from the sunlight up on the street. Meanwhile my father said something, and by the time I opened them, there was Mr. Sütő. Yellowish red light-spots were dancing like bursting pustules all over his round, brownish-skinned features, with the pencil moustache and the tiny gap between his two broad, white front teeth. The next sentence was again spoken by my father, with something about "goods" that "it would be best" if Mr. Sütő "were to take with him right away." Mr. Sütő had no objection, whereupon my father took out from a desk drawer a small package wrapped in tissue paper and tied up with string. Only then did I see what goods they were actually talking about, since I immediately recognized the package from its flat shape: it contained a box. In the box were our more precious jewels and such; indeed, I rather fancy that it was precisely on my account that they had called them "goods," lest I recognize them. Mr. Sütő at once thrust it into his briefcase. After that, however, a minor dispute sprang up between them, because Mr. Sütő took out his fountain pen, with the aim of giving my father a "receipt for the goods" no matter what. He dug in his heels for a fair while, even though my father told him "don't be childish," and "there's no need for that sort of thing between the two of us." I noticed that pleased Mr. Sütő to no end. He said so too: "I'm well aware that you trust me, boss, but in real life there is a right and proper way

6

of doing things." He even appealed to my stepmother for her assistance: "Isn't that so, my dear lady?" With a wan smile, though, she merely said something to the effect that she left it entirely up to the men how the matter was best arranged.

The whole thing was beginning to bore me slightly by the time he eventually tucked the fountain pen away after all, at which they started to chew over the matter of the stockroom here, and what they should do with all the planks of wood in it. I heard my father urging the need for haste, before the authorities "might get round to laying their hands on the business," asking Mr. Sütő to give my stepmother the benefit of his business experience and expertise over this. Turning toward my stepmother, Mr. Sütő at once declared, "It goes without saying, dear madam. We shall be in constant contact in any case over the settling of the accounts." I think he was speaking about the premises that were now in his hands. After an age, he at last began to take leave. He took a long time over his glum-faced shaking of my father's hand. He nevertheless ventured that "long speeches have no place at a moment like this," and so he wished to say just one word of farewell to my father, namely, "See you again soon, boss." My father replied with a quick, wry smile, "Let's hope so, Mr. Sütő." At the same time, my stepmother opened her handbag, pulled out a handkerchief, and straightaway dabbed at her eyes. Strange noises welled up in her throat. There was a hush; the situation was really embarrassing, since I had a feeling that I too ought to do something. But with the whole scene taking me by surprise, nothing sensible occurred to me. I could see that the thing was also making Mr. Sütő uneasy:

7

"My dear lady," he said, "you mustn't. Really not." He looked a tiny bit alarmed. He bowed and virtually fixed his lips to my stepmother's hand to perform his usual hand-kiss. He then at once scurried for the door, barely giving me time to jump out of his way. He even forgot to say good-bye to me. We could still hear his heavy tread on the stairs for a while once he had gone.

After something of a pause, my father said, "Well then, at least that's out of the way." At that, my stepmother, her voice still a bit husky, asked whether it wouldn't have been better if my father had accepted that receipt from Mr. Sütő all the same. My father, though, replied that a receipt like that had no "practical value" at all, besides which it would be even more hazardous to conceal it than the box itself. He explained to her that now "we have to stake everything on a single card," which was to have complete confidence in Mr. Sütő, particularly since right now we had no alternative anyway. My stepmother fell quiet at that, and then she remarked that my father might be right, but all the same she would feel safer "with a receipt in her hand." On the other hand, she was unable to give a satisfactory explanation as to why. At that point, my father urged that they make a start on the job at hand since, as he put it, time was pressing. He wanted to turn the business accounts over to her so that she would be able to find her way around them even in his absence, and so the business need not come to a standstill because he was in a labor camp. In the meantime he exchanged a few fleeting words with me as well. He asked if being let off school had gone smoothly, and so forth. In the end, he told me to sit down and keep quiet until he and my stepmother had done what they had to do with the books.

That, however, took an age. I tried to be patient for a bit, striving to think of Father, and more specifically the fact that he would be going tomorrow and, quite probably, I would not see him for a long time after that; but after a while I grew weary with that notion and then, seeing as how there was nothing else I could do for my father, I began to get bored. Even having to sit around became a drag, so simply for the sake of a change I stood up to take a drink of water from the tap. They said nothing. Later on, I also made my way to the back, between the planks, in order to pee. On returning, I washed my hands at the rusty, tiled sink, then unpacked my morning snack from my school satchel, ate that, and finally took another drink from the tap. They still said nothing. I sat back in my place. After that, I got terribly bored for another absolute age.

It was already noon by the time we got out onto the street. My eyes were again dazzled, this time offended by the light. My father fiddled around a long time with the two gray padlocks— to the point that I had a feeling he was doing it deliberately. He then handed over the keys to my stepmother, given that he would no longer have any use for them. I know that, because he said as much. My stepmother opened her handbag; I feared it was for the handkerchief again, but all she did was tuck the keys away. We then set off in a great hurry. I thought at first we were going home, but no, before that there was still shopping to be done. My stepmother had a rather lengthy list of all the things Father would need in the labor camp. She had already procured some of them yesterday, but now we had to track down the rest. It was a slightly uncomfortable feeling going around with them like that, as a trio, yellow stars on all three of us. The matter is more a source of amusement to me when I am on my own, but together with them it was close to embarrassing. I couldn't explain why that was, but later on I no longer took any notice of it. All the shops were crowded except the one where we bought the knapsack: there we were the only customers. The air was permeated with the pungent smell of proofed canvas. The shopkeeper, a little old man with sallow skin but gleaming false teeth and an oversleeve on one arm, and his plump wife were extremely cordial. They piled up all sorts of items before us on the counter. I noticed that the shopkeeper called the old lady "Lovey," and it was always her he sent off to fetch items. As it happens, I know the shop, because it is situated close to where we live, but I had never been inside before. It is actually a sort of sports goods shop, though they sell other merchandise as well. Of late it has even been possible to get their own make of yellow stars there, given that now there was a big shortage of yellow fabric, of course. (As for our own needs, my stepmother had taken care of that in good time.) As best I could make out, it was their innovative twist to have the material stretched over some cardboard base, so that way, of course, it looked more attractive, plus the arms of the stars weren't cut in such a ludicrously clumsy fashion as some of the homemade ones that were to be seen. I noticed that they themselves had their own wares adorning their chests, but in such a way as to seem that they were only wearing them in order to make them appeal to customers.

By now, though, the old lady was already there with the goods. What had happened before was that the shopkeeper asked if he might inquire whether we were laying in supplies for labor service. My stepmother said yes, we were. The old man nodded disconsolately. He even raised both his wizened, age-blotched hands and let them flop back on the counter in front of him in a gesture of commiseration. It was then that my stepmother mentioned we would need a knapsack and inquired if they had one. The old man hesitated before saying, "For you we have one." He then called out to his wife, "Fetch one out of the stockroom for the gentleman, Lovey!" The knapsack met with immediate approval, but the shopkeeper sent his wife off again for a few other articles that, in his opinion, my father "can't do without where he is going." On the whole, he was very tactful and sympathetic in the way he spoke to us, always doing his best to avoid having to employ the term "labor service." The stuff he showed us was all utilitarian: a mess tin that could be sealed airtight, a penknife with all sorts of tools that folded into the handle, a belt pouch, and so forth, the sort of things, as he pointed out, that tended to be in demand among those "in similar circumstances." My stepmother actually bought the penknife for my father. It took my fancy as well. Then after we had procured what we wanted, the shopkeeper called over to his wife, "Till!" The old lady, her plump body crammed into a black dress, squeezed herself with great difficulty between the cash register and an upholstered armchair. The shopkeeper accompanied us all the way to the door. There he said, "he hoped to have the pleasure another time," then, stooping confidentially toward my father, quietly added, "The way we have in mind, sir, you and I."

Now, at long last, we were indeed headed for home. We live in a big apartment block near a square where the streetcar

11

stops. We were already on the upper floor when it occurred to my stepmother that she had forgotten to redeem the bread coupon. I had to go back to the baker's. Only after a spell of queuing was I able to enter the shop. First of all, I had to present myself to the big-busted, blonde wife; she clipped the appropriate segment from the coupon, after which it was the baker's turn, who weighed out the bread. He did not bother returning my greeting as it is well known in the neighborhood that he could not abide Jews. That was also why the bread he pushed at me was a good half pound short. I have also heard it said this is how more leftovers from the ration stayed in his hands. Somehow, from his angry look and his deft sleight of hand, I suddenly understood why his train of thought would make it impossible to abide Jews, for otherwise he might have had the unpleasant feeling that he was cheating them. As it was, he was acting in accordance with his conviction, his actions guided by the justice of an ideal, though that, I had to admit, might of course be something else entirely.

I rushed home from the baker's, as I was famished by then, so I was only willing to loiter with Annamarie for a quick word, for just as I was making my way up the stairs, she was skipping down them. She lives on our floor, with the Steiners, whom these days we are in the habit of meeting up with every evening at the Fleischmanns'. A while ago we took little notice of the neighbors, but now it has turned out that we are of the same race, which calls for some exchanging of views of an evening on the matter of our mutual prospects. We two, meanwhile, usually talk about other things, which is how I found out that the Steiners are in fact only her uncle

12

and aunt, since her parents are in the process of divorcing, and because they have not yet managed to reach an agreement concerning her, they decided it was better if she were here rather than with either one of them. Before this, for the same reason, she had been at a boarding school, just as I was some time ago. She too is fourteen years old, or thereabouts. She has a long neck and is already starting to round out under her yellow star. She had likewise been sent off to the baker's. She wanted to know whether I fancied a game of rummy that afternoon, four-handed, with her and the two sisters. They live on the floor above us. Annamarie is friends with them, but I know them only casually, from seeing them in the outside corridor and in the air-raid shelter. The younger sister looks to be only eleven or twelve years old; the older one, I know from Annamarie, is the same age as her. From time to time, if I happen to be in our room overlooking the courtyard, I quite often see her hurrying along the outside corridor on her way to or from home. I have even come face-to-face with her a couple of times in the street doorway. I supposed this would be a chance to get to know her better: I would have rather liked that. But right then I remembered my father, so I told the girl not today, because Father had been called up. At that, she immediately remembered that she had already heard about the business with my father at home, from her uncle. She said, "Of course." We fell silent for a short while, after which she asked, "What about tomorrow?" I told her, "The day after, rather." Even so I immediately added, "Perhaps."

When I got home, I found my father and stepmother already at the table. While she busied herself with my plate, my stepmother asked if I was hungry. "Ravenous," I said, on the spur of the moment, not thinking about anything else, since it was the case anyway. She heaped up my plate too, but barely put anything on her own. It was not me but my father who noticed this, and he asked her why. She replied something along the lines that her stomach couldn't tolerate any food right now, which is when I immediately saw my mistake. True, Father disapproved of her doing that, reasoning that she should not neglect herself now, of all times, when her strength and stamina were most needed. My stepmother made no response, but I heard a noise, and when I looked up I saw what it was: she was crying. It was again highly embarrassing, so I tried to keep my eyes fixed just on my plate. All the same, I noticed the movement as my father reached for her hand. A minute later I could hear they were very quiet, and when I again took a cautious glimpse at them, they were sitting hand in hand, looking intently at one another, the way men and women do. I have never cared for that, and this time too it made me feel awkward. Though the thing is basically quite natural, I suppose, I still don't like it, I couldn't say why. It was immediately easier when they started to talk. Mr. Sütő again came up briefly, and of course the box and our other lumberyard; I heard that Father felt reassured to know that at least these were "in good hands," as he put it. My stepmother shared his relief, though she returned, if only in passing, to the matter of "guarantees," in that these were based solely on word of honor, and the big question was whether that was sufficient. Father shrugged and replied that there was no longer any guarantee of anything, not just in business but also "in other areas of life." My stepmother, a sigh breaking from her lips, promptly agreed: she was sorry she had brought the matter up, and she asked my father not to speak that way, not to brood on that sort of thing. But that set him wondering how my stepmother was going to cope with the major burdens that she was going to bear the brunt of, in such difficult times, all alone, without him; my stepmother answered that she was not going to be on her own, since I was here by her side. The two of us, she carried on, would take care of one another until my father was back with us once more. What's more, turning toward me and cocking her head slightly to one side, she asked me if that was how it would be. She was smiling, yet her lips were trembling as she said it. Yes, it would, I told her. My father too scrutinized me, a fond look in his eye. That somehow got to me, and in order again to do something for his benefit I pushed my plate away. He noticed, and asked why I had done that. I said, "I'm not hungry." I saw that this pleased him: he stroked my head. At that touch, for the first time today, something choked in my throat too, though it was not tears, more a kind of queasiness. I would have rather my father had no longer been here. It was a truly lousy feeling, but it came over me so distinctly that it was all I could think of, and right then I became totally confused. I would have been quite capable of crying right then, but there wasn't time for that because the guests arrived.

My stepmother had spoken about them just beforehand: only close family, was how she put it. Seeing my father make a gesture of some kind, she added, "Look, they just want to say good-bye. That's only natural!" No sooner was that said than the doorbell rang: it was my stepmother's older sister

15

and their mama. Soon Father's parents, my grandfather and grandmother, also arrived. We hastened to get grandmother settled on the sofa straightaway, because the thing with her is that even wearing spectacles with bottle-thick lenses she is blind as a bat and just as deaf to boot. For all that, she wants to join in and have a hand in what is going on around her. On these occasions, then, one has one's work cut out, because one has to constantly yell into her ear what's happening while also being smart about stopping her joining in, since anything she might do would only throw things into confusion.

My stepmother's mama arrived wearing a distinctly martial, conical brimmed hat that even had a diagonal feather on the front. She soon took it off, however, which was when her gorgeous, thinning, snow white hair with the straggly bun came into view. She has a narrow, sallow face, enormous dark eyes, and two withered flaps of skin dangling from her neck, which gives her the appearance of a very alert, discerning hunting dog. Her head had a slight continual tremble to it. She was delegated the task of packing up my father's knapsack since she is handy at those sorts of jobs, and she set to work straightaway, following the list that my stepmother provided her.

That left nothing for my stepmother's sister to do, however. She is a lot older than my stepmother and doesn't look like a sibling at all: diminutive, plump, and with a face like an astonished doll. She prattled on endlessly, sobbed, and hugged everyone. I had trouble freeing myself from her springy, powder-scented bosom. When she sat down, all the flesh on her body flopped onto her stumpy thighs. And not to forget my grandpa, he remained standing beside my

16

grandma's sofa, listening to her grumbles with a patient, impassive expression on his face. To begin with, she was in tears on account of my father, but then after a while her own troubles started to displace that worry to the back of her mind. Her head ached, and she moaned about the rushing and roaring that her high blood pressure produced in her ears. Grandpa was well used to this by now; he didn't even bother to respond, but neither did he budge from her side throughout. I didn't hear him speak so much as once, yet whenever I glanced that way I would always see him there, in the same corner, which gradually lapsed into gloom as the afternoon wore on, until just a patch of subdued, yellowish light filtered through onto his bare forehead and the curve of his nose, while the pits of his eyes and the lower part of his face were sunk in shadow. Only from a tiny glint in the eyes could one tell that he was nonetheless following, unnoticed, everything that moved in the room.

On top of that, one of my stepmother's cousins also came by with her husband. I addressed him as Uncle Willie, since that is his name. He has a slight limp, for which he wears a shoe with a built-up sole on one foot; on the other hand, he has this to thank for the privilege of not having to go off to a labor camp. His head is pear-shaped, broad, bulging, and bald on top, but narrowing at the cheeks and toward the chin. His views are listened to with respect in the family because before setting up a betting shop he had been in journalism. True to form, he at once wanted to pass on some interesting pieces of news that he had learned "from a confidential source" that he characterized as "absolutely reliable." He seated himself in an armchair, his gammy leg

17

stretched stiffly out in front, and, rubbing his hands together with a dry rasp, informed us that before long "a decisive shift in our position is to be anticipated," since "secret negotiations" over us had been entered into "between the Germans and the Allied powers, through neutral intermediaries." The way Uncle Willie explained it, even the Germans "had by now come to recognize that their position on the battlefronts is hopeless." He was of the opinion that we, "the Jews of Budapest," were "coming in handy" for them in their efforts "to wring advantages, at our expense, out of the Allies," who of course would do all they could for us; at which point he mentioned what he regarded as "an important factor," which he was familiar with from his days as a journalist, and that was what he referred to as "world opinion," the way he put it being that the latter had been "shocked" by what was happening to us. It was a hard bargain, of course, he went on, and that is precisely what explained the current severity of measures against us; but then these were merely natural consequences of "the bigger game, in which we are actually pawns in an international blackmailing gambit of breathtaking scale"; he also said, however, that, being well aware of "what goes on behind the scenes," he looked on all this as essentially no more than "a spectacular bluff" that was designed to drive the price higher, and he asked us to be just a bit patient while "events unfold." Whereupon Father asked him if any of this might be expected by tomorrow, or was he also to regard his own call-up as "mere bluff," indeed, should he maybe not even bother going off to the labor camp tomorrow. That rattled Uncle Willie a bit. "Ahem, no, of course not," he answered. But he did say that he was quite confident my father would soon be back home. "We are now at the twelfth hour," was how he put it, rubbing his hands all the more. To that he also added, "If I had ever been so sure about any of my tips as I am about this one, I wouldn't be stone broke now!" He was about to continue but my step-mother and her mama had just finished with the knapsack, and my father got up from his seat to test its weight.

The last person to arrive was my stepmother's oldest brother, Uncle Lajos. He fulfills some terribly important function in our family, though I'd be hard put to define exactly what that was. He immediately wanted to talk in pri-vate with my father. From what I could observe, that irked my father, and though phrasing it very tactfully, he sug-gested they get it over with quickly. Uncle Lajos then unex-pectedly drew me into service. He said he would like "a little word" with me. He hauled me off to a secluded corner of the room and pinned me up against a cupboard, face-to-face with him. He started off by saying that, as I knew, my father would "be leaving us" tomorrow. I said I knew that. Next he wanted to know whether I was going to miss his being here. Though a bit annoyed by the question, I answered, "Natu-rally." Feeling this was in some way not quite enough, I immediately supplemented it with, "A lot." With that he merely nodded profusely for a while, a pained expression on his face.

Next, though, I learned a couple of intriguing and sur-prising things from him. For instance, that the time of my life that he said was "the happy, carefree years of childhood" had now drawn to a close for me with today's sadness. No doubt I had not yet considered it like that, he said. I admit-

19

ted that I hadn't. All the same, he carried on, no doubt his words did not come as any great surprise to me. They didn't, I said. He then brought to my attention that with my father's departure my stepmother would be left without support, and although the family "would keep an eye on us," from now on I was going to be her mainstay. To be sure, he said, I would be discovering all too soon "what worry and self-denial are." It was obvious that from now on my lot could not go on as well as it had up till now, and he did not wish to make any secret about that, as he was talking to me "man-to-man." "You too," he said, "are now a part of the shared Jewish fate," and he then went on to elaborate on that, remarking that this fate was one of "unbroken persecution that has lasted for millennia," which the Jews "have to accept with fortitude and self-sacrificing forbearance," since God has meted it out to them for their past sins, so for that very reason from Him alone could mercy be expected, but until then He in turn expects of us that, in this grave situation, we all stand our ground on the place He has marked out for us "in accordance with our strengths and abilities." I, for instance, I was informed, would have to hold my own as head of the family in the future. He inquired whether I sensed the strength and readiness within myself to do that. Though I did not quite follow the train of thought that had led up to this, particularly what he said about the Jews, their sins, and their God, I still grasped somehow what he was driving at. So I said, "Yes." He seemed contented. Good lad, he said. He always knew I was a clever boy, endowed with "profound feelings and a deep sense of responsibility," which in the midst of so many afflictions, to some degree, represented a solace for him, as was clear from what he had said. Grasping my chin with his fingers, the uppers of which were covered in tufts of hair and the undersides slightly moist with sweat, he now tipped my face upward, and in a quiet, slightly trembling voice said the following: "Your father is preparing to set off on a long journey. Have you prayed for him?" There was a hint of severity in his gaze, and it may have been this that awakened in me a keen sense of negligence toward my father, because, to be sure, I would never have thought of that of my own accord. Now that he had aroused it within me, however, I suddenly began to feel it as a burden, like some kind of debt, and in order to free myself of that I confessed, "No, I haven't." "Come with me," he said.

I had to accompany him over to the room on the courtyard side. There we prayed, surrounded by a few shabby pieces of furniture that were no longer in use. Uncle Lajos first placed a little, round black cap with a silky sheen on the back of his head at the spot where his thinning gray hair formed a tiny bald patch. I too had to bring along my cap from the hall. Next he produced a black-bound, red-bordered little book from the inner pocket of his jacket and his spectacles from the breast pocket. He then launched into reading out the prayer, while I had to repeat after him the same portion of text he had preceded me with. It went well at first, but I soon began to flag in the effort, and besides, I was a bit put out by not understanding a single word of what we were saying to God, since I had to recite to Him in Hebrew, a language unknown to me. In order somehow to be able to keep up, I was therefore increasingly obliged to watch Uncle Lajos's lip movements, so in actual fact out of the whole

21

business all that remained with me of what we mumbled was the sight of those moistly wriggling, fleshy lips and the incomprehensible gabble of a foreign tongue. Oh, and a scene that I could see through the window, over Uncle Lajos's shoulder: right at that moment the older sister from upstairs scurried home along the outside corridor, on the far side of the courtyard, a floor above ours. I think I got a bit mixed up over the text as well. Still, when the prayer had come to an end Uncle Lajos seemed to be pleased, and the expression on his face was such that even I was almost convinced we had really accomplished something in Father's cause. When it comes down to it, of course, this was certainly better than it had been before with the weight of that nagging sensation.

We returned to the room on the street side. Evening had drawn in. We closed the windows, with the blackout paper stuck over the panes, on the indigo-hued, humid spring evening. That entirely confined us within the room. The hubbub was by now tiring, and the cigarette smoke also started to sting my eyes. I was driven to yawning a lot. My stepmother's mama set the table. She had brought our supper herself, in her capacious handbag. She had even managed to procure some meat on the black market. She had made a point of relating that earlier, on arrival. My father even promptly paid for it from his leather wallet. We were already eating when, without warning, Uncle Steiner and Uncle Fleischmann also dropped by. They too wanted to take leave of Father. Uncle Steiner launched right away into a "don't anyone mind us." He said: "I'm Steiner. Please, don't get up." As ever, he was in fraying slippers, his rounded paunch poking out from under his unbuttoned waistcoat, the perennial stub of a foul-smelling cigar in his mouth. He had a big, ruddy head, the childlike parting of the hair giving him a distinctly odd impression. Uncle Fleischmann was utterly unnoticeable beside him, being a diminutive man of immaculate appearance, with white hair, ashen skin, owlish spectacles, and a perpetual slightly worried air on his face. He bowed mutely at Uncle Steiner's side, wringing his hands as if in apology for Uncle Steiner, or so it seemed, though I'm not sure about that. The two old codgers are inseparable, even though they are forever bickering, because there is no topic on which they can agree. They shook hands in turn with my father. Uncle Steiner even patted him on the back, calling him "Old boy," and then going on to crack his old quip: "Chin down! Don't lose our disheartenment!" He also said—and even Uncle Fleischmann nodded furiously along with this—that they would continue to look out for me and the "young lady" (as he called my stepmother). He blinked his button eyes, then pulled my father to his paunch and embraced him. After they had gone everything was drowned by the clatter of cutlery, the hum of conversation, and the fumes of the food and the thick tobacco smoke. By now all that got through to me, separating themselves out from the surrounding fog as it were, were disconnected scraps of some face or gesture, especially the tremulous, bony, yellow head of my stepmother's mama as she served each plate; the two palms of Uncle Lajos's hands raised in protest as he refused the meat, since it was pork and his faith forbade it; the pudgy cheeks, lively jaw, and moist eyes of my stepmother's older sister; then Uncle Willie's bald cranium unexpectedly

23

looming pinkish in the cone of the light's rays, and frag-
ments of his latest blithe anatomization; on top of which, I
also recollect Uncle Lajos's solemn words, received in dead
silence, in which he invoked God's assistance in the matter
of "our being able, before long, to gather together again at
the family table, each and every one of us, in peace and love
and good health." I barely saw anything of my father, and all
that I made out of my stepmother was that a great deal of
attention and consideration were being paid toward her—
almost more than toward my father—and that at one point
she complained of a headache, so several of them pressed
her as to whether she would like a tablet or a compress, but
she didn't want either. Then again, every now and then, I
couldn't help noticing my grandmother and how much she
got in the way, how she had to be guided back to the sofa
time and time again, her umpteen complaints, and her blind
eyes, which through the thick, steamed-up, tear-smudged
lenses of her glasses looked just like two peculiar, perspiring
insects. A moment came when everyone got up from the
table. The final farewells ensued. My grandmother and grandfather left separately though, somewhat before my stepmother's family. What stayed with me as maybe the strangest
experience of that entire evening was Grandfather's sole
act to draw attention to himself when he pressed his tiny,
sharply defined bird's head for no more than an instant, but
really fiercely, almost crazily, to the breast of my father's
jacket. His entire body was racked by a spasm. He then hastened quickly to the door, leading my grandmother by the
elbow. Everyone parted to let them through. After that I too
was embraced by several people and felt the sticky marks of

lips on my face. Finally, there was a sudden hush after all of them left.

Then it was time for me too to say good-bye to Father. Or maybe more for him to say good-bye to me. Hard to say. I don't even clearly remember the circumstances; my father must have gone outside with the guests, because for a while I was left on my own at the table, covered as it was with the remains of the supper, and I only came to with a start on Father's return. He was alone. He wanted to say good-bye. There won't be time for that at dawn tomorrow, as he put it. He too recited much the same sorts of things about my responsibility and my growing up as I had already heard before that afternoon from Uncle Lajos, only without God and not so nicely phrased, and much more briefly. He also mentioned my mother, suggesting that she might try now "to lure me away from home to herself." I could see that notion troubled him greatly. The two of them had battled for a long time over my custody until the court eventually ruled in my father's favor, so I found it quite understandable that he would not wish to lose his rights in regard to me now merely as a result of his unfortunate situation. Still, he appealed to my judgment, rather than the law, and to the difference between my stepmother, who had "created a cozy family home" for me, and my mother, who had "deserted" me. I started to prick up my ears at this, because on that particular detail I had heard a different story from my mother: according to her, Father had been at fault. That is why she had felt driven to choose another husband, Uncle "Dini" (or Dénes, to be more correct), who had incidentally gone off just last week, likewise to labor camp. In truth, though, I had never managed to figure out anything more precise, and even this time my father immediately reverted to my stepmother, remarking that I had her to thank for getting out of the boarding school, and that my place "is here, by her side." He said a lot more about her, and by now I had a shrewd idea why my stepmother was not present for these words: they would no doubt have embarrassed her. They began to be a bit wearisome for me, however. I no longer remember now what I promised Father. The next thing was that, all at once, I found myself enfolded between his arms, his hug catching me off guard and somehow unprepared after all he had said. I don't know if my tears stemmed from that or simply from exhaustion, or maybe even because, ever since the first exhortation that I had received that morning from my stepmother, I had somehow been preparing all along to shed them unfailingly; whatever the reason, it was nevertheless good that this was indeed what happened, and I sensed that it also gratified Father to see them. After that he sent me off to bed. By then I was dead tired anyway. All the same, I thought, at least we were able to send him off to the labor camp, poor man, with memories of a nice day.

TWO

Already two months have passed since we said good-bye to Father. Summer is here, but it's been ages since, back in springtime, the grammar school let us out on holiday, adverting to the war that's going on. Indeed, aircraft often come over to bomb the city, and since then they have brought in still newer laws about Jews. For the last two weeks I myself have been obliged to work. I was informed by official letter that "you have been assigned to a permanent workplace." The form of address ran "Master György Köves, trainee ancillary worker," from which I could see straightaway that the Levente cadet movement had a hand in the matter. But then I also heard that people like me who are not yet old enough to be drafted as fully fit for labor service are nowadays being placed in employment at factories and places of that sort. Along with me, for much the same reason, there is a group of eighteen or so boys who are also around fifteen years old. The workplace is in Csepel, at a company called the "Shell Petroleum Refinery Works." As a result, I have actually acquired a privilege of sorts, since under any other circumstances those wearing yellow stars are prohibited from traveling outside the city limits. I, however, was handed legitimate identity papers, bearing the official stamp of the war production commander, which provide that I "may cross the Csepel customs borderline."

The work itself, by the way, cannot be said to be particularly strenuous, and so as it is, given the gang of us boys, is even fairly entertaining, consisting of assisting with bricklaying duties. The oil works was the target of a bombing raid, and it is our job to try and make good the damage done by the aircraft. The foreman whom we have been put under treats us pretty decently as well; at the end of the week he even adds up our wages just like for his regular workforce. My stepmother, though, was thrilled most of all about the identity papers, because up till then every time I set off on any journey, she always got herself worked up about how I was going to vouch for myself should the need arise. Now, though, she has no reason to fret as the ID testifies that I am not alive on my own account but am benefiting the war effort in the manufacturing industry, and that, naturally, puts it in an entirely different light. The family, moreover, shares that opinion. Only my stepmother's sister moaned a little, since it means I have to do manual labor, and with tears all but welling into her eyes, she asked if that was all my going to grammar school had come to. I told her that in my view it was simply healthy. Uncle Willie took my side straightaway, while even Uncle Lajos advised that we must accept God's ordinances in regard to us, at which she held her tongue. Uncle Lajos then drew me aside to exchange a few words of a more serious nature, among which he exhorted me not to forget that when I was at the workplace I was not representing myself alone but "the entire Jewish community," so I must mind my behavior for their sake too, because on that basis judgments would be formed with regard to all of them collectively. That would truly never have occurred to me; still, I realized that he might well be right, of course.

Father's letters also arrive promptly from the labor camp: he is in good health, thank goodness, he is bearing up well under the work, and the treatment is also decent, he writes. The family is also reassured by their tone. Even Uncle Lajos takes the view that God has been with my father so far, urging us to pray daily for Him to continue to look out for him, given that His power has command over all of us. Uncle Willie, for his part, declared that in any case all we had to do now was somehow hang on through "a brief transitional period," because, as he argued, the landings by the Allied powers had now "definitively sealed the fate" of the Germans.

So far, I have been able to get on with my stepmother without any differences of opinion. She, by stark contrast, has been obliged to remain idle as she has been ordered to close the shop, since those who are not of pure blood are forbidden to engage in commerce. Yet it looks as though Father was lucky in placing his bet on Mr. Sütő, for as a result every week he now unfailingly brings round what is due to my stepmother out of the profits of the lumberyard that is now in his hands, just as he promised my father. He was punctual the other day too, counting out a tidy sum of money onto our table, so it seemed to me. He kissed my stepmother's hand and even had a few friendly words for me. He inquired in detail after "the boss's" health, as usual. He was just preparing to say good-bye when one further thing sprang to his mind. He took a parcel out of his briefcase. There was a slightly embarrassed look on his face. "I trust, my dear lady," those were his words, "that this will come in handy for the household." The parcel contained lard, sugar, and other items of that kind. I suspect he must have got them on the black market, perhaps because he too must no doubt have read about the decree that from now on Jews would have to make do with smaller rations in the domain of food supplies. My stepmother tried to protest at first, but Mr. Sütő was very insistent, and in the end, naturally, she could hardly object to the attentiveness. When we were by ourselves, she even asked me whether, in my opinion, she had acted correctly in accepting. She had, I considered, because there was no way she could offend Mr. Sütő by refusing to accept the parcel; after all, he meant well. She was of the same opinion, saying she thought my father would also approve of her course of action. I cannot say I supposed any differently myself, but anyway, she usually knows better than I do.

Twice a week I also visit my mother, as usual, on the afternoons to which she is entitled. I am now having more problems with her. Just as Father predicted, she really is quite irreconcilable to the idea that my place is beside my stepmother, saying that I "belong" to her, my natural mother. But as best I know the court awarded in my father's favor, so in that light his word is surely what goes. Yet this Sunday too

30

my mother was badgering me about what kind of life I want to live, because in her view all that matters are my wishes and whether or not I love her. I told her, of course I love her! But my mother explained that love means being "attached to someone," and as she sees it I am attached to my step-mother. I tried to convince her that she was wrong to see it that way, for after all it wasn't me who was attached to my stepmother but, as she knew full well, that was what Father had decided. Her response to that, though, was that this was about me, my own life, and I should be making that decision for myself, and furthermore, love "is proved by actions, not words." I came away feeling rather troubled: naturally I could not allow her to go on supposing that I didn't love her, but then on the other hand I could not take entirely seri-ously what she had said about the importance of my wishes, and that it was up to me to decide on my own affairs. When all is said and done, it was their quarrel, and it would be embarrassing for me to pass judgment on that. Anyway, I cannot be disloyal to Father, particularly not now, while he is in the labor camp, poor man. All the same, I boarded the streetcar with uncomfortable feelings, for of course I am attached to my mother, and naturally it bothered me that again I could do nothing for her today.

That lousy feeling may perhaps have been the reason why I was none too eager to take leave of Mother. It was she who insisted it would be late, given that those with yellow stars are only permitted to show themselves on the street up to eight o'clock. But I explained to her that now that I have the identification papers, I no longer need to be so dreadfully punctilious about each and every regulation.

31

For all that, I still climbed onto the rearmost platform of the last car of the streetcar as usual, in compliance with the pertinent regulation. It was getting close to eight when I reached home, and although the summer evening was still light, people were already starting to set the black- and blue-colored boards in some windows. My stepmother was also showing signs of impatience, though in her case that was more just out of habit, because I have the ID papers, after all. That evening, as usual, we spent at the Fleischmanns'. The two old codgers are well, still arguing a lot, but even they had been as one in favoring the idea of my going to work, in their case too due to the ID, naturally. In their enthusiasm, they still contrived to quarrel a little. With my stepmother and I not knowing the way out toward Csepel, we asked them for directions the first time we went. Old Fleischmann suggested the suburban train service whereas Uncle Steiner plumped for the bus, because it stops directly by the oil works, he said, but one was still left with a walk from the train—and that is, in fact, the case, as it turned out. We weren't to know that then, however, and Uncle Fleischmann got extremely worked up: "It's always you who has to be right," he groused. In the end, the two fat wives had to step in. Annamarie and I laughed about them a lot.

As to her, by the way, I am now in a somewhat peculiar situation. The incident occurred the day before yesterday, during the alert on Friday night, down in the air-raid shelter, or to be more precise, in one of the deserted, dimly lit cellar passages onto which it opens. Originally, I only wanted to show her that it was more interesting to follow what is happening on the outside from there. But when, about a minute later, we heard a bomb actually go off nearby, she started trembling all over. It was really good, because in her terror she clung to me, her arms around my neck, her face buried in my shoulder. All I remember after that was searching for her lips. I was left with the vague experience of a warm, moist, slightly sticky contact. Well, and also a kind of happy astonishment, for it was my first kiss with a girl after all, besides which I had not been reckoning on it right then.

Yesterday, on the stairwell, it emerged that she too had been very surprised. "It was all because of the bomb," she considered. Basically, she was right. Later on, we kissed again, and that was when she taught me how to make the experience more memorable by also doing certain things with your tongues.

This evening too I was with her in the other room to look at the Fleischmanns' ornamental fish, because in truth we have frequently been in the habit of looking at them at other times anyway. This time, of course, that was not quite the only reason for us to go there. We made use of our tongues as well. Still, we returned quickly, because Annamarie was afraid that her uncle and aunt might suspect something was up. Later on, while we were talking, I learned one or two interesting things as to her thoughts about me: she said she would never have imagined "a time would come when I might mean something else" to her other than merely "a good friend." When she got to know me, she took me, at first, for just another adolescent. Later on, though, she admitted, she had looked a bit closer, and a certain empathy toward me had sprung up in her, maybe, she supposed, due to our similar lot with regard to our parents, while from the

33

occasional remark I made she had also concluded that we think about certain things in a similar way; yet even so, she had not suspected any more than that. She mused a little on how odd that was, and even said, "It seems it was meant to happen this way." She had a strange, almost severe expression on her face, so I didn't argue with her, even though I was more inclined to agree with what she said yesterday about it being because of the bomb. But then, of course, what do I know about anything, and anyway, as far as I could see, this other way was more to her liking. We said good-bye soon after that, as I had to go to work the next day, but when I took her hand, she dug sharply into my palm with her fingernails. I understood it was her way of hinting at our secret, and the look on her face was as if to say "everything's okay."

The next day, though, her behavior was decidedly odd. In the afternoon, having come back from work and first washed myself down, changed shirt and shoes, and run a wet comb through my hair, I went with her to visit the sisters, because Annamarie had in the meantime carried out her original plan of arranging to introduce me to them. Their mama too was pleased to welcome me (their father is away on labor service). They have a fair-sized apartment with a balcony, carpets, a couple of larger rooms, and a separate, smaller room for the two girls. This is furnished with a piano and lots of dolls and other girlish knickknacks. We usually play cards, but today the older sister was not in the mood. She wanted to talk to us first about something that has been preoccupying her recently, since the yellow star has been giving her plenty to puzzle over. In fact, it was "people's looks" that had woken her up to the change, because she finds that people's attitudes toward her have altered, and she can see from their looks that they "hate" her. She had observed that this morning as well, while she was out shopping for her mama. To my way of thinking, though, she was making a bit too much of it. My own experience, at any rate, is not quite the same. At the workplace, for instance, everyone knows that some of the bricklayers there can't stand Jews but they have still become quite friendly with us boys. Not that this does anything to change their views, of course. Then again, the example of the baker came to mind, so I attempted to explain to the girl that they did not really hate her, that is to say not her personally, since they have no way of knowing her, after all—it was more just the idea of being "Jewish." She then said she'd been thinking the same thing right before, because when you get down to it she doesn't even know exactly what "Jewish" is. Annamarie, admittedly, said to her that everyone knows: it's a religion. What interested her, however, was not that but its "sense." "After all, people must know why they hate," she reckoned. She confessed that at first she'd been unable to make any sense of the whole thing, and it had hurt her terribly that they despised her "merely because she is Jewish"; that's when she had felt for the first time that, as she put it, something singles her out from those people, she belongs to some other category. That had started her thinking, and she had tried to find out more about it all from books and conversations, which was how she had come to recognize that they hated her precisely for that. It was her view, in fact, that "we Jews are different from other people," and that difference was the crux of it, that's why people hate Jews. She also remarked how peculiar it was to live "being

35

aware of that differentness," and that sometimes she felt a
sort of pride but at other times more a shame of sorts
because of it. She wanted to know how we felt in regard to
our differentness, whether we were proud of it or rather
ashamed. Her younger sister and Annamarie didn't really
know; I myself hadn't so far been able to find a reason for
these feelings either. Anyway, a person cannot entirely
decide for himself about this differentness: in the end, that
is precisely what the yellow star is there for, as far as I know.
I told her as much, but she dug her heels in: the difference is
"carried within ourselves." According to me, however, what
we wear on the outside is the more crucial. We argued a lot
about this, though I can't think why, because to be honest I
didn't see any of it as being all that important. Still, there
was something in her line of thought that somehow exasperated me; in my opinion it's all a lot simpler. Besides which, I
also wanted to win the argument, naturally. At one point or
another, it seemed that Annamarie wanted to say her piece,
but she didn't get a chance even once, as by then the two of
us were not paying much attention to her.

In the end, I brought up an example. I had already occasionally given some idle thought to the matter, which is how
it entered my head. Then again, I had also read a book, a sort
of novel, not long ago. A beggar and a prince who, leaving
that one difference aside, conspicuously resembled each
other both facially and physically, to the point they could
not be told apart, exchanged fates with each other out of
sheer curiosity, until in the end the beggar turned into a real
prince while the prince became a real beggar. I asked the girl
to try and imagine the same thing about herself. It was not

very likely, of course, but then all kinds of things are possible, after all. What could have happened to her, let's say in very early infancy, when a person is not yet able to speak or remember, it didn't matter how, but suppose she had somehow been swapped or got mixed up with a child from another family whose documents were in perfect order from a racial point of view. In this hypothetical case it would now be the other girl who would perceive the difference and of course wear the yellow star, whereas she, in view of what she knew, would see herself—as of course would others—as being exactly like other people, and she would neither think about nor recognize any difference. As far as I could tell, that had quite an impact on her. At first she merely fell silent, then very slowly, but with a softness I felt as almost palpable, her lips parted as if she were wishing to say something. That was not what happened, however, but something else, much odder: she burst into tears. She buried her head in the angle of her elbow, which was resting on the table, her shoulders shaken by tiny jerks. I was utterly amazed, as that had not been my aim at all, and anyway the sight in itself threw me somehow. I tried leaning over to pat her hair, shoulder, and a bit on her arm, begging her not to cry. But she exclaimed bitterly, in a voice that choked as it went on, something along the lines that if our own qualities had nothing to do with it, then it was all pure chance, and if she could be someone else than the person she was forced to be, then "the whole thing has no sense," and that notion, in her opinion, "is unbearable." I was perturbed, given I was to blame, but I had no way of knowing that this notion could be so important to her. I was almost on the point of telling her not to worry

37

about it, because none of it meant anything to me, I didn't despise her on account of her race; but I sensed right away that this would be a slightly ridiculous thing for me to say, so I didn't say it. Nonetheless, it bugged me not to be able to say it, because that was really what I felt at that moment, irrespective of being in the situation of not being able to say it freely. Though it is quite possible, of course, that in another situation I might perhaps see things differently. I didn't know, and I also realized there was no way to test it. Still, the thing somehow made me feel awkward. I couldn't say exactly why, but now, for the very first time, I sensed something that I suppose indeed slightly resembled shame.

It was only in the stairwell, however, that I learned I had apparently upset Annamarie with this feeling of mine, for that is when she started to behave oddly. I spoke to her, but she didn't even reply. I tried to put my hand on her arm, but she tore herself out of my grasp and left me standing on the stairs.

I also waited in vain for her to appear the next afternoon. As a result, I couldn't go to the sisters' place either, since up till now we had always gone together, so they would undoubtedly have asked questions. Anyway, I was now more inclined to appreciate what the girl had said on Sunday.

She did show up at the Fleischmanns' that evening, however. She was still very stiff about talking to me, her expression only softening a little when, in response to her remark that she hoped I had had a nice afternoon with the sisters, I told her that I hadn't gone up there. She was curious as to why, to which I replied, since it was only the truth, that I hadn't wanted to go without her. I could see that this answer must have pleased her. After some more time, she was even willing to go and look at the fish with me, and by the time we returned from the other room, we had completely patched things up. Later on that evening, she made just one more remark about it all: "That was our first quarrel," she said.

THREE

The next day I had a slightly odd experience. I got up that morning and set off for work as usual. It promised to be a hot day, and as ever the bus was packed with passengers. We had already left the houses of the suburbs behind and driven across the short, unornamented bridge that crosses to Csepel Island, after which the road carries on through open country for a stretch, between fields with, over on the left, a flat, hangarlike building and, over on the right, the scattered greenhouses of market gardeners, when the bus braked very suddenly, and then I heard from outside snatches of a voice issuing orders, which the conductor and several passengers relayed on down to me, to the effect that any Jewish passenger who happened to be on the bus should get off. Ah well, I thought to myself, no doubt they want to do a spot-check on the papers of everyone going across.

Indeed, on the highway I found myself face-to-face with a policeman. Without a word being said, I immediately held out my pass toward him. He, however, first sent the bus on its way with a brisk flip of the hand. I was beginning to think that maybe he didn't understand the ID, and was just on the point of explaining to him that, as he could see, I am assigned to war work and most certainly could not afford to have my time wasted, when all at once the road around me was thronged with voices and boys, my companions from Shell. They had emerged from hiding behind the embankment. It turned out that the policeman had already grabbed them off earlier buses, and they were killing themselves with laughter that I too had turned up. Even the policeman cracked a bit of a smile, like someone who, though more detached, was still joining in the fun to a degree; I could see straightaway that he had nothing against us—nor indeed could he have, naturally. I asked the other boys what it was all about anyway, but they didn't have a clue either for the time being.

The policeman then stopped all subsequent buses running from the city by stepping into their path, from a certain distance away, with a hand upstretched; before that he sent the rest of us behind the embankment. Each and every time, the same scene would be reenacted: the initial surprise of the new boys eventually shifting into laughter. The policeman appeared to be satisfied. Roughly a quarter of an hour passed like this. It was a clear summer morning with the sun already starting to warm the grass, as we could feel when we lay down against it. The fat tanks of the oil plant could readily be made out farther away, amid a bluish haze. Beyond that were factory chimneys and yet farther off, more hazily,

41

the pointed outline of some church steeple. The boys, singly or in groups, turned up one after the other from the buses. One of these arrivals was a popular, very chirpy, freckled kid, his hair cropped in black spikes, "Leatherware" as everyone calls him, because unlike the others, who mostly come from various schools, he has gone into that trade. Then there was "Smoker," a boy you almost never saw without a cigarette. Admittedly, most of the others have the occasional smoke and, not to be outdone, I've recently been trying it out myself, but I've noticed that he panders to the habit quite differently, with a hunger that verges on the truly feverish. Even his eyes have a strange, febrile expression. He's more one of those taciturn, somehow none too sociable types, and is not generally liked by the others. All the same, I once asked him what he found so great about smoking so much, to which he gave the curt reply, "It's cheaper than food." I was slightly taken aback, since such a reason would never have occurred to me. What surprised me even more, though, was the sort of sarcastic, somehow almost censorious look he had when he noticed my discomfiture; it was disagreeable, so I laid off any further probing. Still, I now better appreciated the guardedness the others showed toward him. By then, another arrival was being greeted with a more unconstrained whooping: he's the one known to all his closer pals simply as "Fancyman." That name seemed to me to fit him to a T, given his sleek, dark hair, his big, gray eyes, and the congenial polish of his entire being in general; only later did I hear that the expression actually has quite another meaning, which was why it had been bestowed on him, since back at home he was reputedly very slick in his dealings with girls. One of the buses brought "Rosie" as well—Rosenfeld actually, but everyone uses the shorter nickname. For some reason, he enjoys a degree of respect among the boys, and on matters of common interest we generally tend to go along with his view; he's also always the one who deals with the foreman as our representative. I've heard that he is going through commercial college. With his intelligent, though somewhat excessively elongated face, his wavy blonde hair, and his slightly hard-set, watery-blue eyes, he reminds me of old-master paintings in museums that have titles like "The Infante with Greyhound" and such. Another who turned up was Moskovics, a diminutive kid, with a much more lopsided and what I would call rather ugly mug, the goggles perched on his broad snub nose having pebble lenses as thick as my grandma's . . . and likewise all the others. The general opinion, which was more or less the way I saw it, was that the whole affair was a bit unusual but undoubtedly some kind of mistake. "Rosie," having been egged on by some of the others, even asked the policeman if we would get into trouble for turning up late for work, and when in fact he intended to let us go on about our business. The policeman was not in the least put out by the question, but then again he replied that it was not up to him to decide. As became clear, he really knew very little more than we did: he referred to "further orders" that would replace the older ones, which were to the effect that until then, for the time being, both he and we would have to wait—that was roughly how he explained it. Even if this was not entirely clear, in essence it all sounded, as the boys and I thought, quite reasonable. In any case, we were obligated to defer to the policeman, after all. Then again, we found this all the easier in that quite understandably, safe in the knowledge of our ID cards and the stamp of the war industry authorities, we saw no reason for taking the policeman very seriously. He, for his part, could see—so it emerged from his own words—that he was dealing with "intelligent boys" on whose "sense of discipline," he added, he could hopefully continue to count; as far as I could see, he had decided he liked us. He himself seemed sympathetic: he was a fairly short policeman, neither young nor old, with clear, very pale eyes set in a suntanned face. From a number of the words he used, I deduced he must have come from a rural background.

It was seven o'clock; by now the day shift would be starting in the oil works. The buses were no longer bringing any new boys, and the policeman now asked if any of us were missing. "Rosie" counted us and reported that we were all present. The policeman reckoned it would be better if we didn't hang around there, by the side of the road. He seemed troubled, and I somehow had the impression that he had been just as little prepared for us as we were for him. He even asked, "Now what am I going to do with you guys?" However, there wasn't much we could do to help him on that, of course. We gathered around him exuberantly, giggling, as if he were a teacher on some school excursion, with him in the middle of our group, pensively stroking his chin. In the end, he proposed we go to the customs post.

We accompanied him over to a solitary, shabby, single-story building close by, next to the highway; this was the "Customs House," as a weather-beaten inscription on the front also declared. The policeman produced a bunch of

44

keys and picked out from the many jingling keys the one that fit the lock. Inside we found a pleasantly cool and spacious, though somewhat bare, room furnished with a few benches and a long, rickety table. The policeman also opened the door to a considerably smaller office room of sorts. As best I could see past the gap left by the door, inside were a carpet and a writing desk with a telephone handset on it. We even heard the policeman making a brief call. Though one could not make out what he said, I suppose he must have been trying to hurry the orders along, because when he came out, carefully locking the door behind him, he said, "Nothing. Too bad, we'll just have to wait." He urged us to make ourselves comfortable. He even asked if we knew any party games. One boy—"Leatherware," as far as I recollect—suggested paper, scissors, stone. The policeman, however, was not too keen on that, saying that he had expected better of "such bright kids" like us. For a while he swapped jokes with us, though meanwhile I had the feeling that he was striving at all costs to keep us amused somehow, maybe so we would have no time for any of the unruliness that he had already mentioned out on the highway; but then he proved fairly out of his depth with that sort of thing. Before long, indeed, he left us to our own devices, having noted that he had work to attend to. As he went out we heard him locking the door on us from outside.

There is not much I could tell about what ensued. It seemed we were in for a long wait for the orders. Still, as far as we were concerned, we didn't look on this as the least bit urgent; after all, we were not frittering away our own time. We all agreed it was nicer here, in the cool, than to be sweat-

45

ing at work. There was little shade to be had at the oil plant. "Rosie" had even managed to wangle the foreman's permission for us to strip off our shirts. This did not exactly conform with the letter of the regulations, it's true, since it meant the yellow stars would not be visible on us, but the foreman agreed all the same, out of common decency. The only one to suffer a bit had been Moskovics with his paperwhite skin, as his back had turned red as a lobster in the blink of an eye, and we had a big laugh at the long tatters of skin that he peeled off it afterward.

So we settled down on the benches or on the bare earth of the customs post, but I would find it hard to say exactly how we spent the time. Certainly, plenty of jokes were cracked, cigarettes were brought out, and then, as time went on, packed lunches. The foreman was not forgotten either, with people remarking that he must have been a bit mystified this morning when we didn't turn up for work. Some horseshoe nails were also produced for a game of jacks. It was there, among the boys, that I learned how that goes: each player throws a nail up in the air and the winner is the one who can snatch the most from the nails still in front of him in the time it takes to catch the first nail. "Fancyman," with his slim hands and long fingers, won every round. "Rosie," for his part, taught us a song, which we warbled through several times over. The curious thing about the song was that the lyrics can be rendered in three languages using exactly the same words: by sticking an *es* at the end of the words, it sounds German; an *io*, then Italian; and *taki*, then Japanese. All this stuff was just silly, of course, but it kept me entertained.

After that I took a look at each of the grown-ups as they came in. They too had been rounded up by the policemen from the buses in just the same way as us. That, in fact, is how I realized that when he was not with us, he was out on the highway, engaged in the same pursuit as in the morning. One by one, there must have been seven or eight of them who were collected that way, all men. I could see, however, that they were giving the policeman a tougher time, with their expressions of bewilderment, shaking of heads, explanations, showing of documents, and nitpicking questions. They pumped us too: Who and what were we? Later, though, they tended to keep to themselves; we gave up a couple of the benches for them, and they huddled on or hung around these. They talked about all sorts of things, but I didn't pay much attention. They attempted mainly to figure out what could be behind the policeman's action, and what consequences the episode might have for them; from what I could hear, though, there were about as many different views as there were men. On the whole, as far as I could tell, it depended mainly on what sort of documents they had on them, because as best I could make out, they too all had some paper giving them leave to head for Csepel, some on private business, others—just like us—out of public duty.

I did, however, take note of a few more interesting faces among them. One of them, I noticed, did not join in the conversation, for instance, but instead merely read a book that, it seems, he just happened to have with him. He was a very tall, gaunt guy in a yellow windbreaker, with a sharp slit of a mouth stretching between two deep, ill-tempered-looking furrows in his bristly face. He had chosen a place for himself

47

at the very end of one of the benches, beside the window, legs crossed and back to the others; it was that, perhaps, which reminded me somewhat of a traveler who is so used to railway compartments that he considers every word, query, or the habitual introductory chitchat that accidental travel companions exchange a waste of time, enduring the wait until the destination is reached with bored indifference— that at least was the kind of impression he gave me.

A somewhat older, elegant-looking man with silvered temples and a bald spot on the crown of his head caught my attention the moment he arrived, not long before noon, because he was highly indignant as the policeman ushered him in. He even asked if there was a telephone that "he might make use of." The policeman made it clear, however, that he was very sorry but the device "is reserved purely for official purposes," at which the man fell silent, an angry scowl on his face. Later on, from the answers, laconic though they were, that he gave to inquiries from the others, I gathered that he, like us, also belonged to one of the Csepel manufacturing establishments; he styled himself "an expert," without going into further details. Otherwise he came across as very self-confident and, as far as I could tell, his take on things must have been similar to ours by and large, except that he seemed to be offended at being detained. I noticed that he was invariably disparaging, even somewhat contemptuous, in his pronouncements about the policeman. He said that the policeman, in his view, "may have some general instruction, it appears," that he was probably "executing overzealously." He reckoned, though, that obviously "the competent authorities" would eventually act on the matter, adding that he hoped that was going to be soon. I heard little more from him after that, indeed forgot all about him. It was only getting into the afternoon that he fleetingly attracted my attention again, but by then I was tired too and noticed little more than how impatient he must be, now sitting down, now standing up, now folding his arms over his chest, now clasping them behind his back, now checking his watch.

Then there was also an odd little guy with a very distinctive nose, a large rucksack, dressed in "plus fours" and huge walking boots; even his yellow star somehow seemed larger than usual. He was more of a worrier, moaning especially to everyone about his "bad luck." I more or less registered his case, since it was a simple story and he went over it repeatedly. He was meant to be visiting his "very sick" mother in the Csepel district, as he related it. He had procured a special permit from the authorities; he had it on him and showed it around. The permit was valid for today up till 2:00 p.m. Something had come up, however, a matter that, he said, "could not be put off"—"for business reasons," he added. There had been others in the office, however, so it had taken a very long time before it was his turn. He was by then beginning to think the whole trip was in jeopardy, as he put it. Still, he had hurriedly boarded a streetcar in order to get to the bus terminus, in accordance with his original plan. On the way, though, he had checked the likely duration of the return journey against the permitted deadline and worked out that it would, indeed, be rather risky to set off. But then at the bus terminus he had seen that the noon bus was still waiting there, at which, so we were informed, he thought, "What a lot of trouble I've gone to for that little bit of paper! . . .

49

Besides which," he added, "poor Mama is waiting." He remarked that the old lady was a big concern for him and his wife. They had long ago pleaded with her to move in with them, into the city, but his mama had kept on flatly refusing until it was too late. He shook his head a lot, being of the opinion that, in his view, the old lady was hanging on to her house "at all costs." "Yet it doesn't even have any amenities," he noted. But then, he went on, she was his mother, so he had to be tolerant. On top of which, he added, she was now both ill and elderly. He had felt "he might never be able to forgive himself," he said, if he were to pass up this one opportunity. As a result, he had got onto the bus after all. At that point he fell silent for a minute. He raised, then slowly lowered, his hands in a gesture of helplessness, while a thousand tiny quizzical wrinkles formed on his brow, giving him something of the look of a sad, trapped rodent. "What do you think?" he then asked the others. Might something unpleasant come of the business? Would it be taken into consideration that his overstepping of the permitted deadline had not been his fault? And what, he wondered, must his mama be thinking, whom he had informed about the visit, not to speak of his wife and two small children at home if he failed to get back by two o'clock? Mainly from the direction in which his gaze was pointed, it seemed, as far as I could tell, that he was expecting an opinion or rejoinder on these questions from the aforesaid man with the distinguished bearing, the "Expert." The latter, however, I could see, was not paying much attention; his hand just then was holding a cigarette that he had taken out shortly before, the tip of which he was now tapping on the lid of a gleaming silver case with embossed lettering and engraved lines. I saw from his face that he was absorbed, lost in some distant reflection, giving every sign that he had heard nothing at all of the entire story. At that point, then, the man reverted to his bad luck; if he had reached the terminus just five minutes later, he would not have caught the noon bus, for if he had not found that one still there, he would not have waited for the next, and consequently, assuming this was all through "the difference of just five minutes," then "he would now not be sitting here but at home," he explained over and over again.

Then too I still recall the man with the seal's face: portly, stocky, with a black moustache and gold-rimmed eyeglasses, who was continually seeking "to have a word" with the policeman. Nor did it escape my attention that he always strove to have a go at this separately, a little bit away from the rest, preferably in a corner or by the door. "Constable," I would hear his strangled, rasping voice at these times, "may I have a word with you?" Or: "Please, constable . . . just a word, if I may . . ." In the end, on one occasion the policeman actually asked what he wanted. He then appeared to hesitate, first mistrustfully flashing his spectacles around rapidly. Even though this time they were in the corner of the room quite close to me, I could pick out nothing at all from the ensuing muffled muttering: he was apparently proposing something. A bit later a treacly smile of a more confidential nature also materialized on his features. At the same time, he began to lean just a little closer, until bit by bit, he was right over toward the policeman. In the meantime, as all this was going on, I also observed him make a strange movement. I did not get an entirely clear impression of the thing; at first

51

I thought he was preparing to slip his hand into his inside pocket for something. It even occurred to me, from the evident significance of the movement, that he might be wishing to show an important paper, some remarkable or special document. Only I waited in vain for what might emerge, because in the end he did not complete the movement. All the same, he did not exactly abandon it either, but rather became stalled in it, forgot about it, suddenly somehow aborted it, I might say, just at the climactic moment. As it was, in the end his hand merely fumbled, brushed, and scrabbled for a moment in the general area of his chest, like some big, sparsely haired spider or, even more, some kind of smaller sea monster that was, as it were, seeking the crevice that would allow it to scuttle under the jacket. While that was going on, he himself kept talking, with that particular smile frozen to his face. All this lasted maybe several seconds. After that all I saw was the policeman putting an end to the conversation there and then, very brusquely and with conspicuous decisiveness, even to some extent indignantly, as far as I could see; although I really didn't get much of what it was all about, his behavior struck me too as somehow fishy, in some not readily definable way.

As for the other faces and incidents, I no longer recall much. In any case, as time went by any observations of this kind that I made became increasingly vague. All I can really say is that the policeman continued to be very considerate toward us boys; with the adults, on the other hand, or so I observed, it seemed as if he was just a touch less cordial. By the afternoon, though, he too looked exhausted. By then he would often cool off among us or in his room, paying no attention to any buses that went by in the meantime. I also heard him repeatedly trying the telephone, and every now and then he would even announce the outcome: "Still nothing," but with an almost plainly visible expression of dissatisfaction on his face. There was another incident that I also recall. It happened earlier on, sometime after noon, with one of his pals, another policeman who came by on a bicycle. First of all, he propped the latter against the wall where we were; they then carefully closeted themselves in our policeman's room. It was a long time before they emerged. On parting, there was a lengthy shaking of hands in the doorway. They said nothing, but the way they kept nodding their heads and exchanging glances was something I'd sometimes seen with tradesmen in the old days, back in my father's office, after they'd chewed over the hard times and the sluggishness of business. I realized, of course, that this was not very likely to be the case with policemen, but still, that is the memory their faces conjured up in my mind, that same familiar, somewhat harassed dejection, that same forced sense of resignation so to say, over the immutable order of things. But I was starting to grow tired; all I remember of the remaining time thereafter is that I felt hot, was bored, and even grew a bit drowsy.

All in all, I can report, the day came and went. The order eventually came through, at round about four o'clock, exactly as the policeman had promised. It said that we were to make our way to the "higher authority" for purposes of showing our documents, so the policeman informed us. He, for his part, must have been notified by telephone because prior to that we had heard bustling noises, indicative of a change of some sort, coming from his room: repeated, peremptory ringing of the apparatus, then he in turn sought to be put through to somewhere to dispatch a few terse pieces of business. The policeman also volunteered that although they had communicated nothing absolutely specific to him either, in his view it could be no more than some kind of cursory formality, at least in cases that were as clear-cut and incontestable in the eyes of the law as, for instance, ours were.

Columns, drawn up in ranks of three abreast, set off back toward the city from all the border posts in the area simultaneously, as I was able to establish while we were en route, for at the bridge and at one turnoff or crossroad or another we would meet up with other groups that were similarly made up of a smaller or larger bunch of yellow-star men and one or two—indeed in one case three—policemen. I spotted the policeman with the bicycle too, accompanying one of those groups. I also noticed that on each occasion the policemen invariably greeted one another with the same certain, so to say businesslike briskness, as though they had reckoned on these encounters in advance, and only then did I grasp more clearly the significance of our own policeman's previous phone transactions: it seems that was how they had been able to synchronize the time-points with one another. Finally, it hit me that I was marching in the middle of what was by now a quite sizable column, with our procession flanked on both sides, at sporadic intervals, by policemen.

We proceeded in this manner, spread over the entire road, for quite a long while. It was a fine, clear, summery afternoon, the streets thronged with a motley multitude, as they always are at this hour, but I only saw all this in a haze. I also lost my sense of bearings rather quickly, since we mostly traversed streets and avenues with which I was not all that familiar. Then too my attention was rather taken up and quickly sapped by the ever-growing sea of people, the traffic and, above all, the kind of laboredness that goes together with the progress of a closed column in such circumstances. All I remember of the entire long trek, in fact, was the kind of hasty, hesitant, almost furtive curiosity of the public on the sidewalks at the sight of our procession (this was initially amusing, but after a time I no longer paid much notice to it)—oh, and a subsequent, somewhat disturbing moment. We happened to be going along some broad, tremendously busy avenue in the suburbs, with the honking, unbearably noisy din of traffic all around us, when at one point, I don't know how, a streetcar managed to become wedged in our column, not far in front of me as it happened. We were obliged to come to a halt while it passed through, and it was then that I became alive to the sudden flash of a piece of yellow clothing up ahead, in the cloud of dust, noise, and vehicle exhaust fumes: it was "Traveler." A single long leap, and he was off to the side, lost somewhere in the seething eddy of machines and humanity. I was totally dumbfounded; somehow it did not tally with his conduct at the customs post, as I saw it. But there was also something else that I felt, a sense of happy surprise I might call it, at the simplicity of an action; indeed, I saw one or two enterprising spirits then immediately make a break for it in his wake, right up ahead. I myself took a look around, though more for the fun of it, if I may put it that way, since I saw no other reason to bolt, though I believe there would have been time to do so; nevertheless, my sense of honor proved the stronger. The policemen took immediate action after that, and the ranks again closed around me.

We went on for a while longer, after which everything happened very quickly, unexpectedly, and in a slightly astonishing fashion. We turned off somewhere and, as best I could see, we had arrived, because the road carried on between the wide-open wings of a gateway. I then noticed that from the gate onward a different set of men stepped into the places of the policemen on our flanks, in much the same uniforms as soldiers but with multicolored feathers in their peaked caps: these were gendarmes. They led us on into a maze of gray buildings, ever farther inward, before we suddenly debouched onto a huge open space strewn with white gravel—some sort of barracks parade ground, as I saw it. I immediately glimpsed a tall figure of commanding appearance striding directly toward us from the building opposite. He was wearing high boots and a tight-fitting uniform jacket with gold buttons and a diagonal leather strap over his chest. In one of his hands I saw he had a thin crop, rather like the ones used by horse riders, which he was continually tapping against the lacquered polish of his boot uppers. A minute later, with us by then waiting in stationary ranks, I was also able to make out that he was handsome in his fashion, fit, and all in all with something of the movie star about him, given his manly features and narrow brown moustache, fashionably clipped, which went very well with his sun-bronzed face. When he got nearer, a command from the gendarmes snapped us all to attention. All that has stayed with me after that are two almost simultaneous impressions: the stentorian voice of the riding-crop wielder, akin to that of a market stall-keeper, which came as such a shock after his otherwise immaculate appearance that maybe this is why I did not take in much of what he actually said. What I did grasp, however, was that he did not intend to conduct the "investigation"—that was the term he used—into our cases until the next day, upon which he turned toward the gendarmes, ordering them, in a bellow that filled the entire square, to take "the whole Jewish rabble" off to the place that, in his view, they actually belonged—the stables, that is to say—and lock them in for the night. My second impression was the immediately ensuing indecipherable babble of commands, the bellowed orders with which the abruptly reanimated gendarmes herded us away. I didn't even know offhand which way I was supposed to turn, and all I remember is that in the thick of it I felt a bit like laughing, in part out of astonishment and confusion, a sense of having been dropped slap in the middle of some crazy play in which I was not entirely acquainted with my role, in part because of a fleeting thought that just then flashed across my mind, which was my stepmother's face when it finally dawned on her that it would be pointless to count on seeing me for supper this evening.

FOUR

On the train, it was water that was missed most of all. Food supplies, taking everything into account, appeared to be sufficient for a substantial period; but then there was nothing to drink with them, which was disagreeable, that's for sure. Those on the train immediately declared that the initial spasms of thirst soon pass. Eventually we would almost forget about it, after which it would reemerge, only by then it would allow no one to forget it, they explained. The length of time that someone could last out, for all that, should the need arise, taking into account the hot weather and assuming he was healthy, did not lose too much water as sweat, and ate no meat or spicy food, if at all possible, was six or seven days, according to those in the know. As things were, they reassured us, there was still time; it all depended on how long the journey was going to last, they added.

Quite. I too was curious about that; they did not inform us at the brickyard. All they announced was that anyone inclined to do so could present himself for work, specifically in Germany. Just like the rest of the boys and many others in the brickyard, I found that idea immediately attractive. In any case, we were told by the men, identifiable from their armbands as belonging to a body called the "Jewish Council," one way or another, willingly or forcibly, everyone would sooner or later be resettled from the brickyard to Germany, and the better places, not to speak of the concession of being able to travel no more than sixty per carriage, would be granted to those who volunteered first, whereas later at least eighty would have to be fit in, due to the shortage of wagons—the way they laid it all out to everyone did not really leave too much to consider, I had to agree.

Nor was I able to deny the validity of the other arguments, which concerned the shortage of space in the brickyard and its possible sanitary consequences, as well as the growing concern over food supplies: that was how it was, I could attest to all that. By the time we arrived from the gendarmerie (many of the grown-ups had registered that the barracks were called the "Andrássy Gendarme Casern") every cranny of the brickyard had already been filled to overflowing with people. I saw among them both men and women, children of all ages, as well as countless old people of both sexes. Wherever I stepped, I would stumble over blankets, rucksacks, all manner of suitcases, bundles, and other impedimenta. Naturally enough, I too was soon tired of that, not to mention the myriad petty nuisances, annoyances, and vexations that, it appears, are inevitably bound up with communal life of that kind. Contributing further to that was the inaction, the senseless feeling of idleness, not to speak of the boredom; that too is why I don't remember distinctly a single one of the five days that I spent there, and barely even the occasional detail in aggregate, though certainly the relief at having the boys there around me: "Rosie," "Fancyman," "Leatherware," "Smoker," Moskovics, and all the rest. As far as I could tell, not one of them was missing: they too had all been honest. Nor did I personally have that much to do anymore with gendarmes in the brickyard; I saw them more just standing guard on the other side of the fencing, mixed up with the occasional policeman here and there. The latter were in fact later talked about in the brickyard as being more considerate than the gendarmes, readily inclined to be decent, particularly in return for certain negotiated terms, whether in the form of money or any other valuables. Above all, so I heard, many commissioned them to pass on letters and messages; indeed, some insisted opportunities were even open through them—albeit rare and risky, they admitted—for escaping, though it would have been hard for me to know anything really definite about that. But then I recalled, and in doing so also came to a somewhat more precise understanding, I believe, what the seal-faced fellow at the customs post must have been wanting so much to have a word about with the policeman. That is how I realized that our policeman, by contrast, had been honest, which may well have explained how it was that every now and then, while knocking about the yard or waiting for my turn in the area of the communal kitchen, I would spot the seal-faced guy in the melee of unfamiliar faces in the brickworks.

Of the rest of the customs post crowd, I also saw the man with the bad luck again; he often sat around with us "young people," so as "to cheer himself up," as he put it. He too, it seems, must have found a place to camp somewhere close to us, in one of the many identical shingle-roofed but open-sided structures in the yard that had in fact originally served, so I heard, for drying bricks. He looked a bit the worse for wear, with mottled blotches of swelling and bruising on his face. We learned from him that these had all been the outcome of the gendarmes' investigation, since they had come across medicines and food in his knapsack. His attempt to explain it was stuff that had come from older stocks and was intended purely for his very ill mother was useless: they alleged that he was obviously dealing on the black market. Similarly useless was his permit, and equally unavailing the fact that he, for his part, had always held the law in respect, never violating so much as a single letter of it, he related. "Have you heard anything? What's going to happen to us?" he asked regularly. He would again bring up his family, not to speak of his bad luck. How much he had run around after the permit, how delighted he had been to get it, he recalled with a morose head-shaking; he would never have believed the business "would come to this," that was for sure. It had all hinged on those five minutes. If he hadn't had the bad luck . . . If the bus back then had . . .—those were the reflections I heard. He seemed largely content, however, with the beating. "I was left to the last, and that may have been my good fortune," he recounted: "They were in a hurry by then." All in all, he "could have come off worse," was how he summed it up, adding that he had "seen uglier cases" at the gendarmerie, which was no more than the truth, as I too recalled. No one should think, the gendarmes had warned us on the morning of the investigation, that he would be able to conceal his crimes, money, gold, or other valuables from them. When it was my turn, I too had to lay out money, watch, pocketknife, and all my other belongings on a table before them. A stocky gendarme even frisked me, with brisk and what somehow seemed like practiced movements, from my armpits all the way down to the legs of my short trousers. Behind the table I also saw the lieutenant again, for by then it had already transpired from words the gendarmes exchanged with one another that the officer with the riding-crop was actually called Lt. Jackl. Towering next to him, on his left, I also immediately took note of a shirt-sleeved, walrus-moustached gendarme looking like a butcher, who had in his hand a cylindrical implement that basically struck me as being a bit of a joke, somewhat reminding me as it did of a cook's rolling pin. The lieutenant was pretty friendly, asking me if I had any documents, though I saw not the slightest sign, not even the slightest glimmer, of my papers then producing any impression on him. That surprised me, but—most particularly in light of an abrupt gesture of dismissal from the walrus-moustached gendarme, with its unmistakable implicit assurance of the alternative—I considered it more prudent, it stands to reason, not to raise any objections.

After that, the gendarmes had led us all out of the barracks and, first of all, crammed us into the carriages of a special local train service then, at some spot on the banks of the Danube, transferred us onto a ship and finally, after that had berthed, took us a farther stretch on foot, which was how I had got to the brickyard—the "Budakalász Brick Works" to be more specific, as I was to learn there, on the spot.

There were plenty of other things that I also heard about the journey on the afternoon we had to register. The men with armbands were omnipresent, ready to answer any questions. They were primarily on the lookout for youngsters, the venturesome and those who were on their own, though they were assuring inquirers, as I heard, that there would also be room for women, infants, and the elderly, and they would also be able to bring along all their luggage. In their opinion, however, the cardinal issue was were we going to sort the matter out among ourselves, and thus with all possible humanity, or would we rather wait for the gendarmes to make the decision for us? As they explained, the consignment would have to be made up one way or another, and insofar as their lists fell short, the gendarmes would make up the enrollment from among us; so most people, myself included, saw it as obvious that we might do better for ourselves, naturally enough, the first way.

A great diversity of views about the Germans also came to my attention right away. Many people, particularly the older ones with experience to look back on, professed that whatever ideas they might hold about Jews, the Germans were fundamentally, as everybody knew, tidy, honest, industrious people with a fondness for order and punctuality who appreciated the same traits in others, which did indeed, by and large, roughly correspond with what I myself know about them, and it occurred to me that no doubt I might also derive some benefit from having acquired some fluency in their language at grammar school. What I could look forward to from working, though, was above all orderliness, employment, new impressions, and a bit of fun—all in all, a more sensible lifestyle more to my liking than the one here in Hungary, just as was being promised and as we boys, quite naturally, pictured it when we talked among ourselves, though alongside that it crossed my mind that this might also be a way of getting to see a bit of the world. To tell the truth, when I reflected on some of the events of recent days, such as the gendarmes and, most of all, on my ID, and on justice in general, then even patriotism, when it came time to examine that emotion, did not offer much to hold me back.

Then there were the more skeptical types who were differently informed, claiming to be acquainted with other sides of the German character; still others who asked them, in that case, what better suggestion they had; and yet others again who, instead of that kind of bickering, came out in favor of the voice of reason, of showing by example, of being seen as worthy in the eyes of the authorities—all of which arguments and counterarguments, along with a whole lot of other bits of news, information, and counsel, were debated inexhaustibly by knots of people, small and large, incessantly breaking up and re-forming all around me in the yard. I even heard mention of God, among other things, and "His inscrutable will," as one person expressed it. Like Uncle Lajos had done once, he too spoke about fate, the fate of the Jews, and he too, like Uncle Lajos, considered that "we have abandoned the Lord," and that explained the tribulations that were being inflicted upon us. He aroused my interest a little bit all the same, because he was a man of vigorous presence and physique, with a somewhat unusual face, characterized by a thin but sweepingly curved nose, a very bright, misty-eyed gaze, and a fine, grizzled moustache that merged into a short, rounded beard. A lot of people were standing around him and curious about what he had to say, I could see. Only then did I become aware that he was a priest, because I heard him being addressed as "rabbi." I even registered one or two of the more unusual words or expressions he used, such as the point where he admitted that, "through the eye that sees and the heart that feels," he was bound to concede that "we here on Earth might, perhaps, dispute the severity of the sentence"—and here his voice, otherwise so clear and far-carrying, faltered and broke down for a minute, while his eyes became somehow even more misted over than usual, at which point, I don't know why, I had the odd feeling he had actually been preparing to say something else and in some way he might have been a little bit surprised himself by those words. Still, he carried on, "he did not wish to delude himself," he confessed. He was well aware, for it was enough to look around "this atrocious place and these tormented faces"—that was how he put it, and his compassion rather took me aback, since he himself was in exactly the same situation, after all—to realize how difficult a task he had. Yet it was not his goal, because there was no need, "to win souls for the Eternal Father," for all of our souls were from Him, he said. He urged us all: "Don't live in strife with the Lord!"—and not even primarily because it was sinful to do so, but because that path would lead "to denial of the sub-

65

lime meaning of life"; in his opinion, however, we could not live "with that denial in our hearts." A heart like that might be at ease, but only because it was empty, like the barrenness of the desert, he said; hard though it might be, the sole path to consolation, even in the midst of tribulation, was to glimpse the infinite wisdom of the Eternal Father, because, as he continued, word for word: "His moment of victory will come, and those who have been unmindful of His power shall be repentant and shall call out to Him from the dust." If, therefore, he were now to say that we must believe in the advent of His ultimate mercy ("and may that belief be our succor and unfailing source of strength in this hour of afflictions"), then he was at the same time pointing out the sole manner in which it was possible for us to live at all. And he called that manner "the denial of denial," since without hope "we are lost"; on the other hand, hope was to be derived from faith alone, from an unbroken assurance that the Lord would take pity on us, and that we should be able to gain his mercy. The reasoning, I had to acknowledge, seemed clear, though I did notice that he failed to say, at the end of it all, anything more precise about how we might actually achieve this; nor was he truly able to supply any good advice to those who were pressing him for an opinion on whether they should register for the journey now, or rather stay. I saw the man with the bad luck there too, on several occasions, bobbing up first with one group, then with another. Still, I noticed that while he was doing this the restless gaze of his beady, slightly bloodshot eyes was in constant motion, tirelessly darting on to other groups and other people. Every now and then, I also heard his voice as he stopped people, his face tensely inquisitive, wringing and fumbling with his hands while he was at it, to inquire: "excuse me, but are you also going to make the trip?" and "why?" and "do you think that will be better, if you don't mind my asking?"

Right then, I recall, another familiar figure from the customs post also showed up: the "Expert." I had already caught sight of him more than once during the days at the brickyard. Though his suit was by now crumpled, his necktie had vanished, and his face was covered in a gray stubble, on the whole, even so, all the indisputable signs of his former distinguished bearing were still apparent. His arrival immediately attracted attention, as a whole ring of excited people gathered round, and he was almost overwhelmed by the myriad questions with which they besieged him. As I soon gathered, he had been given the chance to speak directly with a German officer. The incident had taken place up front, in the area of the offices of the commander, the gendarmes, and other investigating authorities, where during the days here I too had noticed, every now and then, the hurried popping up or vanishing of one or another German uniform. Prior to that, as I managed to hear, he had also had a go at the gendarmes, trying, as he put it, "to get in touch with his firm." We learned, however, that the gendarmes were "continually denying" him that right, even though "it concerns a defense company" and "management of production was inconceivable without him," which the authorities themselves had acknowledged, though at the gendarmerie they had "expropriated" the document stating this, like everything else—all of which I was only just about able to follow, because he related it in dribs and drabs, in response to the hail of cross-questioning. He appeared to be extremely irate, but he remarked that he did "not want to go into the matter in detail." That, though, was precisely why he had approached the German officer. The officer had been just about to leave. Quite by chance, we learned, the "Expert" happened to be close by at the time. "I stepped up to him," he said. There were, in fact, several present who had been witnesses to the event, and they remarked on his audacity. With a shrug of the shoulders, he responded by saying that nothing ventured, nothing gained, and anyway he had wished to speak "to someone in authority at last." "I am an engineer," he went on, "with perfect German," he added. He had related all this to the German officer as well, telling him how "his work here had been made impossible, both in point of moral principle and in practice," and what was more, in his own words, "without any cause or legal foundation, even under the currently prevailing regulations." "But who profits from that?" he had asked the German officer. He told him, just as he was now telling us: "I am not seeking any advantages or privileges. Nevertheless, I am a somebody, and I know a thing or two; I simply want to work, in accordance with my capabilities—that's all I'm after." The advice he had then received from the officer was to sign on as one of the volunteers. He had not made any "grand promises," he said, but assured him that in its present endeavors Germany had need of everyone, especially the expertise of trained people like himself. For that reason, we were informed by him, for the officer's "objectivity," he felt that what had been said was "fair and realistic"—that was how he characterized it. He even made particular mention of the officer's "manner": in contrast to the "coarseness" of the gendarmes, he described it as "sober, measured, impeccable in every respect." In response to another question, he also conceded that "naturally there is no other guarantee" than the impression he had formed of this officer; he noted, however, that he would have to make do with that for the moment, but he did not think he was mistaken. "Assuming I am not a bad judge of human character," he added, though in such a manner that, at least as far as I was concerned, one was left feeling the likelihood of that being the case was, indeed, rather remote.

After he had departed, what should I see but, hey presto, the man with the bad luck spring like a jack-in-the-box out of the remaining group and hare off at an angle after him, or rather to cut him off. It even struck me, from the visible agitation and a kind of resolve on his face: well now, this time he's going to speak to him, not like at the customs post. In his haste, though, he stumbled into one of the armbanded types, a burly, gangling fellow bearing a list and pencil who just happened to be heading that way. That stopped him in his tracks; he recoiled in surprise, looked him up and down, then leaned forward and asked something, but I don't know what happened after that because right then "Rosie" called across: it was our turn.

All I remember next is that by the time I was making my way back toward our quarters with the boys on that last day it was a notably tranquil summer evening, the sky ruddy over the hills. On the far side, over toward the river and above the wooden fencing, I could see the roofs of the green carriages of the local suburban train as it sped by; I was tired and also, very naturally after the registration process, a little bit curious. The other boys likewise seemed, on the whole, satisfied. The man with the bad luck had also somehow managed to slip in among us, telling us, with a sort of solemn, though at the same time somehow inquisitive expression, that he too was now on the list. We approved, which, as far as I could tell, went down well, but then I did not listen much to what he said after that. The brickyard was quieter back here, toward the rear. Though here too I could still see smaller groups conferring with one another, others were already preparing for the night or eating supper, keeping an eye on their baggage, or simply sitting around just so, mutely, in the evening air. We came up to a married couple. I had seen them plenty of times and knew them well by sight: the petite, frail wife with her delicate features and the gaunt, bespectacled husband with a few teeth missing here and there, ever on the move and at the ready, a film of perspiration constantly on his brow. He was very busy right then as well, squatting on the ground and, with the wife's sedulous assistance, feverishly gathering their bags and strapping all the items together, seemingly preoccupied with this task to the exclusion of all else. The fellow with the bad luck, though, came to a halt behind him, and it looked as if he too must have recognized him, because a minute later he asked if that meant they too had decided in favor of traveling. Even at this, the husband only cast a quick glance behind and up at him, squinting from behind his spectacles, sweaty, his drawn face troubled in the evening light, and merely offered a single astonished question as a rejoinder: "We have to, don't we?" Simple as it was, I felt that this observation, in the end, was no more than the truth.

The next day we were sent on our way early in the morning. The train set off in brilliant summer weather from the platform of the local branchline, in front of the gates—a sort of freight train made up solely of brick red, covered boxcars with locked doors. Inside were the sixty of us, our luggage, and a consignment of food for the journey given by the men in armbands: piles of bread and large cans of meat—stuff of real rarity, looked at from the perspective of the brickyard, I had to admit. But then ever since the previous day I had been able to experience the attentiveness, the signal favor and, I might say, almost a certain degree of respect that had generally enveloped those of us who were making the journey, and this abundance too, so I sensed, might perhaps have been a form of reward, as it were. The gendarmes were there as well, with their rifles, surly, buttoned up to the chin, looking somehow as if they were watching over enticing goods but weren't really supposed to touch them—no doubt, it crossed my mind, on account of an authority even mightier than them: the Germans. The sliding door was closed on us, with something being hammered onto it on the outside, then there was some signaling, a whistle, busy railwaymen, a lurch, and—we were off. We boys made ourselves comfortable in the rear third of the wagon, which we took over as soon as we boarded. It had a single windowlike aperture on each side, placed fairly high up and carefully covered with tangles of barbed wire. It was not long before the matter of water and, along with that, the duration of the journey was raised in our wagon.

Other than that, there is not much I can say about the journey as a whole. Just as before, at the customs post, or more recently at the brickyard, we had to find ways of somehow passing the time. Naturally, here that was, perhaps, made all the more difficult by the circumstances. On the other hand, the consciousness of a goal, the thought that every completed section of the journey, slow and tiresome as it might be, what with all the bumping, shunting, and stop-pages, was in the end bringing us closer—that helped one through the troubles and difficulties. We boys did not lose patience either. "Rosie" kept on reassuring us that the trip would last only until we got there. "Fancyman" was ragged a lot over a girl—here with her parents, the boys reckoned—whose acquaintance he had made in the brickyard and for whose sake he often vanished, especially to start with, into the depths of the wagon, with all sorts of rumors about this circulating among the others. Then there was "Smoker"; even here some sort of dubious, crumbling twist of tobacco, a scrap of paper of some sort, and a match would emerge from his pocket, and he would bend his face to the flame, sometimes even during the night, with all the avidity of a bird of prey. The occasional cheerful word or remark was to be heard, even on the third day, from Moskovics (incessant streams of sweat and grime trickling from his brow—as they did on all of us, myself included, it goes without saying—to run down his spectacles, his snub nose, and his thick lips) and from all the others, as well as the odd flat joke, albeit with a stutter, from "Leatherware." One of the adults even managed, I don't know how, to discover that the destination of our journey was, more specifically, a place by the name of "Waldsee," and whenever I was thirsty or it was hot, the implicit promise held by that name in itself promptly gave a degree of relief. For those who complained about the lack of space there were plenty who reminded them, quite rightly, to remember that the next time there would be eighty of them. And basically, if I thought about it, when all was said and done, there had been times when I was more tightly packed: in the gendarmerie stable, for instance, where the only way we had been able to resolve the problem of fitting ourselves in was by agreeing that we should all squat cross-legged on the ground. My seat on the train was more comfortable than that. If I wanted, I could even stand up, indeed take a step or two—over toward the slop bucket, for example, since that was situated in the rear right-hand corner of the wagon. What we initially decided about that was to use it as far as possible only for purposes of taking a leak; but as time passed, entirely predictably of course, it was forcibly brought home to many of us that the demands of nature were more powerful than any vow, and we boys acted accordingly, just like the men, to say nothing of the women.

The gendarme did not, in the end, cause too much unpleasantness either. The first time, he startled me a bit, his face popping up at the window opening on the left, just above my head and shining his flashlight in among us on the evening of the first day, or rather the night by then, during what was one of our longer halts. It soon became clear that he had been impelled by good intentions, coming merely to impart the news: "Folks, you have reached the Hungarian frontier!" He wished to take the opportunity to address an appeal, a request one might say, to us. His behest was that insofar as there were any monies or other valuables still left on any of us, we should hand them over to him. "Where you're going," so he reckoned, "you won't be needing valuables anymore." Anything that we might still have the Germans would take off us anyway, he assured us. "Wouldn't it be better, then," he carried on, up above in the window slot, "for them to pass into Hungarian hands?" After a brief pause that struck me as somehow solemn, he then suddenly added, in a voice that switched to a more fervent, highly confidential tone which somehow offered to forgive and forget all bygones: "After all, you're Hungarians too when it comes down to it!" After a flurry of whispering and consultation, a voice, a deep male voice from somewhere in the wagon, acknowledged the force of this argument, provided we could get some water from the gendarme in exchange, to which the latter seemed amenable, despite its being "against orders," as he noted. Even so, they were unable to reach agreement as the voice wished to be given the water first, but the gendarme said it had to be the articles, and neither would budge from his own sequence. In the end, the gendarme took great umbrage, snapping: "Stinking Jews! You make a business out of the holiest of matters!" In a voice nearly choking with indignation and loathing, he threw this wish at us: "Die of thirst, then." That did indeed come to pass later on—that at least was what they said in our wagon. There is no denying that, from about the afternoon of the second day on, I too was constantly subjected to a particular voice coming from the wagon behind us: not exactly pleasant. The old woman, so they said in our wagon, was ill and had presumably gone mad, undoubtedly from thirst. That explanation seemed credible. Only now did I realize how right were those who had declared at the very start of the journey how fortunate it was that neither small infants nor the extremely elderly had landed up in our wagon. The old woman finally fell silent on the morning of the third day. Among our lot, it was said at the time that she had died because she could get no water. But then, we were aware that she was also sick and old, which is how everyone, including me, found the case understandable, all things considered.

I am in a position to declare that waiting does not predispose to joy—that at least was my experience when we did indeed finally arrive. It may have been that I was tired, then again perhaps the very keenness with which I had been looking forward to the destination ended up making me forget that thought to some degree, but it was more that I was left somehow indifferent. I slightly let the entire event slip by. What I remember is that I awoke suddenly, presumably at the demented shrieking of nearby sirens; the faint light that was filtering in from outside signaled the dawn of the fourth day. The base of my spine, where it had been in contact with the wagon floor, ached a little. The train was idling, as it had often done at other times, invariably so during air raids. The window spaces were taken up, as they always were at this time. Everyone was claiming to see something—that too is how it was nowadays. After a while, I myself managed to get a place: I could see nothing. The dawn outside was cool and fragrant, with wraiths of gray mist lying on wide stretches of meadow, from somewhere behind which, a bit later, a sharp, thin, red shaft of light appeared unexpectedly, like a trumpet blast, and I grasped that I was looking at the sunrise. It was pretty and, on the whole, intriguing: back home, I was usually still asleep at this time. I also glimpsed, directly in front and to the left, some building, a godforsaken railway halt or possibly the signal box for some larger terminal. It was minuscule, gray, and, as yet, completely deserted, its small windows closed and with one of those ridiculously steep-pitched roofs that I had already seen in this region yesterday: it first solidified before my eyes into its true contours, then mutated from gray to mauve, and at that moment its windows also gleamed ruddily as the first rays of sunlight struck them. Others also spotted this, and I too gave a commentary to the inquisitive crowd behind me. They asked if I could see a place-name on it. In the strengthening light, on the narrower gable end of the building, facing the direction in which we were traveling, on the surface below the roof, I could in fact make out two words: "Auschwitz-Birkenau" was what I read, written in spiky, curlicued Gothic lettering, joined by one of those wavy double hyphens of theirs. For my own part, though, I cast around my geographical knowledge in vain, and others proved no wiser than me. I then sat down because others behind me were already asking to have my place, and since it was still early and I was sleepy, I quickly dropped off again.

The next thing, I was wakened by a bustling and flurry of excitement. Outside, the sun was by now blazing in full brilliance. The train was again in motion as well. I asked the boys where we were, and they said we were still in the same place but had just now begun to move on; this time, it seems, the lurch must have awoken me. There was no question however, they added, that factories and settlements of sorts could be seen up ahead. A minute later, those who were at the window reported, and I myself also noticed from a fleeting change in the light, that we had slipped under the arch of some form of gateway. After a further minute had passed, the train came to a halt, at which they informed us in great excitement that they could see a station, soldiers, and people. At this, many started to gather their things together or button up their clothes, while some, women especially, hastily freshened up, smartened themselves, combed their hair. From outside I heard an approaching banging, a clattering-back of doors, the commingling hubbub of passengers swarming from the train; I had to concede there could be no doubt about it, we were indeed at our destination. I was glad, very naturally, though in a different way, I sensed, than I would have been glad yesterday, say, or still more the day before that. Then a tool snapped on the door of our wagon, and somebody, or rather several somebodies, rolled the heavy door aside.

I heard their voices first. They spoke German, or some language very close to that, and from the way it sounded, all at once. As far as I could make out, they wanted us to get off. Instead, though, it seemed they were pushing their way up among us; I could still see nothing as yet. The news was already going around, however, that suitcases and baggage were to be left here. Everyone, needless to say, so it was explained, translated, and passed on from mouth to mouth around me, would get their belongings back later, but first disinfection awaited all articles and a bath for us—and none too soon, I considered. They then got closer to me in the hurly-burly, and I finally got my first glimpse of the people here. It was quite a shock, for after all, this was the first time in my life that I had seen, up close at any rate, real convicts, in the striped duds of criminals, and with shaven skulls in round caps. Naturally enough, I immediately recoiled from them a bit. Some were answering people's questions, others were taking a look around in the wagon, yet others were already starting to unload the luggage with the practiced skill of porters, and all with a strange, foxlike alacrity. On the chest of each one, apart from the customary convict's number, I also saw a yellow triangle, and although it was naturally not too hard to work out what that color denoted, it still somehow caught my eye; during the journey I had, in a way, all but forgotten about that entire business. Their faces did not exactly inspire confidence either: jug ears, prominent noses, sunken, beady eyes with a crafty gleam. Quite like Jews in every respect. I found them suspect and altogether foreign-looking. When they spotted us boys, I noticed, they became quite agitated. They immediately launched into a hurried, somehow frantic whispering, which was when I made the surprising discovery that Jews evidently don't only speak Hebrew, as I had supposed up till now: "*Rayds di yiddish, rayds di yiddish, rayds di yiddish?*"[1] was what they were asking, as I gradually made out. "*Nein,*" we told them, the boys and me too. I could see they weren't too happy about that. Then suddenly—on the basis of my German, I found it easy to figure out—they all started to get very curious about our ages. We told them, "*Vierzehn*" or "*Fünfzehn,*" depending on how old each of us was. They immediately raised huge protestations, with hands, heads, their entire bodies: "*Zestsayn!*" they muttered left, right, and center, "*zestsayn.*" I was surprised, and even asked one of them:

---

[1] "Do you speak Yiddish?"

"Warum?" "Willst di arbeiten?"—Did I want to work, he asked, the somehow blank stare of his deep-set, drawn eyes boring into mine. *"Natürlich,"* I told him, since that was after all my reason for coming, if I thought about it. At this, he not only grabbed me by the arm with a tough, bony, yellow hand but gave it a good shake, saying then in that case *"Zestsayn! . . . vershtayst di? Zestsayn!"* I could see he was exasperated, on top of which the thing, as I saw it, was evidently very important for him, and since we boys had by then swiftly conferred on this, I somewhat cheerfully agreed: all right, I'll be sixteen, then. Furthermore, whatever might be said and quite irrespective of whether it was true or not, there were also to be no brothers, and particularly—to my great amazement—no twins; above all, though, *"jeder arbeiten, nist kai mide, nist kai krenk"*[2]—that was about the only other thing I learned from them during the possibly not quite two whole minutes it took as I moved in the crush from my place to the door, finally to take a big leap out into the sunlight and fresh air.

The first thing I noticed was a vast expanse of what looked like flat terrain. I was immediately a little blinded by the sudden spaciousness, the uniformly white, eye-stabbing brilliance of the sky and the plain. I did not have much time to look around, though, what with the bustling and teeming, the cries, tiny incidents, and sorting-out going on all around me. We would now, I heard, have to separate from the women for a short while, for after all we could not bathe together with them under the same roof; however, there were

---

[2]"Everyone work, no being tired, no being sick!"

motor vehicles waiting a bit farther away for the elderly, the weak, mothers with infants, and those who had been exhausted by the journey. We were given to understand all this by a new set of prisoners, though I noticed that out here there were now German soldiers, in green forage caps and with green collars on their tunics, who were keeping an eye on everything and making eloquent hand gestures to indicate directions; I was even a bit relieved to see them, since they struck me as smart and trim, the sole anchors of solidity and calm in the whole tumult. I immediately heard, and moreover agreed with, the exhortation from many of the adults among us that we should try to do our bit by cutting questions and good-byes short, within reason, so as not to give the Germans the impression of such a rabble. As to what followed, it would be hard to recount: I was caught up and swept along by a damply seething, swirling tide. A woman's voice behind me kept on squawking about a certain "small bag" that she was letting someone know had stayed with her. An old, disheveled-looking woman kept getting in the way in front of me, and I heard a short young man explaining: "Do what you're told, Mama, we'll be meeting up again before long anyway. *Nicht wahr, Herr Offizier?*"[3] turning, with a knowing and, in a way, somewhat grown-up conspiratorial smile toward the German soldier who happened to be giving orders right there, "*wir werden uns bald wieder . . .*" But my attention was already being taken up by a hideous squealing from a grubby, curly-haired little boy, dressed up a bit like a shopwindow dummy, as he tried with

---

[3]"Isn't that so, officer?"

peculiar jerks and wriggles to free himself from the grasp of a blonde woman, evidently his mother. "I want to go with Daddy! I want to go with Daddy!" he screamed, bellowed, and howled, stamping and drumming his feet, incongruously shod as they were in white shoes, on the white gravel and white dust. In the meantime I was also attempting to keep up with the boys, following the intermittent calls and signals that "Rosie" was giving, while a stout matron in a sleeveless, floral-patterned summer dress forged a path through everybody, myself included, in the direction where they had pointed out the vehicles were. After that, a tiny old man with a black hat and black necktie bobbed, twisted, and jostled around for a while, looking anxiously this way and that and shouting out, "Nellie! Nellie!" Then a tall, sharp-featured man and a woman with long, black hair clung to one another, faces, lips, their entire bodies locked together, causing everyone a flash of irritation, until the ceaseless buffetings of the human tide finally detached the woman, or rather girl, carrying her away and swallowing her up, though even as she receded I saw her a few times more, struggling to remain in view and waving a sweeping farewell from where she was.

All these images, voices, and incidents in this maelstrom flustered me and made my head swim slightly, jumbling them into what was ultimately a single, strange, colorful, and, I might almost say, crazy impression; that was one reason why I was less successful in being able to keep track of other, possibly more important things. I would find it hard to say, for instance, whether it was as a result of our own efforts or those of the soldiers or the prisoners, or all together, that in the end one long column was formed around me, now made up solely of men, all in regularly ordered ranks of five, which moved forward in step with me, slowly but at last steadily. Up ahead, it was again confirmed, was a bath, but first, I learned, a medical inspection was awaiting all of us. It was mentioned, though naturally I did not find it hard to appreciate, that this was obviously a matter of grading, of screening for suitability for work.

That gave me a chance to catch my breath until then. Along with the other boys beside, in front of, and behind me, we shouted across and signaled to one another that we were still here. It was hot. I was also able to take a look around me and orient myself a little as to where, in fact, we were. The station was smart. Under our feet was the usual crushed-stone covering of such places, a bit farther off a strip of turf in which yellow flowers were planted, and an immaculate white asphalt road running as far as the eye could see. I also noticed that this road was separated from the entire vast area that began behind it by a row of identically recurved posts, between which ran strands of metallically glinting barbed wire. It was easy to work out that over there, clearly, must be where the convicts lived. Maybe because this was the first chance I had to spare the time for it, they now began to intrigue me for the first time, and I would have been curious to know what offenses they had committed.

The scale, the full extent of the plain, also astounded me as I looked around. Yet, what with being among all those people and also in that blinding light, I was not really able to gain a truly accurate picture; I could hardly even discern the distant low-lying buildings of some sort, a scattering of raised platforms here and there that looked like game-shooting hides, a corner, a tower, a chimney. The boys and adults around me were also pointing at something up there, lodged in the milky vapors of a sky that, though cloudless, was nevertheless almost bleached of color, an immobile, elongated, severely gleaming body—a dirigible, to be sure. The explanations of those around generally agreed on its being a barrage balloon, at which point I recalled that dawn siren wail. Still, I could see no sign of concern or fear on the features of the German soldiers around us here. I remembered the air raids at home, and now this air of scornful composure and invulnerability all at once made the kind of respect with which the Germans were normally spoken of back there more clearly comprehensible to me. Only now did two forked lines on their collars catch my eye. From that I was able to establish that this must mean they belonged to that celebrated formation of the SS about which I had already heard so much at home. I have to say they did not strike me as the slightest bit intimidating: they were ambling up and down in leisurely fashion, patrolling the entire length of the column, answering questions, nodding, even cordially patting some of us on the back or shoulder.

There is one other thing I noticed during these idle minutes of waiting. I had already seen German soldiers often enough in Hungary, naturally. On those occasions, however, they had always been hurrying, always with uncommunicative, preoccupied expressions, always in immaculate dress. Here and now, though, they were somehow moving in a different manner, more casually and in a way—so I observed— more at home. I was even able to detect some minor disparities: caps, boots, and uniforms that were softer or stiffer, shinier or merely, as it were, workaday. Each had at his side a weapon, which is only natural, of course, when it comes down to it, given that they were soldiers, yet I saw many also had a stick in their hand, like a regular hooked cane, which slightly surprised me, since they were, after all, men without any problems walking, and manifestly in prime condition. But then I was able to take a closer look at the object, for I observed that one of them, up ahead with his back half-turned toward me, all at once placed the stick horizontally behind his hips and, gripping it at both ends, began flexing it with apparent boredom. Along with the row, I came ever-closer to him, and only then did I see that it was not made of wood but of leather, and was no stick but a whip. That was a bit of an odd feeling, but then I did not see any instance of them having recourse to it, and after all there were also lots of convicts around, I realized.

Meanwhile I heard but barely paid heed to calls being made for those with relevant experience—one, I recollect, for mechanical fitters—to step forward, while others were for twins, the physically disabled, indeed—amid a degree of merriment—even any dwarfs who might be among us. Later it was children they were after, because, it was rumored, they could expect special treatment, study instead of work, and all sorts of favors. Several adults even urged us to line up, not to pass up the opportunity, but I was still mindful of the warning that had been given by the prisoners on the train, and anyway I was more inclined to work, naturally, rather than lead a child's life.

While all that had been going on, though, we had moved a fair bit farther forward. I noticed that the numbers of soldiers and prisoners around us had, all of a sudden, multiplied considerably. At one point, our row of five transformed into a single file. At the same time we were called on to remove our jacket and shirt so as to present ourselves to the doctor stripped to the waist. The pace, I sensed, was also quickening. At the same time, I spotted two separate groupings up ahead. A larger one, a highly diverse bunch, was gathering over on the right, and a second, smaller, somehow more appealing, in which moreover I could see several boys from our group were already standing, over on the left. The latter instantly appeared, to my eyes at least, to be made up of the fit ones. Meanwhile, and at gathering speed, I was heading directly toward what, in the confusion of the many figures in motion, coming and going, was now a fixed point, where I fancied I could see an immaculate uniform with one of those high-peaked German officer's caps, after which the only surprise was how swiftly it was my turn.

The inspection itself can only have required roughly around two or three seconds. Moskovics just in front of me was next, but for him the doctor instantly extended a finger in the other direction. I even heard him trying to explain: "*Arbeiten . . . Sechzehn . . . ,*" but a hand reached out for him from somewhere, and I was already stepping up into his place. The doctor, I could see, took a closer look at me with a studied, serious, and attentive glance. I too straightened my back to show him my chest, even, as I recall, gave a bit of a smile, coming right after Moskovics as I was. I immediately felt a sense of trust in the doctor, since he cut a very fine figure, with sympathetic, longish, shaven features, rather narrow lips, and kind-looking blue or gray—at any rate pale—eyes. I was able to get a good look at him while he, resting his gloved hands on my cheeks, pried my lower eyelids down a bit on both sides with his thumbs in an action I was familiar with from doctors back home. As he was doing that, in a quiet yet very distinct tone that revealed him to be a cultured man, he asked, though almost as if it were of secondary importance, "*Wie alt bist du?*" "*Sechszehn*,"[4] I told him. He nodded perfunctorily, but somehow more at this being the appropriate response, so to speak, rather than the truth—at least that was my impression offhand. Another thing I noticed, though it was more just a fleeting observation and perhaps mistaken at that, but it was as if he somehow seemed satisfied, almost relieved in a way; I sensed that he must have taken a shine to me. Then, still pushing against my cheek with one hand while indicating the direction with the other, he dispatched me to the far side of the path, to the fit group. The boys were waiting there, exultant, chortling gleefully. At the sight of those beaming faces, I also understood, perhaps, what it was that actually distinguished our group from the bunch across on the opposite side: it was success, if I sensed it correctly.

So I then pulled on my shirt, exchanged a few words with the others, and again waited. From here I now watched the entire business that was proceeding on the other side of the road from a new perspective. The flood of people rolled along in an unbroken stream, was constrained in a narrower channel, accelerated, then branched in two in front of the doctor. Other boys also arrived, one after the next, and now I too was able to join in the greeting they received, naturally. I caught a glimpse of another column farther away: the women. There too they were surrounded by soldiers and prisoners, there too

---

[4]"How old are you?" "Sixteen."

was a doctor before them, and there too everything was proceeding in exactly the same way, except that they did not have to strip off their upper garments, which was understandable, of course, if I thought about it. Everything was in motion, everything functioning, everyone in their place and doing what they had to do, precisely, cheerfully, in a well-oiled fashion. I saw smiles on many of the faces, timid or more self-confident, some with no doubts and some already with an inkling of the outcome in advance, yet still essentially all uniform, roughly the same as the one I had sensed in myself just before. It was the same smile with which what, from here, looked to be a very pretty, brown-skinned woman with rings in her ears, clutching her white raincoat to her chest, turned to ask a soldier a question, and smiled in the same way as a handsome, dark-haired man stepping up right then in front of the nearer doctor: he was fit. I soon figured out the essence of the doctor's job. An old man would have his turn—obvious, that one: the other side. A younger man—over here, to our side. Here's another one: paunchy but shoulders pulled stiffly back nonetheless—pointless, but no, the doctor still dispatched him this way, which I was not entirely happy about as I, for my part, was disposed to find him a shade elderly. I also could not help noting that the vast majority of the men were all terribly unshaven, which did not exactly make too good an impression. Thus, I was also driven to perceive through the doctor's eyes how many old or otherwise unusable people there were among them. One was too thin, the other too fat, while yet another I judged, on the basis of an eye tic and the way his mouth and nose twitched incessantly rather in the manner of a sniffing rabbit, to be some kind of nervous case, yet he too dutifully gave a wholehearted smile even as he diligently hurried over, with an oddly waddling gait, to join the unfit group. Yet another—already clutching his jacket and shirt, his suspenders dangling on his thighs, the skin on his arms and chest flabby, to the point of wobbling here and there. On coming before the doctor, who instantly indicated his place among the unfit, naturally, a certain expression on the shabbily bearded face, a sort of smile on the parched, chapped lips, identical though it may have been, was nevertheless more familiar, ringing a distant bell in my memory: as if there were still something he wished to say to the doctor, or so it seemed. Only the latter was no longer paying attention to him but to the next one, at which point a hand—presumably the same one as with Moskovics before—now yanked him out of the way. He made a move and turned around, an astonished and indignant expression on his face—that was it! The "Expert"; I hadn't been mistaken.

We waited around for another few minutes. There were still a great many people in front of the doctor, while there must have been something like forty of us, approximately, in our bunch here, boys and men, I estimated, when the word came: we were setting off for a bath. A soldier stepped up to us (on the spur of the moment, I couldn't see from where), a short, placid-looking man, getting on a bit in years, with a big rifle—I took him for a common soldier of some kind. "*Los, ge' ma' vorne!*"[5] he announced, or something like that, not quite in accordance with what books of grammar taught, I ascertained. However that may be, it was music to my ears, since the boys and I were by now just a bit impa-

---

[5]"Right, move it!"

tient, though not so much for the soap, to tell the truth, as, above anything else, for the water, of course. The road led through a gate of woven barbed wire to somewhere farther inside the area behind the fence where, it appeared, the bathhouse must be: we set off along it in slack clusters, not hurrying but chatting and looking around, with the soldier, not saying a word, listlessly bringing up the rear. Under our feet there was again a broad, immaculately white, metaled road, while in front of us was the whole rather tiring prospect of flat terrain in air that all around was by now shimmering and undulating in the heat. I was even anxious about its being too far, but as it transpired the bathhouse was located only about ten minutes away. From what I saw of the area on this short walk, on the whole it too won my approval. A football pitch, on a big clearing immediately to the right of the road, was particularly welcome. Green turf, the requisite white goalposts, the chalked lines of the field of play—it was all there, inviting, fresh, pristine, in perfect order. This was latched onto straightaway by the boys as well: Look here! A place for us to play soccer after work. Even greater cause for joy came a few paces later when, on the left-hand border of the road, we spotted—no doubt about it—a water faucet, one of those roadside standpipes. A sign in red letters next to it attempted to warn against it: "*Kein Trinkwasser,*"[6] but right then that could do little to hold any of us back. The soldier was quite patient, and I can tell you it had been a long time since water went down so well, even if it did leave a peculiar stinging and a nauseating aftertaste of some

---

[6]"Not for drinking."

chemical in my mouth. Going farther, we also saw some houses, the same ones that I had already noticed from the station. Even close up, they were oddly shaped buildings indeed, long, flat, and of an indeterminable shade, with some sort of apparatus for ventilation or lighting protruding from the roof along the entire length. Each one had a little garden path of red gravel running round it, each one a well-tended patch of lawn to separate it from the metaled road, and between them, to my delighted wonder, I saw small seedbeds and cabbage patches, with flowers of assorted colors being grown in the plots. It was all very clean, tidy, and pretty—truly, I had to reflect, we had made the right choice back in the brickyard. Just one thing was rather missing, I realized: the fact that I saw no sign of movement, of life, around them. But then it occurred to me that this must be only natural, since it was, after all, during working hours for the inhabitants.

At the bathhouse too (which we reached after a left turn, a farther barbed-wire fence, and again a barbed-wire gate into a yard), I could see they were already set to receive us, happily explaining everything to us well in advance. We went first of all into some sort of stone-flagged anteroom. Inside there were already a great many people whom I was able to recognize as coming from our train. From that I gathered that the work here too was presumably pushing ahead unremittingly, with people being continuously brought in groups from the station to bathe, it would appear. Here too a prisoner was again of assistance, an exceedingly fastidious convict, I could not help noticing. He too wore a striped outfit like other prisoners, that was true, but it had padded shoulders and was tapered at the waist, tailored and pressed, I would even say, in almost conspicuous conformity with the highest fashion, and just like us, free persons, he had a full head of carefully combed, darkly glossy hair. In greeting us, he stood at the opposite end of the room, and to his right, seated behind a small desk, was a soldier. The latter was very squat, of jovial appearance, and exceedingly fat, his belly beginning at his neck, his chin rippling in a circle over his collar, and no more than funny slits for eyes in his crumpled, hairless, sallow features; he put me a little in mind of those so-called dwarfs whom they had been looking for at the station. Nevertheless, he had an imposing cap on his head, a gleaming, evidently brand-new attaché case on the desk, and next to it what I had to admit was a beautifully crafted lash, braided from white leather, that was obviously his personal property. I was able to observe all this at leisure through gaps between the many heads and pairs of shoulders while we newcomers did our best to squeeze ourselves in and somehow come to rest in the already cramped room. During this same period the prisoner slipped out then hastily back through a door opposite in order to communicate something to the soldier, leaning down very confidentially, almost right down to the latter's ear. The soldier seemed to be satisfied, and straightaway his piping, penetrating, wheezing voice, more reminiscent of a child's or perhaps a woman's, was audible as he spoke a few sentences in reply. Then the prisoner, having straightened up and raised a hand, at once requested "silence and attention" from us—and now, for the first time, I tasted that oft-cited joyful experience of unexpectedly hearing the familiar strains of one's own language abroad: it meant I was confronted with a compatriot. I immediately felt a bit sorry for him too, for I could not help but notice and be forced to admit that despite his being a rather young, intelligent convict, the man had a charming face, and I would dearly have liked to have found out from him where, how, and for what offense he had been imprisoned; however, for the time being all he told us was that he intended to instruct us about what we had to do, to acquaint us with what "*Herr Oberscharführer*"[7] required of us. Provided we did our best—as was indeed expected of us in any event, he added—then it would all be accomplished "quickly and smoothly," and although that, in his opinion, was above all in our own interest, he assured us it was equally the wish of "*Herr Ober*," as he now called him for short, somewhat dispensing with the formal title and also, I felt, somehow more familiarly.

We were then informed of a few simple and, in the circumstances, obvious matters, which the soldier also endorsed with vigorous nods, as it were confirming for us the truth of what, after all, were a prisoner's words, and meanwhile turning his friendly face and jolly gaze first toward him, then toward us. We were given to understand, for instance, that in the next room, the "changing room," we were to undress and hang all our clothes neatly on the hooks that would be seen there. We would also find a number on each hanger. While we were bathing, our clothes would be disinfected. Now, it maybe went without saying, he ventured (and I reckoned he was right), why it was important for everyone to commit the

---

[7]SS NCO rank, roughly master sergeant.

number of their hanger firmly to memory. Equally it wasn't hard for me to see the point of his suggestion that it would be "advisable" for us to tie our shoes together as a pair "in order to avoid any potential mix-ups," as he added. After that, he promised, barbers would attend to us, then the turn could finally come for the bath itself.

Before that, however, he continued, all those who still had any money, gold, jewels, or other valuables on them should step forward and place these voluntarily "on deposit with *Herr Ober,*" as this was the last opportunity they would have "still to get rid of such belongings with impunity." As he went on to explain, trading, buying, and selling of any description, and consequently also possessing and bringing in any articles of value, were "strictly forbidden in the *Lager*"—and that was the expression he used, which was new to me but at once readily comprehensible from the German term. After bathing, every person, so we learned, would be "roentgenographed," and "in a special, purpose-built apparatus" at that, and with an expressive nod, conspicuous jollity, and unmistakable assent the soldier gave particular emphasis to the word "roentgenograph," which he obviously must have understood. It also crossed my mind that it looked as if the gendarme's tip-off had been correct after all. The only further comment the prisoner could make for his part, he said, was that any attempt at smuggling—for which the perpetrator would incidentally place himself at risk of "the gravest punishment" and all of us would put at stake our honor in the eyes of the German authorities—would therefore, in his view, be "pointless and senseless." Though the issue had little to do with me, I supposed he must no doubt be right. That was followed by a brief hush, a stillness that toward the end, so I felt, became a touch uncomfortable. Then there was a shuffling up toward the front: someone asked to be let through, and a man made his way out, placed something on the tabletop, then scurried back again. The soldier said something to him, laudatory by the sound of it, and immediately thrust the object—something tiny that I was unable to get a good look at from where I was—into the desk drawer, having first inspected it, appraised it so to speak, with a quick glance. As best I could tell, he was satisfied. Then there was another pause, shorter than the previous one, again a shuffling, again another person, after which people sprang forward ever more fearlessly and with growing alacrity, by now uninterruptedly, proceeding one after the other to the table and setting down on it some shining, chinking, twanging, or rustling object in the small free space between the whip and the attaché case. Except for the footsteps and the sound of the articles, not to forget the soldier's occasional terse, piping, but unfailingly jovial and encouraging comments, this all went ahead in complete silence. I also noticed that the soldier adopted exactly the same procedure with every single object. Thus, even if someone set down two items at once, he still looked at each one separately, at times giving an appreciative nod: first the one, separately pulling the drawer out for that, separately placing it in there, then again closing the drawer, usually with his belly, before turning to the next item and repeating exactly the same thing with that. I was utterly flabbergasted at all the stuff that still came to light in this way—after the gendarmes and everything. But I was also a bit surprised by the hastiness, this sudden burst of enthusiasm, on the part of the people there, given that hitherto they had accepted all the troubles and cares that went with possession of these articles. Maybe that was the reason why the same slightly embarrassed, slightly solemn yet, all in all, to a certain extent somehow relieved expression was to be seen on virtually every face returning from the table. But then, in the end, here we all were, standing at the threshold to a new life, and that, after all, I realized, was of course an entirely different situation from the one at the gendarmerie. All this, the whole business, must have taken up roughly around three or four minutes, if I wish to be strictly accurate.

There is not much that I can say about what ensued: in essence, it all went the way the prisoner had instructed. The door opposite opened, and we went into a room that was indeed fitted out with long benches and hooks above them. I found the number straightaway and repeated it a number of times lest I somehow forget it. I also tied my shoes together, just as the prisoner had advised. Next came a large, low-ceilinged, very brightly lit room; along the walls all around razors were at work in earnest, electric hair-clippers buzzing, barbers—convicts to a man—bustling about. I passed to one on the right-hand side. I should take a seat, he must presumably have said, because I didn't speak his language, on the stool in front of him. By then he had already pressed the machine against my neck and shorn my hair right off—every last hair, leaving me totally bald. He then picked up a razor: I was to stand up and raise my arms, he demonstrated, and he then proceeded to scrape a bit in my armpits with the blade. Next he himself sat down on the stool in front of me.

Not to mince words, he grasped me by that most sensitive of all my organs and, with his razor, scraped the whole bush off there as well, every single strand, my entire scrap of virile pride, though it hadn't sprouted all that long before. Foolish though it may be, that loss somehow pained me even more than that of the hair on my head. I was taken aback, and maybe also somewhat angry, but then I realized it would be ridiculous for me to get hung up over such a trifle, when it came down to it. Anyway, I could see that everyone else, including the other boys, got the same treatment, and what's more we immediately began ragging "Fancyman": so, where's this going to leave you with the girls now?

We had to move on, though: the bath was next. At the door, a prisoner pressed a small lump of brown soap into "Rosie's" hand, just ahead of me, both saying and signaling that it was for three persons. In the bathroom itself we found that underfoot were slippery wooden slats and overhead a network of pipes on which there were masses of shower-heads. Lots of naked and, to be sure, not exactly agreeably smelling men were already in there. What I also found inter-esting was that the water started flowing of its own accord, quite unexpectedly, after everyone, including me, had searched around in vain for a tap somewhere. The jet of water was none too generous, but I found its temperature refreshingly cool, exactly to my liking in that sweltering heat. Before anything else, I took a long swig from it, again encountering the same taste as before at the faucet; after that I was only able to enjoy the feel of the water on my skin for a short while. Around me too were all manner of happy noises of slopping, sneezing, and blowing: a cheerful, carefree moment. With the other boys, we teased one another plenty over our bald heads. It turned out that the soap did not, sad to say, lather much but contained a lot of sharp, gritty specks that grazed the skin. Nonetheless, one plump man near me laboriously scrubbed away with earnest, even ceremonious actions at his back and chest, the black curls of hair on which had evidently been left on him. To my eyes, though, something was missing—apart from the hair on his head, naturally. Only then did I notice that the skin on his chin and around his mouth was indeed whiter than elsewhere, and also covered with fresh, reddish nicks. I recognized him as being the rabbi from the brickyard: so he too had come along. Without his beard, he now looked less remarkable to me: a simple, basically ordinary-looking man with a slightly prominent nose. He was soaping away on his legs as it happened, when, with the same unexpectedness as it had started, the water suddenly stopped flowing: he cast a startled glance upward then immediately down again before gazing ahead, but now somehow resignedly, like someone who registers, understands, and at the same time bows his head, as it were, before the will of a higher dispensation.

Not that I could do anything else myself: we were already being carried along, pushed and squeezed out. We passed into a dimly lit room where a prisoner placed into each hand, mine as well, a handkerchief—not, as became clear, a towel—indicating that it was to be given back after use. Simultaneously, but quite out of the blue and with extremely rapid and deft strokes, my skull, armpits, and that certain sensitive spot were coated by another prisoner, using some sort of flat brush, with a liquid that, judging from its suspect color, the itching it produced, and its foul smell, was ostensibly a disinfectant. A corridor came next, with two illuminated hatches on the right and finally a third, doorless room, at each of which a prisoner was standing and distributing clothing. Like everyone else, I was given a buttonless, collarless, no doubt once blue, white-striped shirt of my grandfather's vintage, some long johns that were likewise only suitable, at best, for old men, with a split at the ankles and two genuine cords to secure them; a worn-looking outfit, an exact copy of that worn by the convicts, with blue and white stripes and made of burlap—regulation prison duds, from whatever angle I might look at them; and then in the open room I was allowed to choose for myself from among a pile of strange wooden-soled sandals with canvas uppers, provided with three buttons on the side rather than laces, a pair that, in the heat of the moment, approximately fitted my feet. Not to forget two gray pieces of cloth that, I assumed, were obviously intended as handkerchiefs and, last but not least, an indispensable accessory: a round, battered, and cross-striped convict's forage cap. I hesitated slightly, but of course, in the midst of voices at every hand urging people to step on it, and with the hasty, frantic donning of clothes going on all around me, I had no time to waste if I did not wish to see myself left behind the others. Since the trousers were too big, and there was no belt or other form of fastening, I was obliged to knot them hurriedly, while one unforeseen feature of the shoes that now became clear was that the soles did not flex. Meanwhile, in order to free up my hands, I placed the cap on my head. The other boys had also all finished by then: we just looked at one another, not knowing whether to laugh or be dumbstruck. There was no time for either; in an instant we were outside, in the open air. I don't know who saw to it, or even what happened—all I recollect is a pressure of some kind weighing heavily on me, a momentum of some kind carrying and jostling me along, still stumbling a little in my new shoes, a cloud of dust, behind me strange thwacking noises that sounded rather as if someone was being slapped on the back, and ever onward, in what ultimately became a blurred and confused jumble of new courtyards, new barbed-wire gates, barbed-wire meshes, fences opening and closing.

FIVE

There can be no prisoner, I suppose, who would not be astounded, just a little, to start with in this situation. So, in the yard which we finally reached after the bath, the boys and I for a long time at first just examined and stared in wonderment at one another, turning each other around. But I also noticed a young-looking man nearby who at length and with absorbed attention, yet somehow hesitantly, was inspecting and patting his clothes from top to toe, as though he wished merely to convince himself about the quality of the material, its genuineness, so to say. After that, he glanced up, like someone who suddenly has a remark to make, but then, seeing all at once only clothes of the same kind around him, finally says nothing after all—that was my impression, right then at least, though that might have been mistaken, of course. Bald though he was, and in a convict outfit that was a little bit short on his tall frame, I still recognized him from his bony features as the lover who, approximately an hour before—because that was how much time must have passed from our arrival right up to our metamorphosis—had found it so hard to let go of the black-haired girl. One thing, however, bothered me quite a lot here. Back at home, I had once taken down at random from the bookshelf, as I recall, one of the more tucked-away volumes that was gathering dust there, unread since God knows when. The author had been a prisoner, and I didn't read it right to the end either, because I wasn't really able to follow his thinking, and then the characters all had dreadfully long names, in most cases three of them, all totally unmemorable, and in the end also because I was not the least bit interested in, indeed to be frank was somewhat repelled by, the prisoners' life; consequently, I was left ignorant in my hour of need. The only bit that had stuck in my mind out of the whole thing was that the prisoner, the book's author, claimed to recollect the early days of his imprisonment—that is to say, the ones most distant from him—better than he did the following years, which were, after all, closer to him when he was writing. At the time, I had found that rather hard to credit, even in some ways a bit of an exaggeration. Yet I now think he could well have written the truth after all, for I too recall the first day most precisely, and more precisely indeed, when I think about it, than I do the days that followed.

At the very beginning, I still considered myself to be what I might call a sort of guest in captivity—very pardonably and, when it comes down to it, in full accordance with the propensity to delusion that we all share and which is thus, I suppose, ultimately part of human nature. The courtyard, the sun-beaten area we had here, seemed rather barren, with no trace of a football pitch, seedbed, turf, or flowers to be found anywhere. The only thing standing there was an undecorated wooden building, outwardly resembling a large barn: manifestly our home. Entry, so I learned, was only permitted to us when the time came to turn in for the night. In front of and behind it, as far as the eye could see, was a long row of similar barns, and over to the left as well there was an absolutely identical row, at regular distances and intervals in front, behind, and to the side. Beyond that was that broad, dazzling, metaled road—or another metaled road like it, that is to say, since on that vast, completely flat terrain it had no longer really been possible, at least in my eyes, to keep track of the paths, squares, and identical build-ings on our way from the bathhouse. Free passage along the radial road at the point it would have intersected with the crossroad between the barns was blocked by a very neat, fragile, toylike red and white pole barrier. On the right was one of those now familiar barbed-wire fences—electrically charged as I learned to my surprise, and indeed it was only then that I spotted the many white porcelain knobs on the concrete posts, just like those on power lines and telegraph posts at home. Its shock, I was assured, was lethal; apart from that, one only needed to step on the loose sand of the narrow path running along the foot of the fence for them to shoot one down, without a sound or word of warning, from the watchtower (this was pointed out and I duly recognized it as being what, at the station, I had taken to be a hunters' hideout). In a short while, the corvée of volunteers arrived, amid a great clatter, staggering under the burden of brick red cauldrons. Before that, you see, a rumor had gone around, which was immediately discussed, commented on, and spread up and down the entire yard: "We'll soon be getting some hot soup!" Needless to say, I reckoned it was high time too, but all the same, the sight of all those beaming faces, the gratitude, the singular, somehow almost childish delight with which this news was received slightly amazed me, and maybe that was why I had the feeling it might well have been chiefly directed not so much toward the soup but rather, in some way, toward the solicitude itself, coming at last after the sundry initial surprises, as it were—that, at least, was my feeling. I also considered it very likely that the information might well have derived from that prisoner who had immediately appeared to become our guide, not to say host, at this place. He too, just like the prisoner at the bathhouse, had a snugly fitting outfit, a head of hair, which to me in itself already seemed truly unusual, and on his head a soft cap of dark blue felt, what one would call a beret, on his feet elegant tan shoes, and on his arm a red band to give his authority immediately visible expression, and I began to realize that it seemed I ought to revise a notion I had been taught back home to the effect that "clothes do not make the man." He likewise had a red triangle on his chest, and that too showed everyone straightaway that he was not here on account of his bloodline but merely for his way of thinking, as I was able to learn not much later. Though perhaps a trifle formal and laconic, he was amiable enough toward us, readily explaining all that was necessary, which I didn't find at all odd at the time, since he had been here longer, after all, so I thought to myself. He was a tall man, on the thin side, a bit wrinkled, a bit haggard, but nice-looking on the whole. I also noticed that he frequently held himself aloof, and once or twice I caught sight of him with a kind of disdainful, baffled look on his face, the corner of his mouth fixed in a kind of head-shaking smile of dismissal, so to say, as if he were a little nonplussed by us, though I don't know why. People said later on that he was of Slovak extraction. A few of our group who spoke the language themselves often formed a small huddle around him.

It was he who served out the soup to us, with a strange long-handled ladle rather like a funnel, while two other men, assistants of some type and likewise not from among us, handed out red enameled bowls and battered spoons—one each between two of us, since the stock was limited, they told us, which was also why, they added, we should return the bowls as soon as they had been emptied. I had to share the soup, bowl, and spoon with "Leatherware," which I wasn't too happy about as I had never been used to eating with someone else from a single plate and with the same utensils, but then there's no knowing, I realized, when needs may bring a person even to this. He took a taste first then promptly passed it to me. He had a slightly peculiar expression on his face. I asked him what it was like, and he told me to try it for myself. By then, however, I could see that the boys around us were all looking at one another, some aghast, some choking with laughter, so I had a taste too: I had to admit that it was indeed, unfortunately, inedible. I asked "Leatherware" what we should do, and he replied that for all he cared I could tip it out if I wanted. At that moment my ears caught a snatch of enlightenment from a cheerful voice behind my back: "This is what they call *dörrgemüze*," it was explaining. I glimpsed a squat man, already getting on in years, a whiter patch beneath his nose in the place of a former square of moustache, his face wreathed with well-meant learning. A few people making sour faces were still standing around us, clutching mess tin and spoon, and he told them that he had already played a part in the first world war, the one before this, as a military officer. "That gave plenty of opportunity," he related, "to become closely acquainted with this dish," particularly among the German comrades in arms on the front line "whom we were then fighting alongside," as he put it. According to him, it was actually nothing other than "dried vegetable stew." "A bit unaccustomed for Hungarian stomachs, of course," he added, accompanying this with a somehow sympathetic and a slightly forbearing smile. He maintained, however, that it was possible to become accustomed to it—indeed necessary, he reckoned, since it contained plenty of "nutrients and vitamins," as guaranteed, he explained, by the method of dehydration and the Germans' expertise in this. "In any case," he noted with a renewed smile, "the first rule for a good soldier is to eat up everything that is put in front of one, because there's no knowing what tomorrow will bring"—that's what he said. At which, true to his word, he spooned up his portion, calmly, steadily, and without a grimace, right down to the last drop. All the same, I still spilled my own portion away at the foot of the barracks wall, exactly as I had already seen a number of other grown-ups and boys do. I was taken aback, though, when I spotted the eyes of our superior looking at me and worried whether I might possibly have upset him; however, that peculiar expression, that indeterminate smile, was all that I thought I detected for a moment on his face again. After that I took the bowl back, receiving in return a thick slab of bread and upon that a blob of white stuff that resembled a toy building brick and was of roughly the same size: butter—or rather, margarine, as we were told. That I did eat up, though I had never before come across bread like this either: rectangular, with crust and inner crumb seemingly both baked from black sludge, embedded in which were bits of chaff and particles that crunched and crackled under the teeth; still, it was bread, and after all I had grown pretty hungry during the long journey. For want of any better means, I smeared the margarine on with my fingers, Robinson Crusoe fashion so to say, which in any case was just what I saw the others were doing. I would have looked for water next, but unfortunately it turned out there was none; hell, I fumed, don't say we'll have to go thirsty again after all this, just like on the train.

It was then that we were obliged to pay attention—basically, more seriously than we had thus far—to the smell. I would find it difficult to pin down: sweetish and somehow cloying, with a whiff of the now familiar chemical in it as well, but altogether enough to almost make me fear the bread of a moment ago might be regurgitated. It was not hard to establish that the culprit was a chimney over to the left, in the direction of the metaled road but a fair way beyond that. It was a factory chimney, that was immediately apparent, and that is what people were also told by our superior; specifically a tannery chimney, as many had recognized straight-

106

away. To be sure, it reminded me that on the occasional Sunday back then I had sometimes gone with my father to watch football matches in Újpest, and the streetcar had taken us past a leather works, where there too I had always had to hold my nose on that stretch of the route. For all that, the rumor went, we would not, fortunately, be working in that factory; all being well, and providing there was no outbreak of typhus, dysentery, or other infection among us, we would soon be moving off for another—and, we were assured, friendlier—place. That was also why until then we would not be carrying a number on our jacket and on our skin in particular, like our superior, or "block chief," as they were now calling him. Many had seen this number for themselves: it was inscribed in light green ink, so the rumor went, on his forearm, indelibly stained or tattooed into the skin with pricks of a specially designed needle. It was at roughly the same time that a conversation between the volunteers who had brought the soup also reached my ears. They too had seen the numbers, likewise imprinted in the skin of the older prisoners in the kitchens. One response above all that did the rounds from mouth to mouth, its significance being furiously probed and repeated around me, was what one of those prisoners had said in reply to an inquiry from one of our own people as to what it was: "*Himmlische Telephonnummer*"—"a celestial telephone number," the prisoner was alleged to have said. I could see the matter was giving everyone a lot of food for thought, and although I could not make much of it, I too found the phrase unquestionably odd. Anyway, that is when people started scrambling around the block chief and his two assistants, coming and going,

107

interrogating them, veritably besieging them with questions, and hastily exchanging information with one another—for instance, about whether there was an epidemic raging. "There is," was the word on that. What happens to the patients then? "They die." And the dead? "They're burned," we learned. In truth, it slowly became clear that the chimney stack over the way, though I did not catch precisely how, was not actually a tannery but the chimney of a "crematorium," a place where corpses are reduced to ashes, as we were told the word meant. I certainly took a harder look at it after that. It was a squat, square, widemouthed stack that looked as if it had been brusquely chopped off at its top. I can only say that I did not sense much else than a certain respect—apart from the stench, naturally, in which we were well and truly mired as in some fetid swamp. But then in the distance too, to our repeated astonishment, we were able to make out one more, then another, and again, right on the very horizon of the bright sky, yet another identical stack, two of which were right at that moment billowing out smoke similar to ours, and maybe people were also right to become suspicious of a puff of smoke from behind some sort of sparsely wooded park, and for the question to form in their minds, again rightly in my opinion, as to whether the outbreak could really be such as to produce so many dead.

I can state that even before dusk fell on that first day I fully understood just about everything, by and large. True, in the meantime we had also paid a visit to the latrine barracks, a place that comprised three sort of raised platforms along its entire length in each of which were two holes, so six altogether, over or into which one had to perch or aim, depending on what business one had. Little time was allowed, that's for sure, as an appearance was soon made by an angry prisoner, this one with a black armband and what looked like a hefty club in his hand, and everyone had to make it scarce just as they were. A couple of other longtime prisoners were also still loitering around; they were more docile, though, even obliging enough to offer a few bits of information. Following the block chief's directions, we had a considerable trek there and back, the path taking us by an interesting settlement: there were the usual barns behind the barbed-wire fence and between them these strange women (I promptly turned away from one, since dangling out of her unbuttoned dress right at that moment was something to which a bald-headed infant, its cranium glistening in the sun, was tenaciously clinging) and even stranger men in clothes that, threadbare as they were in general, were in the end nevertheless like those worn by people outside, in the free world so to say. By the time we were on the way back, though, I was clear that this was the Gypsies' camp. I was a bit surprised, since although, guarded as almost everyone back home, myself included, was in their opinion of Gypsies, naturally enough, up till now I had never heard it said that they were actually criminals. Right then a cart arrived on their side of the fence, drawn by small children with harnesses on their shoulders, just like ponies, while alongside them walked a man with a big moustache and a whip in his hand. The load was covered with blankets but there was no mistaking the bread, white loaves at that, peeping through the many gaps and the rags, from which I concluded that they must have a higher status than us after all. Another sight from that walk also stuck in my mind: coming the other way along the path was a man in a white jacket, white trousers with a broad red stripe down the sides, and a black artist's cap of the kind painters used to wear in the Middle Ages, a stout gentleman's walking stick in his hand, constantly looking to both sides as he went, and I found it very hard indeed to believe that this distinguished person was, as it was asserted, merely a prisoner, the same as us.

I would be prepared to swear that I didn't exchange a word with any stranger on the walk, yet it was to this that I can truly ascribe my more precise grasp of the facts. There across the way, at that very moment, fellow passengers from our train were burning—all those who had asked to be taken by car, or who up in front of the doctor had proved unfit due to old age or other reasons, along with little ones and the mothers who were with them and expectant women, so it was said. They too had proceeded from the station to the baths. They too had been informed about the hooks, the numbers, and the washing procedure, just the same as us. The barbers were also there, so it was alleged, and the bars of soap were handed out in just the same way. Then they too had entered the bathroom itself, with the same pipes and showerheads, so I heard, only out of these came, not water, but gas. This did not come to my notice all in one go but piecemeal, each time bringing further details, some disputed, others allowed to stand and added to. All along, I hear, everyone is very civil toward them, swaddling them with solicitude and loving-kindness, and the children play football and sing, while the place where they are suffocated to death lies in a very picturesque area, with lawns, groves of trees, and flower beds,

which is why, in the end, it all somehow roused in me a sense
of certain jokes, a kind of student prank. Adding to this, if
I thought about it, was the crafty way in which, for instance,
they had induced me to change clothes simply with the ruse
of the hook and the number on it, or had frightened people
carrying valuables with the X-rays, for example, which in the
end had been no more than empty words. Of course, I was
well aware that it was not altogether a joke, looked at from
another angle, as I was in a position to convince myself of
the outcome, if I may put it that way, with my own eyes and,
above all, my increasingly queasy stomach; nevertheless that
was my impression, and fundamentally—or at least so I
imagined—that must have been pretty much the way it happened. After all, people would have had to meet to discuss
this, put their heads together so to say, even if they were not
exactly students but mature adults, quite possibly—indeed,
in all likelihood—gentlemen in imposing suits, decorations
on their chests, cigars in their mouths, presumably all in
high command, who were not to be disturbed right then—
that is how I imagined it. One of them comes up with the
gas, another immediately follows with the bathhouse, a third
with the soap, then a fourth adds the flower beds, and so on.
Some of the ideas may have provoked more prolonged discussion and amendment, whereas others would have been
immediately hailed with delight, the men jumping up (I
don't know why, but I insisted on their jumping up) and
slapping one another's palms—this was all too readily imag-
inable, at least as far as I was concerned. By dint of many
zealous hands and much to-ing and fro-ing, the command-
ers' fantasy then becomes reality, and as I had witnessed,

111

there was no room for any doubt about the stunt's success. Doubtless that is how they had all proceeded from the railway station: the old lady dutifully following her son's wishes, the little boy with the white shoes and his blonde mother, the stout matron, the old gentleman in the black hat, or the nervous case up in front of the doctor. The "Expert" also crossed my mind: he would most likely have been utterly amazed, I suppose, the poor man. "Rosie" himself said "Poor old Moskovics" with a commiserating shake of the head, and we were all with him on that. Even "Fancyman" let out a cry of "Sweet Jesus!" for, as we were able to worm out of him, the boys' hunch had been correct: he and that girl at the brickyard had indeed "gone all the way," and he was now thinking of the possible consequences of that act which might show on her body over time. We recognized that the concern was justified, yet all the same, beyond anxiety, it was as if some other, less readily definable emotion were reflected in his face, and the boys themselves looked on him right then with a certain measure of respect, which I didn't find so very difficult to understand, naturally.

Another thing that somewhat set me thinking that day was the fact that, as I was informed, this place, this institution, had already been in existence for years, standing here and operating exactly the same way, day after day, but nevertheless, as it were—and I admit this notion may, perhaps, contain a certain element of exaggeration—ready and waiting for me. In any event, our own block chief—more than a few people referred to this with distinct, one could say awestruck, admiration—had already been living here for four years. It occurred to me that that had been a year of particular significance for me, being when I enrolled at the grammar school. The occasion of the opening ceremony for the school year was still lodged firmly in my memory: I too was there in a dark blue, braided, Hungarian-style uniform, a so-called "Bocskai" suit. Even the headmaster's words had registered, he himself being a man of distinguished and, now I think back on it, somewhat commanding presence, with severe eyeglasses and a majestic white handlebar moustache. In winding up he had made reference, I recollected, to an ancient Roman philosopher, quoting the tag *"non scolae sed vitae discimus"*—"we learn for life, not school." But then in light of that, really, I ought to have been learning all along exclusively about Auschwitz. Everything would have been explained, openly, honestly, reasonably. The thing was, though, that over the four years at school I had heard not a single word about it. Of course, that would have been embarrassing, I conceded, nor indeed did it belong to education, I realized. The drawback, however, was that now I would have to be edified here—to learn, for example, that we are in a *"Konzentrationslager,"* a "concentration camp." Not that these were all the same, it was explained. This one, for example, is a *"Vernichtungslager,"* that is to say an "extermination camp," I was informed. An *"Arbeitslager"* or "work camp," on the other hand, it was immediately added, was something quite different: life there was easy, the conditions and food, the rumors went, bore no comparison, which is natural enough as the aim, after all, is also different. Now, given all that, we too would eventually be going to a place like that, unless something should intervene, which indeed it well might in Auschwitz, those around me acknowledged. At all events, under no circumstances was it advisable to report sick, the nuggets of instruction went on. The hospital camp, incidentally, was over that way, right at the foot of one of the chimneys, "Number 2," as the better-informed were by now casually referring to it in shorthand among themselves. The hazard was concealed in the water, unboiled water—like that, for instance, from which I too had taken a drink on the way from the station to the baths, but there had been no way of knowing that then. To be sure, there had been a notice there, I could not dispute that, but all the same, the soldier ought maybe to have said something as well, I reckoned. But it then occurred to me that, hang on, what mattered was the end result; as best I could tell, I was feeling fine, thank goodness, and so far I had heard no complaints from the boys either.

Later that day, I made my first acquaintance with a number of other particulars, sights, and customs. I might say that, by the afternoon at any rate, in general I heard more information, and there was more talk around me, about prospects and possibilities regarding our future than about the chimney here. There were times when it might not have been there, we did not catch so much as a whiff of it; it all depended which way the wind was blowing, as many discovered. That day I also saw the women too for the first time. A group of men congregating and excitedly swarming around by the barbed-wire fence pointed them out: there they were, true enough, though I found it hard to pick them out in the distance, on the far side of the clayey field that stretched before us—and, above all, to recognize them as being women. They scared me a little, and I noticed that after the initial delight, the excitement at the discovery, the people around me here all fell very quiet. Just one observation, which rang hollow and a little tremulously, reached my ear from nearby: "They're bald." In the big hush, I too picked out for the first time, carried by the occasional wafts of a light summer-evening breeze, thinly, squeakily, and barely audibly, but beyond any doubt, the soothing, joyous sound of music, which, combined as it was with the sight, somehow hugely astounded everyone, myself included. I also stood for the first time, without knowing as yet what we were waiting for, in one of the rear rows of the ranks of ten that were drawn up before our barracks—in the same way as all the other prisoners were waiting before all the other barracks, to the side, in front, and behind, as far as the eye could see—and for the first time, on the order to do so, snatched my cap from my head while outside, on the main road, gliding slowly and noiselessly on bicycles in the balmy dusk air, there materialized the figures of three soldiers: a somehow majestic and, I was made to feel, austere sight. It crossed my mind even then: amazing, how long it had been since I had actually come across any soldiers. Only I had to wonder how difficult it would be to recognize the members of that politely spoken, good-humored corps who had greeted us this morning at the train in these men, who listened so coldly, frigidly, and as it were from an unapproachable exaltedness on the far side of the barrier, with one of them making notes in an elongated notebook of some description, to what on this side our block chief (he too with cap in hand) said to them, these somehow almost ominous potentates, who then glided on farther without so much as a single word, sound, or nod. At the same time, a faint noise, a voice, came to my attention, and to my right I noticed a profile straining forward and the protuberant curve of a chest: it was the former army officer. He was whispering in such a way that his lips barely even moved: "Evening roll call," giving a tiny nod, with a smile and the knowledgeable expression of a man for whom this was all happening in a fashion that was readily comprehensible, perfectly lucid, and in a certain sense, almost—hard to credit—to his satisfaction. It was then that I saw for the first time, with the darkness overtaking us where we stood, the night sky's hues and also one of its spectacles: Greek fire, a veritable pyrotechnic display of flames and sparks around the entire rim of the sky off to the left. Many of the people around me were whispering or muttering, reiterating: "The crematoriums! . . ." though by now this was little more than the wonder that accompanies what I might call some kind of natural phenomenon as it were. Later, "*Abtreten*," the order to fall out, and I would have been hungry, but then I learned that the bread had, in fact, been our supper, and after all, I had already eaten that this morning. As for the barracks, the "block," it turned out that it was completely bare inside, a concrete-floored place without any furniture, fittings, or even lights, where it again proved, as in the gendarmerie stable, that a night's rest could only be accomplished by propping my back against the legs of some boy sitting behind me, while the one sitting in front of me rested against my knees; and since I was by then tired out by the host of new events, experiences, and impressions, and moreover drowsy, I soon dropped off to sleep.

Of the days that followed, much as with those at the

brickyard, fewer details have stayed with me—more just their tone, a sense, what I might call a general impression, only I would find that difficult to define. During these days too there was always still something new to learn, see, and experience. During these days too, every now and then, I would still be brushed by a chill of that peculiar sense of strangeness that I first encountered at the sight of the women; every now and then it still happened that I would find myself in a circle of incredulous, drawn faces, people staring at one another and asking one another, "What do you say to that? What do you say to that?" and the answer on such occasions being either nothing or almost invariably: "Ghastly." But that is not the word, that is not precisely the experience—for me at any rate, naturally—with which I would truly characterize Auschwitz. Among the several hundred inmates of our block, it turned out, the man with the bad luck was also there. He looked a bit odd in his loosely hanging prison uniform, his oversized cap constantly slipping down over his forehead. "What do you say to that?" he too would ask, "What do you say to that? . . ."—but of course there was not much we could say. And then I would not have much joy trying to follow his hurried and muddled words. He mustn't think about, or rather that is to say he could and indeed had to think all the time about just one thing, those whom "he had left at home" and for whose sake "he had to be strong," since they were waiting for him: his wife and two children—that, roughly speaking, is about all I could make out, the gist of it. So anyway, his only main concern, even here, was basically the same as it had been at the customs post, on the train, or in the brickyard: the length of

117

the days. They now started very early indeed, just a fraction after the midsummer sunrise. That is also when I learned how cold the mornings were at Auschwitz; pressed close together to warm one another up, the boys and I would huddle by the side of our barracks opposite the barbed-wire fence, facing the still obliquely lying, ruddy sun. A few hours later, however, we would rather have been seeking some shade. In any event, time passed here too; "Leatherware" was with us here too, and the occasional joke would be cracked; here too, if not horseshoe nails, there were bits of gravel for "Fancyman" to win from us time after time; here too "Rosie" would speak up every now and then: "Now let's have it in Japanese!" Apart from that, two trips a day to the latrines, in the morning coupled with that to the washroom barracks (a similar place, the sole difference being that instead of the platforms down its length there were three lines of zinc-lined troughs, with a parallel iron pipe fitted over each, through the tiny, closely set holes in which the water trickled), the issuing of rations, roll call in the evening, and not forgetting, of course, the bits of news—I had to make do with that; that was a day's agenda. Added to that were events such as a "*Blocksperre,*" or "confinement to barracks," on the second evening—the first time I saw our chief looking impatient, indeed I might even say irritated— with the distant sounds, an entire jumble of sounds, that filtered across at that time, in which, if one listened very hard in the somewhat stifling darkness of the barracks, one might imagine one could pick out a shriek, a dog barking, and the cracks of shots; or again the spectacle, again from behind the barbed-wire fence, of a procession of those returning from work so it was said, and I had to believe them, because

118

that is how I too saw it, that lying on the makeshift stretchers being dragged over there by the returnees in the rear, those really were dead people, as those around me asserted. For a while, all this constantly gave plenty of work for my imagination, naturally, but not enough, I can affirm, to fill an entire long and inactive day. That is in part how I came to realize: even in Auschwitz, it seems, it is possible to be bored—assuming one is privileged. We hung around and waited in actual fact, if I think about it, for nothing to happen. That boredom, together with that strange anticipation: I think that is the impression, approximately, yes, that is in reality what may truly denote Auschwitz—purely in my eyes, of course.

Something else I have to admit: the next day I ate the soup, and by the third day was even looking forward to it. The meal system in Auschwitz, I have to say, was most peculiar. At the crack of dawn, a liquid of some kind—coffee they called it—would arrive quite soon. Lunch—soup, that is to say—was dished out astonishingly early, around nine o'clock. After that, though, there was nothing at all in this regard right up to the bread and margarine that came at dusk, before *Appell*; consequently, by the third day I had already struck up a rather close acquaintance with the tormenting sensation of being hungry, and the others all complained about it too. Only "Smoker" made the observation that the sensation was nothing new to him, it was more the cigarettes that he missed, and there was yet another expression on his face, besides his customary laconic air—almost a sense of satisfaction, which was rather irritating at the time, and this, I think, is why the boys dismissed it so quickly.

Amazing as it seemed when I tallied it up afterward, the

truth is that I actually spent only three whole days in Auschwitz. By the evening of the fourth day I was again sitting in a train, in one of those by now familiar freight cars. The destination, so we were informed, was "Buchenwald," and although I was somewhat cautious by now about such promising names, a certain unequivocal tinge of cordiality and even warmth one might say, a hint of a certain tender, dreamy, envious kind of sentiment, on the faces of some of the prisoners who said good-bye to us could not have been altogether misplaced, I felt. I also could not help noticing that many of them were highly knowledgeable old lags, and Prominents at that, as shown by their armbands, caps, and shoes. It was they who saw to everything at the trains; there were only a couple of soldiers whom I saw, farther off by the edge of the ramp, more middle-ranking officer types, and at this quiet place, in the gentle hues of this tranquil evening, nothing at all, or at most only the vastness, reminded me of the station, seething with activity, lights, sounds, and vitality, vibrating and throbbing at every point, where I had once—three-and-a-half days previously, to be precise—disembarked.

There is even less I can now say about the journey: everything happened in the accustomed manner. There were not sixty of us now, but eighty, though now there was no luggage with us, and then again we didn't have to worry about women either. Here too there was a slop bucket, here too we were hot, and here too we were thirsty; on the other hand, we were also subjected to less temptation in the matter of food: the rations—a larger than usual hunk of bread, a double dollop of margarine, and also a piece of something else, so-called "wurst," which in appearance was somewhat reminiscent of the sausages back home—were issued to us alongside the train, and I wolfed them down straightaway on the spot, first because I was hungry, then because there would have been nowhere to store them anyway, and also because, as before, they did not tell us that the trip would last three days.

We arrived at Buchenwald likewise in the morning, in clear, sunny weather that was kept cool and fresh by patches of scudding cloud and flurries of light wind. The railway station here, after Auschwitz at any rate, struck one as no more than a sort of cozy country halt. The reception alone was less cordial, for the doors were dragged aside by soldiers rather than prisoners; indeed, it occurred to me this was actually the first genuine and, so to say, overt occasion on which I had come into such proximity, such close contact, with them. I just watched the expeditiousness, the methodical precision, with which it was all accomplished. A few brusque barks: "*Alle 'raus!*"—"*Los!*"—"*Fünferreihen!*"— "*Bewegt euch!*"[1] a few blows, a few whip cracks, an intermittent swing of the boot, an intermittent rifle jab, a number of muffled cries of pain, and our column had been formed and was already on the march, as if it had only taken some pulls on a string, to be joined at the end of the platform, always with the same about-face, by one soldier on each flank for every fifth row—that is, two for every twenty-five striped-uniform men—at roughly one-yard intervals, not dropping their gaze for so much as a second, but now mutely setting

---

[1]"Everyone out!"—"Get going!"—"Five abreast!"—"Move yourselves!"

direction and pace merely by their tread, keeping in constant life, as it were, every segment of the whole continually moving and undulating column, which somewhat resembled one of those caterpillars in a matchbox that as a child I had guided with the aid of slips of paper and prods, all of which somehow slightly intoxicated, even utterly fascinated, me. I also had to smile a bit as a recollection of the sloppy, practically sheepish escort that the police had supplied back at home that day, going to the gendarmerie, suddenly sprang to mind. And even all the excesses of the gendarmes, I recognized, could only be considered a form of noisy officiousness in comparison with this tight-lipped expertise, perfectly dovetailing in every detail. For all that I could clearly see, for example, their faces, the color of their eyes or hair, this or that individual feature and even blemish, the odd pimple, I was nevertheless somehow unable quite to get a hold on all this, somehow almost had to doubt it: were these beings proceeding here by our side deep down, despite everything, basically similar to ourselves, fashioned, when it came down to it, from much the same human material? But then it occurred to me that my way of looking at it might be flawed, since I myself was not, of course, one and the same.

Even so, I noticed that all the time we were steadily climbing on a gently sloping incline, again on a superb highway, though one that was twisting and not, as at Auschwitz, straight. In the vicinity, I saw a lot of natural greenery, pretty buildings, villas hidden farther back among trees, parks, gardens; the whole area, the scales, all the proportions, striking me, if I may be so bold, as benign—at least to an eye conditioned to Auschwitz. I was surprised by a regular small zoo suddenly appearing on the right-hand side of the road; there were deer, rodents, and other animals as residents, among which a shabby brown bear, greatly excited on hearing our tread, immediately adopted a begging pose and even promptly showed off a few clownish gestures in its cage; on this occasion, though, its efforts were naturally fruitless. We later passed by a statue that stood on the green sward of a clearing wedged between the two forks that the road took here. The work itself, resting on a white plinth and hewn from the same soft, dull, grained white stone, had in my judgment been executed with somewhat rough-and-ready, slapdash artistry. From the stripes carved into its clothing and its bald cranium, but above all from the whole demeanor, it was immediately apparent that this was seeking to portray a prisoner. The head was thrust forward and one leg kicked out high behind in imitation of running, while the two hands, in a cramped grip, were clasping an incredibly massive cube of stone to the abdomen. At first glance, I looked at it merely the way one appraises a work of art, which school too had taught, what I might call totally disinterestedly, but then it crossed my mind that it no doubt also carried a message, though that message could not be considered exactly auspicious, if one thought about it. But then above an ornate iron gate, between two squat stone columns set in the dense barbed-wire fencing, I caught sight of, and soon passed beneath, a structure somewhat reminiscent of the captain's bridge on a ship: I had arrived at Buchenwald concentration camp.

Buchenwald lies on the crest of one of the elevations in a region of hills and dales. Its air is clear, the countryside varied, with woods all around and the red-tiled roofs of the village houses in the valleys down below delightful to the eye. The bathhouse is situated off to the left. The prisoners are mostly friendly, though somehow in a different way from in Auschwitz. On arrival, here too one is greeted by bathhouse, barbers, disinfectant, and a change of clothes. The stock of the clothes depot, as far as that goes, is exactly the same as at Auschwitz, though the bathhouse here is warmer, the barbers are more careful in carrying out their work, and the storeman at least tries, if only with a cursory glance, to assess your size. Afterward you find yourself in a corridor, in front of a glazed sliding window, and they ask whether you happen to have any gold teeth. Then a compatriot, a longer-term resident with hair, records your name in a big register and hands you a yellow triangle as well as a broad strip, both of linen. In the middle of the triangle, as a sign that you are, after all, a Hungarian, is a big letter "U," while on the strip you can read a printed number—64921 in my own case, for example. It would be advisable, I was informed, to learn as soon as possible how this was to be pronounced in German, clearly, intelligibly, and in a distinctly articulated fashion, thus: "*Vier-und-sechzig, neun, ein-und-zwanzig,*" since from now on that was to be the answer I must always give when anyone asks me to identity myself. Here, though, they do not inscribe that number in your skin, and if you were to have been worried on that score and had inquired about it beforehand, in the bathhouse area, the old prisoner would raise his hands and, rolling his eyes to the ceiling in protest, say: "*Aber Mensch, um Gotteswillen, wir sind doch hier nicht in Auschwitz!*"[2] Nevertheless both number and triangle must be affixed to the breast of the jacket by this evening, specifi-

---

[2]"For God's sake, man, this isn't Auschwitz!"

cally with the assistance of the tailors, the sole possessors of needle and thread; if you should get really bored with queuing until sundown, you will be able to put them more in the mood with a certain fraction of your bread or margarine ration, but even without that they will do it willingly enough as, in the end, they are obliged to, so it is said. The Buchenwald climate is cooler than that at Auschwitz, the color of the days gray, and rain often drizzles down. But at Buchenwald it can happen that they spring on you the surprise of a hot, thickened soup of some sort for breakfast; and furthermore I learned that the bread ration is normally one-third of a loaf, but on some days might even be one-half—not the usual one-quarter and on some days one-fifth as at Auschwitz, while the midday soup may contain solid scraps, and in these may be red shreds or even, if you are lucky, an entire chunk of meat; and it was here that I became acquainted with the notion of the *"Zulage,"* an extra that you can requisition—the term used by the army officer, likewise present here and looking mightily pleased with himself on such occasions—in the form of wurst or a spoonful of jam along with the margarine. At Buchenwald we lived in tents, in the *"Zeltlager"*—"Tent Camp," or *"Kleinlager"*—"Little Camp"—as it was also called, sleeping on hay strewn on the ground, not separately and somewhat tightly packed maybe, but at least horizontally, while here the barbed-wire fence at the back is not, as yet, electrified, though anyone who might step outside the tent at night would be ripped apart by Alsatian dogs, they warned, and if that warning might perhaps surprise you at first hearing, don't doubt its seriousness. At the other barbed-wire fence, marking the start of the cobblestoned paths, neat green barracks and single-story, stone-built blocks of the main camp proper, sprawling all around farther up the hill, every evening offers good opportunities for bargains in the shape of spoons, knives, mess tins, and clothing from the local, indigenous prisoners who trade there at that hour; one of them offered me a pullover for the price of altogether half a bread ration, as he demonstrated, signaled, and explained, but in the end I didn't buy it as I had no need of a pullover in summer, and after all, winter, I supposed, was still a long way off. I also saw then just how many variously colored triangles and different letterings they wore, to the point that I ended up not always being able to figure out where a person's homeland might actually be. Even here, in my immediate surroundings, I picked out lots of dialect words from the speech of the Hungarians, and indeed more than a few times the strange language that I had first heard on the train at Auschwitz, from the odd-looking prisoners who had greeted us. At Buchenwald there was no *Appell* for the inmates of the *Zeltlager*, and the washroom was in the open air, or to be more precise beneath the shade of the trees: essentially much the same structure as the one at Auschwitz, except the trough was of stone and, most of all, water trickled, spurted, or at least oozed all day long through the holes in the pipe, and for the first time since I had entered the brickyard, I experienced the miracle of being able to drink when I was thirsty, or even merely when the fancy took me. At Buchenwald too there is a crematorium, naturally, but merely one, and even that is not the camp's purpose, its essence, its soul, its sense, I make so bold as to declare, for the only people who are burned up

126

here are those who die in the camp, under the ordinary circumstances of camp life so to say. At Buchenwald—so went the rumor that reached my ears, probably originating from old prisoners—it was most particularly advisable to steer clear of the stone quarry, although, it was added, that was now hardly in operation, unlike in their time, as they put it. The camp, I am instructed, has been functioning for seven years, though there are some here from even older camps, among which I heard the names of a certain "Dachau" as well as "Oranienburg" and "Sachsenhausen," which is when I understood why at the sight of us there was a touch of indulgence in the smiles on the faces of some of the well-dressed Prominents on the other side of the barbed-wire fence, on whom I spotted numbers in the twenty and ten thousands, indeed four- and even three-digit numbers. Close to our camp, I learned, lies the culturally celebrated city of Weimar, the fame of which I had already learned about back home, naturally: here had lived and worked the man who wrote the poem beginning *"Wer reitet so spät durch Nacht und Wind?"*[3] that even I know by heart, while somewhere within the area of our camp, so they say, marked with a commemorative plaque and protected from us prisoners by a fence, is a now nobly spreading tree that he planted with his own hand. All things considered, it wasn't at all difficult to understand those faces at Auschwitz: it is fair to say that I too soon came to like Buchenwald.

Zeitz, or to be more precise the concentration camp named after this place, lies a night's ride by freight train

---

[3]"Who rides so late through night so wild?"—Goethe's *Erl-king*.

from Buchenwald, then a farther twenty or twenty-five minutes' march, under military escort, along a highway fringed
by plowed fields and well-cultivated rural land, as I myself
had the chance to find out. This would at least be the final
place of residence, we were assured, for those from our
ranks whose names came before the letter "M" in the alpha-
bet; for the rest the destination was to be a work camp in the
city of Magdeburg, which from its historical renown had a
more familiar ring to it—so we were informed, while still at
Buchenwald, again on the evening of the fourth day, on a
monstrous parade ground lit with arc lamps, by various
high-ranking prisoners holding long lists in their hands. The
only thing I felt sorry about was that it meant I would finally
be parted from many of the boys, "Rosie" above all, and
then, unfortunately, the sheer vagary of the names by which
we were boarded onto the train separated me from all the
others too.

I can tell you there is nothing more tiresome, more
exhausting, than those exasperating strains that, so it seems,
we must undergo each time we arrive at a new concentration camp—that was my experience at Zeitz anyway, after
Auschwitz and Buchenwald. I could see straightaway that
this time I had arrived at what was no more than some kind
of small, mediocre, out-of-the-way, so to say rural concentration camp. It would have been pointless looking for a
bathhouse or even a crematorium here: it seems those are
trappings only of the more important concentration camps.
The countryside too was again a monotonous flatland, with
some distant blue range—the "Thuringian Hills," I heard
someone say—visible only from the far end of the camp.

The barbed-wire fence, with a watchtower at each of the four corners, stretches right alongside the highway. The camp itself is square in plan—in essence, a large, dusty space that is open over toward the gateway and the highway beyond, while the other sides are enclosed by huge tents the size of an airfield hangar or a circus big top; as it turned out, the only point of the protracted counting, column formation, harassment, and pushing around was to assign the prospective inmates to each and every tent, or "Block" as they called them, and line them up, ten abreast, in front of it. I too finished up at one of them, to be absolutely precise, the tent on the far right in the hindmost row, if one were to take bearings from where I was standing, face to the gate and back to the tent, and for a very long time too, to the point of numbness under the unending burden of that now ever more disagreeable day. It was useless casting glances around in search of the boys; the people around me were all strangers. To my left was a tall, thin, slightly peculiar neighbor, continuously muttering something to himself and rocking his upper body rhythmically to and fro, while to my right was a broad-shouldered man, more on the short side, who spent his time directing tiny spitballs, tersely and highly accurately, at regular intervals into the dust in front of him. He likewise looked at me, the first time just fleetingly but then the next time more searchingly, with his crooked, sparkling, button eyes. Under those I saw a comically small, seemingly almost boneless nose, while he wore his prison cap jauntily tilted to one side of his head. So, he asked on the third occasion, and I noticed that all his front teeth were missing, where did I come from, then? When I told him Budapest, he became

129

quite animated: was the Grand Boulevard still there, and was the No. 6 streetcar still going as it had been when he "last left it," he immediately inquired. Sure, I told him, everything was the same; he seemed happy at that. He was also curious as to how I "got mixed up in this here," so I told him: "Simple: I was asked to get off the bus." "And then?" he quizzed, so I told him that was all: then they transported me here. He seemed to wonder a little at that, as if he were maybe not quite clear about the course life had taken back home, and I was about to ask him . . . but by then I was unable to do so because at that instant I received a clout on the face from the other side.

I was virtually already sprawling on the ground before I heard the smack and its force began to sting my left cheek. A man was standing in front of me, in black riding dress from head to toe, with a black beret on his head of black hair, even a black pencil moustache on his swarthy features, in what, to me, was a billow of an astonishing odor: no doubt about it, the sweetish fragrance of genuine cologne. All I could pick out from the confused ranting were repeated reiterations of the word "*Ruhe*," or "silence." No mistaking it, he appeared to be a very high-ranking functionary, which the preeminent low number and green triangle with a letter "Z" on his left breast, the silver whistle dangling from a metal chain on the other side, not to speak of the "LÄ" in white lettering sported by his armband, each in itself, only appeared to reinforce. All the same, I was extremely angry as, after all, I was not used to being hit, and whoever it might be, I strove to give expression—decked though I might be, and if only on my face—to passable signs of that rage. He must have spotted it too, I suppose, because I noticed that even as he carried on with his incessant bawling the look in those big, dark eyes, seemingly almost swimming in oil, meanwhile took on an ever-softer and, in the end, well-nigh apologetic air as he ran them attentively over me, from my feet right up to my face; that was somehow an unpleasant, embarrassing feeling. He then rushed off, people stepping aside to make way for him, in the same stormy haste with which he had materialized just beforehand.

After I had picked myself up, the neighbor to the right soon inquired whether it had hurt. I said to him, deliberately loud and clear: no chance. "So it won't do you any harm to mop your nose, then," he supposed. I touched the spot, and there was indeed red on my fingers. He showed me how I should tip my head back to stem the bleeding, and made this comment about the man in black: "Gypsy," then, following a brief pause for reflection, as an afterthought: "The guy's a homo, that's for sure." I didn't quite understand what he was trying to say, and indeed asked him what the word meant. He chuckled a bit and said: "Like—queer!" That clarified the notion a bit better for me, or near enough, I think. "By the way," he went on to note, stretching out a hand sideways, "I'm Bandi Citrom," whereupon I told him my name as well.

He for his part, I later learned, had reached here from a labor camp. He had been conscripted as soon as Hungary entered the war because he had just turned twenty-one: so he was fitted for labor service by virtue of age, race, and condition, and he had not been back home even once in the last four years. He had even been in the Ukraine, on mine-clearing

131

work. "What happened to the teeth, then?" I asked. "Knocked out," he replied. Now it was my turn to be surprised: "How come . . . ?" But he simply said it was "a long story," and did not give much else away about the reason. At all events, he "had a run-in with the sergeant of his corps," and that was when his nose, besides other bones, had been broken: that was all I could get out of him. He was no more forthcoming about the mine-clearing: it took a spade, a length of wire, plus sheer luck, as he put it. That is why very few were left in the "punishment company" at the end, when Germans arrived to replace the Hungarian troops. They had been glad too, because they were immediately offered a prospect of easier work and better treatment. They too, naturally, had stepped off the train at Auschwitz.

I was just about to take the prying a bit further, but right then the three men returned. About ten minutes before that, more or less the only thing I had registered from what was going on up front was a name, or to be more precise an identical bawl from several voices up front, all yelling out "Doctor Kovács!" at which a plump, dough-faced man, with a head shorn by hair-clippers at the sides, but naturally bald in the middle, shyly, reluctantly, and merely in deference to the urgent call as it were, stepped forward, then himself pointed to another two. The three of them had immediately gone off with the man in black, and only subsequently did the news get back to me here, in the last rows, that we had in fact elected a leader, or *"Blockältester"*—"senior block inmate"—as they called it, and *"Stubendiensts,"* or "room attendants," as I roughly translated it for Bandi Citrom, since he did not speak German himself. They now wanted to

132

instruct us in a few words of command and the actions that went along with these, which—the leaders had been warned, and they warned us in turn—they were not going to go through this more than once. Some of these—the cries of "*Achtung!*" "*Mützen . . . ab!*" and "*Mützen . . . auf!*"[4]—I was basically already familiar with from my previous experiences, but new to me was "*Korrigiert!*" or "Adjust!"—the cap, of course, and "*Aus!*" or "Dismiss!" at which we were supposed to "slap hands to thighs," as they said. We then practiced all these a number of times over. The Blockältester, we learned, had one other particular job to do on these occasions, which was to make the report, and he rehearsed this several times over, there in front of us, with one of the Stubendiensts, a stocky, ginger-haired man, with slightly purplish cheeks and a long nose, standing in for the soldier. "*Block fünf,*" I could hear him yell, "*ist zum Appell angetreten. Es soll zweihundert fünfzig, es ist . . . ,*" and so on, from which I discovered that I too must therefore be an inmate of Block 5, which has a roll of two hundred and fifty men. After a few repetitions this was all clear, comprehensible, and could be performed without error, so everyone reckoned. After that, there followed more minutes with nothing to do, and since in the meantime I noticed, on a piece of empty ground to the right of our tent, some sort of mound with a long pole above it and what could be surmised to be a deep trench behind it, I asked Bandi Citrom what purpose it might serve, in his opinion. "That's a latrine," he announced straight off after one swift glance. He then shook his head

---

[4]"Attention!" "Caps off!" "Caps on!"

when it emerged that I wasn't familiar with that term either. "It's obvious that you must have been tied to Mummy's apron strings up till now," he reckoned. All the same, he explained it in a few pithy words, then added something which, to quote him in full, went: "By the time we fill that with shit, we'll all be free men!" I laughed, but he kept a serious face, like someone who was really convinced, not to say determined, about this. Nevertheless, he wasn't given the chance to say anything more about that belief, since right at that moment, all of a sudden, there appeared the severe, very elegant figures of three soldiers who were making their way across from the gateway, without haste but obviously very much at ease, at which the Blockältester yelled out, in a voice that acquired a new edge, a keen and screeching timbre that I had not discerned in it even once during the rehearsals: "*Achtung! Mützen . . . ab!*" at which, like everyone else, me included, he too, naturally, snatched his cap from his head.

SIX

Only in Zeitz did I come to realize that even captivity has its mundane round; indeed, true captivity is actually nothing but a gray mundane round. It was as if I had been in a roughly comparable situation already, that time in the train on the way to Auschwitz; there too everything had hinged on time, and then on each person's individual capabilities. Except in Zeitz, to stay with my simile, the feeling I had was that the train had come to a standstill. From another angle, though—and this is also true—it rushed along at such speed that I was unable to keep up with all the changes in front of and around me, or even within myself. One thing I can say at least: for my own part, I traveled the entire route, scrupulously exploring every chance that might present itself on the way.

At all events, in any place, even a concentration camp, one gets stuck into a new thing with good intentions, at least

135

that was my experience; for the time being, it was sufficient to become a good prisoner, the rest was in the hands of the future—that, by and large, was how I grasped it, what I based my conduct on, and incidentally was pretty much the same as I saw others were doing in general. I soon noticed, it goes without saying, that those favorable opinions I had heard when still at Auschwitz about the institution of the Arbeitslager must certainly have been founded on somewhat exaggerated reports. As to the entire extent of that exaggeration, and above all the inferences that stemmed from it, however, I did not—nor, in the end, could I—immediately take fully accurate account of this myself, and that was again pretty much what I perceived to be the case with others, indeed I dare say with everyone else, all of the approximately two thousand other prisoners in our camp—the suicides excepted, naturally. But then those cases were uncommon, in no way the rule nor in any way exemplary, everyone recognized. I too got wind of the occasional occurrence of that kind, hearing people arguing and exchanging views about it, some with undisguised disapproval, others more sympathetically, acquaintances with sorrow, but on the whole always in the way of someone striving to form a judgment of a deed that was exceedingly rare, remote to our experience, in some ways hard to explain, maybe slightly frivolous, maybe even slightly honorable, but in any case premature.

The main thing was not to neglect oneself; somehow there would always be a way, for it had never yet happened that there wasn't a way somehow, as Bandi Citrom instilled in me, and he in turn had been instructed in this wisdom by the labor camp. The first and most important thing under all

136

circumstances was to wash oneself (before the parallel rows of troughs with the perforated iron piping, in the open air, on the side of the camp over toward the highway). Equally essential was a frugal apportioning of the rations, whether or not there were any. Whatever rigor this disciplining might cost you, a portion of the bread ration had to be left for the next morning's coffee, some of it indeed—by maintaining an undeflectable guard against the inclination of your every thought, and above all your itching fingers, to stray toward your pocket—for the lunch break: that way, and only that way, could you avoid, for instance, the tormenting thought that you had nothing to eat. That the item in your wardrobe I had hitherto regarded as a handkerchief was a foot cloth; that the only secure place to be at roll call and in a marching column was always the middle of a row; that even when soup was being dished out one would do better to aim, not for the front, but for the back of the queue, where you could pre-dict they would be serving from the bottom of the vat, and therefore from the thicker sediment; that one side of the handle of your spoon could be hammered out into a tool that might also serve as a knife—all these things, and much else besides, all of it knowledge essential to prison life, I was taught by Bandi Citrom, learning by watching and myself striving to emulate.

I would never have believed it, yet it is a positive fact that nowhere is a certain discipline, a certain exemplariness, I might even say virtue, in one's conduct of life as obviously important as it is in captivity. It suffices merely to take a little look around the area of Block 1, where the camp's native inmates live. The yellow triangles on their chests tell you all you really need to know, while the letter "L" in them discloses the incidental circumstance that they have come from distant Latvia, more specifically from the city of Riga, I was informed. Among them one can see those peculiar beings who at first were a little disconcerting. Viewed from a certain distance, they are senilely doddering old codgers, and with their heads retracted into their necks, their noses sticking out from their faces, the filthy prison duds that they wear hanging loosely from their shoulders, even on the hottest summer's day they put one in mind of winter crows with a perpetual chill. As if with each and every single stiff, halting step they take one were to ask: is such an effort really worth the trouble? These mobile question marks, for I could characterize not only their outward appearance but perhaps even almost their very exiguousness in no other way, are known in the concentration camps as "*Musulmänner*" or "Muslims," I was told. Bandi Citrom promptly warned me away from them: "You lose any will to live just looking at them," he reckoned, and there was some truth in that, though as time passed I also came to realize it takes much more than just that.

For example, your first device is stubbornness: it may have come in varying forms, but I can tell you there was no lack of it at Zeitz, and at times it can be of immense assistance, so I observed. For instance, I found out more from Bandi Citrom about that weird band, collection, breed, or whatever one should call them, a specimen of which—on my left in the row—had already somewhat astonished me on my arrival. It was he who told me that we call them "Finns." Certainly if you ask them where they are from, they really

138

do reply—if they see fit to give you any answer at all, that is—something like "*fin Minkács,*" for example, by which they mean they are from Munkachevo, or "*fin Sadarada,*" which, for example (and you have to guess), is Sátoral-jaújhely. Bandi Citrom already knows their organization from labor camp and doesn't speak very highly of it. They can be seen everywhere, at work, while marching or at *Appell*, rocking rhythmically back and forth as they unflaggingly mutter their prayers to themselves, like some unrepayable debt. When meanwhile they speak out of the corner of the mouth to whisper across something like, "Knife for sale," you don't pay any attention. All the less so, however tempting it may be, especially in the morning, when it is "Soup for sale," because, however strange it may sound, they don't touch soup nor even the sausage that we occasionally get—nothing prescribed by their religion. "So what do they live on?" you might well ask, and Bandi Citrom would reply: you don't have to worry about them, they look after themselves. He would be right too because, as you see, they stay alive. Among one another and with the Latvians they use Yiddish, but they also speak German, Slovakian, and a smattering of who knows what, only not Hungarian—unless it's a question of doing business, of course. On one occasion (there was no getting out of it), as luck would have it, I ended up in their work *Kommando.* Their first question was "*Rayds di yiddish?*" When I told them that, no, unfortunately I didn't, that was it as far as they were concerned, I became a nonperson, they looked at me as if I were thin air, or rather didn't exist at all. I tried to speak, get myself noticed, but to no avail. "*Di bisht nisht kai yid, d'bisht a shaygets*,"[1] they shook their heads, and I could only wonder at how people who after all were reputedly at home in the business world could cling so irrationally to something from which the harm to them was so much more, the losses so much greater, than any gains with regard to the end result. That day I learned that the discomfiture, the skin-crawling awkwardness which at times took hold between us was already familiar to me from back home, as if there had been something not quite right about me, as if I did not quite measure up to the proper ideal, in short as if I were some-how Jewish—a rather odd feeling to have after all, I reckoned, in the midst of Jews, in a concentration camp.

At other times it was Bandi Citrom who slightly amazed me. Whether at work or during a break, I often heard, and quickly learned from him, his favorite song, which he had brought with him from his labor service days in the punish-ment company: "We clear mines from land in the Uk-raine, / But even there we're never chicken . . ." was how it began, and I was specially fond of the closing lines, which go: "If a com-rade, a good bud-dy, should be lost, / For those back home our ri-poste / Is: / Come of us what may, / Our dear old home-land, / We'll not de-ceive you, at any cost." A noble sentiment, undeniably, and the somber tune, more on the slow side than snappy, along with the ditty as a whole, did not fail to exert their influence on me too, naturally— only somehow they merely jogged my memory of the gen-darme, that time back on the train, when he reminded us of our being Hungarian; only in the end, strictly speaking, the

---

[1] "You're not a Jew, you're a Gentile kid."

homeland had punished them too. I mentioned this to him once, what's more. He did not come up with any counterargument either, yet he seemed to be just a little put out, even annoyed one could say. On some occasion the next day, though, very wrapped up in something, he again started whistling, humming, and finally singing it as if any recollection of that had been clean forgotten. Another frequently repeated refrain was that he would again "set foot on the pavements of Forget-me-not Road," that being where he lived back home, and he mentioned the street, even the number of the house, so many times and in so many ways that finally I too knew all its attractions by heart, almost longed to go there myself, even though in my own recollections I actually knew it only as a fairly secluded backstreet somewhere in the neighborhood of the Eastern Railway Terminal. He often spoke about, evoked, and also reminded me of other places too, squares, avenues, houses, as well as certain well-known slogans and advertising signs that blazed on their roofs and in various shopwindows—"the lights of Budapest" as he called them, though here I had to correct him, being obliged to point out that those lights no longer existed on account of the blackout regulations, and the bombing, to be sure, had knocked the city's panorama about a bit here and there. He fell silent, but as far as I could make out the news was not very much to his liking. The next day, though, as soon as the opportunity presented itself, he again started to go on about the lights.

But then, could anyone be acquainted with all the variants of stubbornness? For I can assure you, had I but known, there were many variants I could have chosen from

141

in Zeitz. I heard about the past, the future, and a lot, a very great deal, about freedom above all; indeed, I can safely say, nowhere does one hear as much about it, it seems, as among prisoners, which naturally makes a lot of sense after all, I suppose. Yet others took some strange pleasure in an adage, a joke, a wisecrack of sorts. I heard this one myself, naturally. There is an hour of the day which falls between returning from the factory and the evening *Appell*, a distinctive, always bustling, and liberated hour that I, for my part, always looked forward to and enjoyed the most while in the Lager; as it happened, this was generally also supper time. I was just pushing my way through the milling, trading, and chatting knots of people when someone bumped into me, and a pair of tiny, worried eyes above a singular nose gazed at me from under the loose-fitting convict's cap. "I don't believe it," we both said almost simultaneously, as he had recognized me and I him, the man with the bad luck. He immediately appeared to be delighted and inquired where my quarters were. Block 5, I told him. "Pity," he said regretfully, since he was lodged elsewhere. He complained that he didn't "get to see familiar faces," and when I told him that I didn't either he somehow looked crestfallen, though I don't know why. "We're becoming split up, all split up," he observed with an implication in his words and the shaking of his head that was somewhat lost on me. Then his face brightened all of a sudden, and he asked, "Do you know what this here," pointing to his chest, "this letter 'U,' signifies?" Sure I did, I told him: "*Ungar*, Hungarian." "No," he answered, "*Unschuldig*," meaning "innocent," then gave a snort of laughter followed by prolonged nodding of the head with a

142

brooding expression, as if the notion were somehow highly gratifying, though I have no idea why. Subsequently, and quite often in the beginning, I saw the same on others in the camp from whom I also heard that wisecrack, as if they derived some warming, fortifying emotion from it—that at least is what was suggested by the unfailingly identical laugh and then that same softening of features, the dolefully smiling and yet somehow euphoric expression with which they told and hailed this witticism each and every time they told it, in much the same sort of way as when a person hears music that deeply touches his feelings or some particularly moving story.

Yet all the same, with them too what I noticed was the same endeavor, the same good intention: they too wanted merely to be seen as good prisoners. Make no mistake about it, that was in our interest, that is what the conditions called for, that is what life there, if I may put it this way, compelled us to do. If the rows were perfectly in line and the numbers tallied, for instance, the roll call did not last so long—at least to start with. If one was diligent at work, for example, then one might avoid a beating—usually, at any rate.

Even so, at least to start with, I believe the thinking of each and every one of us cannot have been guided entirely by that gain alone, not exclusively by that kind of benefit alone, I can honestly say. Take work, for example, the first afternoon of work, to start with that straightaway: the task was to unload a wagon of gray gravel. If, after Bandi Citrom and I—naturally having sought permission beforehand from the guard: on this occasion, a soldier who was getting on in years and, at first glance, more docile-looking—had stripped down to the waist (that was the first time I saw his golden-brown skin with the big, smooth muscles lithe under it and the darker patch of a birthmark below the left breast), he said, "Now then, let's show these guys what Budapesters can do!" then he meant that perfectly seriously. And I tell you, considering it was after all the first time in my life that I had handled a pitchfork, that both the guard and the foreman-type guy, no doubt from the factory, who would nose around every now and then seemed rather satisfied, which only made us reintensify our efforts, naturally. If, on the other hand, a stinging sensation declared itself on my palms after a time, and I saw blood all around the base of my fingers, and then our guard in the meanwhile called over: "*Was is denn los?*"[2] so I laughed and held up my palm to show him, whereupon he, abruptly turning surly, even giving a jerk on his rifle strap, demanded: "*Arbeiten! Aber los!*"[3]—then it was only natural, in the end, that my own interests should also turn to other things. From then on, I paid attention to just one thing: the times when he did not have his eyes on me, so I could steal the occasional quick breather, or how I might put as little as possible on my spade, shovel, or pitchfork; and I can tell you, later on I made very considerable progress in such tactics, at any rate gaining a great deal more expertise, schooling, and practice with them than in the performance of any job of work that I completed. And anyway, who profits from it, after all?—as I recall the "Expert" once asking. I maintain there was some problem here, some obstacle, some mistake, some breakdown. A word, a sign, a glim-

---

[2] "What's the matter?"
[3] "Work! Snap to it!"

144

mering of appreciation now and again, nothing more, just a scintilla, might have proved more efficacious, for me at any rate. For what malice do we in fact have to bear against one another at the individual level, if one thinks about it? And then, after all, one retains a sense of pride even in captivity, so who would not, in the final analysis, lay claim, in his heart of hearts, to a drop of kindness, to say nothing of getting further with a considerate word, so I found.

Still, at bottom, experiences of that kind could not truly shake me as yet. Even the train was still running; if I looked ahead, I dimly sensed the destination somewhere in the distance, and in the initial period—the golden days, as Bandi Citrom and I later dubbed them—Zeitz, along with the conduct it required and a dash of luck, proved a very tolerable place—for the time being, that is, in the interim, until a time to come should secure release from it, naturally. Half a loaf of bread twice a week, a third of a loaf—three times, a quarter—twice only, fairly regular Zulage, boiled potatoes once a week (six spuds, doled out in one's cap, though more than likely there would be no Zulage to go with them), noodle milk pudding once a week. One is soon made to forget any initial annoyance at the early reveille by dewy summer dawns, the unclouded sky, and then a steaming mug of coffee too (and you need to be smart at the latrines, as the cry of *"Appell! Antreten!"* will soon resound). The morning muster, in all likelihood, is bound to be short: after all, work beckons, presses. One of the factory side-gates that we prisoners are also allowed to use lies off to the left of the highway, down a sandy footpath about ten to fifteen minutes' walk from our camp. Already from a long way off, there is a rumbling, clat-

tering, throbbing, panting, a hacking cough of three or four
iron throats: the greetings of the factory, though more a veritable town, what with its main and side roads, slowly
trundling cranes, earth-grabbing machines, profusion of rail
tracks, its labyrinth of flues, cooling towers, piping, and
workshop buildings. The many pits, ditches, ruins, and cave-
ins, the mass of ripped-up conduits and spilled-out cables,
attest to visitations by aircraft. Its name, as I learned as soon
as the first lunch break, is "Brabag," which is "the shorthand formerly used even on the stock market" to refer to the
"Braun-Kohl-Benzin Aktiengesellschaft"[4] so I heard; moreover a burly man who was just then resting his weight on
one elbow with a weary sigh as he fished a nibbled hunk of
bread from his pocket was pointed out as the one who was
the source of that information and, it was subsequently
rumored in the camp, always accompanied by a touch of
glee, and who had also formerly owned a few shares in the
company, I gathered (though I never heard him personally
say as much)—and the smell alone may well have reminded
me of the oil works in Csepel—that here too they are hard at
work producing gasoline, though by dint of some ingenious
trick that allows them to extract it from lignite rather than
oil. I thought this was an interesting concept, even though I
was well aware that wasn't what they were looking for from
me, naturally. The options offered by the work squads, the
Arbeitskommandos, are always a matter of lively debate.
Some swear by spades, others by pitchforks for choice; some
proclaim the advantages of cable-laying work, yet others pre-

---

[4]Lignite-Petroleum Corporation.

fer being assigned to the cement mixers, while who could divine what hidden motive, what dubious predilection, makes certain individuals particularly attached to work on the drains of all things, up to their waists in yellow slime or black oil, though no one doubts the existence of such a motive since most of them happen to be from among the Latvians, plus of course their like-minded friends, the Finns. Only once a day does the word "*Antreten*,"[5] wafting down from on high, have a long, drawn-out, and inviting bittersweet lilt, and that is in the evening, when it signals the time to return home. Bandi Citrom squeezes through the throng around the washbasins with a shout of "Move over, Muslims!" and no part of my body can be kept hidden from his scrutiny. "Wash your pecker too! That's where the lice lodge," he'll say, and I comply with a laugh. This marks the start of that particular hour, that hour of odd matters to attend to, of jokes or complaints, visits, discussions, business deals, and exchanges of information that only the homely clatter of cauldrons, the signal that galvanizes everyone, stirs everyone into quick action, is capable of breaking. Then "*Appell!*" and it's a matter of sheer luck how long for. But then, after a lapse of one, two, or, tops, three hours (with the arc lights going on in the meantime), the great rush along the narrow gangway of the tent, hemmed in on both sides by rows of three-tier bunk-bedding spaces, here called "boxes." After that, for a while yet, the tent is all semidarkness and whispering; this is the time for spinning yarns, tales about the past, the future, freedom. I got to learn that back

---

[5]"Fall in!"

home everyone had been a very model of happiness, usually wealthy as well. It was also at this time that I could get an idea what people used to have for their supper, and even, from time to time, certain other topics of what, between men, sounded like a confidential nature. It was then that speculations were debated (though I never heard anything more about it later on) that a form of sedative, a "bromide," was being mixed into the soup for some particular reason— that's what was alleged at any rate, amid exchanges of knowing and always slightly enigmatic looks. Bandi Citrom too could always be relied on at this time to bring up Forget-me-not Road, the lights or—particularly in the early days, though there were not that many observations of my own that I could make on the subject, naturally—the "Budapest girls." At other times, I would become aware of a suspicious muttering, a quiet, stifled chanting and shaded candlelight coming from one of the corners of the tent, and I heard that it was Friday night, and across there was a priest, a rabbi. I scrambled over the tops of the plank-beds to take a look for myself, and in the middle of a group of men it actually was him, the rabbi I already knew. He was going through the devotions just as he was, in prison garb and hat, but I did not watch him for long since I yearned more for sleep than prayers. I am berthed with Bandi Citrom on the uppermost tier. We share our box with two more bedfellows, both young, likable, and also from Budapest. Wooden planks with straw on them and sacking over the straw serve for bedding. We have one blanket between two, though in the end even that is too much in summertime. We don't exactly have a terrific abundance of space: if I turn over, my neighbor has to do the same, and if my neighbor draws his legs up, I have to do the same; still, even so, sleep was deep and expunged all memories. Those were golden days, indeed.

I began to notice the changes a bit later on—in the matter of rations, first and foremost. I and the others could only speculate how the era of half-loaves could have flown by so swiftly; into its place, at all events, irreversibly stepped the era of thirds and quarters, even the Zulage was no longer always an absolute certainty. That is also when the train began to slow down and eventually came to a standstill altogether. I tried to look ahead, but the prospect stretched only to tomorrow, while tomorrow was an identical day, that is to say, another day exactly the same as today—in the best case, of course. My zest dwindled, my drive dwindled, every day it was that little bit harder to get up, every day I turned in for sleep that little bit wearier. I was that little bit hungrier, found it took that little bit more effort to walk, somehow everything started to become harder, with me becoming a burden even to myself. I (all of us, I dare say) was no longer absolutely always a good prisoner, and we were soon able to recognize the reflections of this, of course, in the soldiers, not to speak of our own functionaries, and among these, if only by virtue of his rank, the *Lagerältester*.

He is still only ever to be seen, anytime and anywhere, in black. It is he who shrills the morning whistle for reveille, he who inspects everything last thing in the evening, and all sorts of things are said about his living quarters somewhere up at the front. German by language, Gypsy by race—even among ourselves he is only known as "the Gypsy"—which is also the primary reason why a concentration camp was designated as his abode, the other being the deviant streak in his nature that Bandi Citrom had immediately sized up at first glance. The green triangle, on the other hand, was a warning to all that he had robbed and killed a lady who allegedly was older and also, so the rumor goes, very rich, and had in fact been his means of support, so it was said; this was therefore the first time in my life I had the chance to see a genuine murderer in person. His duty was the law; his job, to enforce order and justice in our camp—not exactly a particularly comforting thought at first hearing, everyone reckoned, myself included. On the other hand, I was made to see that at a certain point nuances can be deceptive. I personally, for instance, had more trouble with one of the Stubendiensts, even though he is an irreproachably honest man. That is indeed why he was elected by the same close acquaintances who chose Dr. Kovács the Blockältester (that title, I gathered, denotes his status as a lawyer, not a physician), all of them being from the same place, so I hear, the picturesque area around Siófok on the southern shore of Lake Balaton. I mean the ginger-headed guy known universally as Fodor. Now, whether it is true or not, there is general agreement: the Lagerältester uses his club or fist for fun, because, according to camp gossip at any rate, he supposedly derives a certain pleasure from that, something related to what he is also after, the better-informed profess to know, with men, boys, and sometimes even women. With Fodor, though, order is not a pretext but a veritable precondition, and should necessity compel him to act in a similar manner, that is in the general interest—as he never omits to mention. Still, order is never total, indeed ever less so. That may be why he feels obliged to lash out with the long handle of the ladle among those pushing in the queue, and this is how—should one fail by some accident to know the way to approach the soup vat, placing one's bowl precisely at a defined spot on its rim—one may join the ranks of the ill-starred out of whose hands mess tin and soup might easily go flying on such an occasion, because—no question, and the approving murmur behind one indeed signals as much—one is thereby holding him up in his work and therefore also us, those next in line, and also why he pulls Seven Sleepers down from the bunks by the legs, for after all, the sins of one will be visited upon the innocent others. A distinction in intention has to be drawn, naturally, but what I am saying is that such nuances can become blurred at a certain point, while the end result, in my experience, was the same, whichever way I looked at it.

Apart from them, another one here is the German *Kapo*,[6] with his yellow armband and always immaculately ironed striped outfit, whom I did not see much of, fortunately, but later on, to my utter amazement, the occasional black armband with the humbler inscription of *"Vorarbeiter"*[7] upon it also began to appear in our ranks. I happened to be there when one person from our block, until then not particularly conspicuous as far as I was concerned, nor, to the best of my recollection, particularly highly regarded by or well-known to others, but otherwise a vigorous, hefty man, appeared at

---

[6]Head of a work detachment or branch of the camp organization (kitchen, infirmary, etc.).
[7]Foreman.

supper for the very first time with his brand-new armband. But now, I could not help noticing, he was no longer that anonymous person: friends and acquaintances could hardly get near him, what with all the words and hands of rejoicing, congratulation, and good wishes on his promotion that were being offered from all sides, which he accepted from some but not, I noticed, from others, who then hastily made themselves scarce. Eventually the most ceremonious moment of all, for me at least, occurred when, with all eyes on him and in the midst of a form of respectful and even, I might say, reverential hush, very dignified, not hurrying a bit, not hastening a bit, he stepped up in a barrage of amazed or envious looks for the second helping that now befitted his rank, and one from the very bottom of the vat at that, which the Stubendienst ladled out for him with the discrimination now due to those granted that right.

On another occasion, the letters flaunted themselves at me from the arm of a man with a haughty stride and puffed-up chest whom I immediately recognized as the former army officer from Auschwitz. One day I even found myself under his charge, and I can confirm: it's true that he would go through fire and water for his good men, but loafers and shirkers who got others to do the dirty work could expect no laurels from him, as he himself announced, in those very words, when work started. Still, the next day Bandi Citrom and I considered it better to slip into another work-gang.

One other change also caught my eye, interestingly enough with the outsiders most of all, the men in the factory, our guards, but particularly one or another of the Prominents within our camp: they altered, I noticed. I did not quite know what this could be put down to at first: somehow they all looked very splendid, at least in my eyes. It was only later, from one piece of evidence and another, that I realized it was us who had changed, naturally; only this had been harder to spot. If I looked at Bandi Citrom, for example, I would notice nothing odd about him. But when I tried to think back and compare him with his initial appearance, back then, on my right in the row, or the very first time at work, his sinews and muscles still rippling, bulging, dimpling, lithely flexing, or ruggedly straining, like an illustration in a biology text-book as it were, then, to be sure, I found it a little hard to credit. Only then did I understand that time can sometimes play tricks on one's eyes, it seems. That is also how this process, readily measurable though its results were, could escape my notice with an entire family, the Kollmann family, for instance. Everyone in the camp knows them. They hail from a small town in eastern Hungary by the name of Kisvárda, from which many others here have come, and I deduced from the way that people spoke to or about them that they must no doubt have been people of some standing. There are three of them: the father, bald and short, a taller and a shorter son, their faces dissimilar to their father's but spitting images of each other (and thus, I assume, quite probably of their mama's), with identical fair whiskers, iden-tical blue eyes. The three of them always go about together, whenever possible, hand in hand. But then, after a while, I noticed that the father kept falling behind, and the two sons had to help him, tugging him along with them by the hand. After yet another while, the father was no longer between them. Soon after that, the bigger one had to tow the smaller

one in the same manner. Later still he too vanished, with the
bigger one merely dragging himself along, though recently I
have not seen even him around anywhere. Like I say, I saw all
that, only not the way that I was now able, if I thought about
it, to review it, to reel through it like a film so to say, but only
frame by frame, becoming habituated to each single image
again and again, and so consequently not actually noticing at
all. Yet it seems I myself may have changed, since "Leatherware," whom I spotted one day looking very much at home as
he stepped out of the kitchen tent—and I learned that he
had indeed found a position for himself among the enviable
dignitaries of the potato-peelers—was initially not at all willing to believe it was me. I protested that it really was me,
from "Shell," then went on to ask whether, seeing as it was
the kitchen, there happened to be any scraps to eat, some
leftovers perhaps, possibly something from the bottom of
the cauldrons. He said he would have a look, and though he
was not seeking anything for his own part, did I have a cigarette by any chance, since the kitchen Vorarbeiter was "dying
for smokes," as he put it. I admitted that I had none, then he
went away. Not too long after, I realized that I would be wasting time to hang around anymore, and that even friendship
evidently has its limits, with the boundaries being set by the
laws of life—and quite naturally so, no two ways about it.
Another time it was me who didn't recognize a strange crea-
ture who was just then coming my way, presumably stumbling along toward the latrines. His convict's cap slipping
down onto his ears, his face all sunken, pinched, and peaky, a
jaundiced dewdrop on the tip of his nose. "Fancyman!" I
called out: he did not so much as look up. He just shuffled on,

one hand holding his trousers up, and I thought to myself: Can you beat that! Who'd have thought it! On yet another occasion, only this time even more jaundiced, even skinnier, the eyes even a touch larger and more feverish, I think it was "Smoker" I caught sight of. It was around then that the Blockältester's reports at evening and morning roll calls started to include an occasional phrase that was subsequently to become a permanent feature, changing only in respect of the numbers: *"Zwei im Revier,"* or *"Fünf im Revier," "Dreizehn im Revier,"*[8] and so on, and later on also the new notion of shortfalls, the missing, losses, the *"Abgang"* that is to say. No, under certain circumstances not even good intentions are enough. When I was still back at home, I had read that in time, and of course with the requisite effort, a person can become accustomed even to a prisoner's life. That may well be so, I don't doubt it: for instance, in Hungary let's say, in some kind of regular, proper civilian prison, or whatever I am supposed to call it. Only in a concentration camp, going by my experience, there is not much chance of that, to be sure. I can confidently say that, in my case at least, it was never for want of effort, for want of good intentions; the trouble is that they simply don't allow enough time.

I know of (because I saw, heard of, or experienced them for myself) three means of escape in a concentration camp. I personally availed myself of the first, though perhaps, I admit, the most modest of the three—but then, there is a corner of one's nature that, as indeed I came to learn, is a person's accepted and inalienable possession. The fact is, one's

---

[8]"Two (five, thirteen . . .) in sick bay."

imagination remains unfettered even in captivity. I contrived, for instance, that while my hands were busy with a spade or mattock—sparingly, carefully paced, always restricted to just the movements that were absolutely necessary—I myself was simply absent. Still, even the imagination is not completely unbounded, or at least is unbounded only within limits, I have found. After all, with the same effort I could equally have been anywhere—Calcutta, Florida, the loveliest places in the world. Yet that would not have been serious enough, all the same, for me that was not credible, if I may put it that way, so as a result I usually found myself merely back home. True, make no mistake about it, I was no less audacious in doing that than I would have been with, say, Calcutta; only here I hit upon something, a certain modesty and, I might say, a kind of work that compensated and thereby, as it were, promptly authenticated the effort. I soon realized, for example, that I had not been living properly, had not made good use of my days back home; there was much for me to regret, far too much. Thus, I could not help recalling, there had been dishes that I had been fussy about, had picked at then pushed aside, simply because I didn't like them, and right at the present moment I regarded that as an irreparable omission. Then there was the whole senseless tug-of-war between my father and mother over me. When I get back home, I reflected, just like that, with this simple, self-explanatory turn of phrase, not even so much as pausing over it, like someone who can be interested in nothing but the issues that ensued from this all-surpassingly natural fact—when I get back home I shall put a stop to that at any rate, there has to be a truce, I decided. Then there were

156

156

matters back home over which I had fretted, indeed—
however silly it may sound—had been scared of, such as certain subjects in the curriculum, the teachers of those subjects,
being quizzed on them and maybe coming to grief in my
answers, and lastly my father when I reported the outcome
to him: now I would summon up these fears purely for the
diversion of picturing them to myself, living through them
again, and smiling over them. But my favorite pastime was
always, however often, to visualize an entire, unbroken day
back home, from the morning right through the evening if
possible, while still, as before, keeping it purely on the modest scale. After all, it would have taken an effort for me to
conjure up even some kind of special or perfect day, but
then I normally only envisaged a rotten day, with an early rising, school, anxiety, a lousy lunch, the many opportunities
they had offered back then that I had missed, rejected, or
indeed completely overlooked, and I can tell you that now,
here in the concentration camp, I set them all right to the
greatest possible perfection. I had already heard, and now I
can also attest: the confines of prison walls cannot impose
boundaries on the flights of one's fantasy. The only snag was
that if they meanwhile went so far as to make me forget even
my hands, the nonetheless still all-too-present reality might
reassume its rights very swiftly, with the most cogent and
explicit of all rationales.

Around that time, there were occasions at the camp when
it happened that the roll at the morning *Appell* did not
tally—like the other day in Block 6, next to us. Everyone was
perfectly well aware what might have occurred, since reveille
in a concentration camp does not awaken anyone who can no

longer be awakened, and there are such cases. But then that is the second method of escape, and who has not felt that temptation, if only the once, a single time at least; who could remain unfalteringly steadfast, most especially in the morning, when one awakes to—no, has dawn on one—yet another new day in the environs of an already noisy tent, neighbors already making preparations to go: I, for one, could not, and I would undoubtedly have made an attempt, had Bandi Citrom not prevented me from doing so time after time. Coffee is not so important in the end, and anyway you will be there for *Appell*, you think to yourself, as indeed did I. Naturally, you do not stay in your bunk—no one is that infantile after all—but get up, properly, honorably, just like the rest, but then . . . you know of a place, an absolutely safe nook, you would stake a hundred to one on it. You had picked it out, spotted it, or it caught your eye yesterday or maybe even longer ago, quite by chance, without any plan or premeditation, doing no more than vaguely intimating it to yourself. Now it comes to mind. You might squeeze beneath the lowest boxes, for example. Or seek out that hundred-percent-sure crevice, hollow, niche, or nook, then cover yourself well with straw, litter, blankets. All the time with the thought continually in your head that you are going to attend *Appell*. Yes, there was a time, I tell you, when I understood that well, very well indeed. The bolder ones may even suppose that a single person will somehow pass unnoticed; there might be a miscount, for example—people are only human after all: a single shortfall, just today, just this morning, is not necessarily going to be conspicuous, and anyway, by the evening the numbers will add up, you'll make sure of that; the even more reckless, that there is no way or means by which anyone will ever be able to find them in that safe place. But those who are really determined will not think even of that, as they simply consider—and there have been times when I too supposed the same—that an hour or so's good sleep, in the end, is worth any risk, any price.

But then there is not much chance of them getting that much, for in the morning everything unrolls swiftly. Look! A search party is already forming up in great haste, the Lagerältester in black, freshly shaven, fragrant, with dashing moustache at its head, the German Kapo close behind, and behind him a couple of senior block inmates and Stubendiensts, with clubs, bludgeons, and hooked sticks all grasped at the ready, and they turn straight into Block 6. From inside a clamor, pandemonium, and just a couple of minutes later—listen to that!—the triumphant, strident jubilation of those who have found the trail. A sort of squeaking is mingled into that, ever feebler and eventually stilling altogether, and before long the hunters themselves emerge. That thing they are lugging along out of the tent—from here it looks by now like no more than a motionless pile of inanimate objects, a tangle of rags—is tossed down at the very end of the row and left lying there: I do my best not to look over. Yet a shattered detail, a contour, lineament, or distinctive feature that can be made out even so, would draw, compel me to look across, and I did indeed recognize it as the man who had bad luck. After which: "*Arbeitskommandos antreten!*"—and we can depend on it that the soldiers are going to be stricter today.

Finally, the third, the literal, and true mode of escape can also come into play, it seems; there was a single instance of this too in our camp, a one-off occasion. There were three escapees, all three Latvians, seasoned prisoners, well equipped with German and local knowledge, sure of themselves—that was the whispered rumor doing the rounds, and I can tell you that after the initial realization and secret glee—even, here and there, awe—at the expense of our guards and a nascent burst of enthusiasm as we contemplated emulating the example and weighed up the chances, we were also pretty incensed about them, every one of us, by that night, around two or three a.m., when we were still standing (though tottering would be the more accurate word for it) at *Appell* in punishment for their action. The evening of the next day, on marching back, I again had to do my best not to look over to the right. Three chairs were placed there, and on them were seated three men, or men of sorts. Precisely what kind of sight they may have presented, and what may have been inscribed in clumsy big letters on the paper sign hanging from their necks—I felt it simpler not to ask about all that (I got to know anyway, because it was a topic of conversation in the camp for a long time after: "*Hurrah! Ich bin wieder da!*"—or in other words, "Hooray, I'm back again today!"), apart from which I also saw another piece of gimcrackery, a stand which reminded me a bit of the carpet-beating racks in the courtyards of apartment blocks back home, on which there were three ropes tied in nooses—and thus, I realized, a gallows. Naturally, there could be no question of supper, but right away "*Appell!*" and then: "*Das ganze Lager: Achtung!*" [9] as the Lagerältester in person, up front, bellowed at

---

[9]"Attention, everyone in the camp!"

the top of his lungs. The customary punishment squad assembled, then, after a further wait, the representatives of the military authorities made their appearance, after which everything went ahead in due form, if I may put it that way—fortunately, up front near the washroom, far from where we were, not that I watched anyway. My attention was drawn rather to my left, from where all at once came a sound, a muttering, some sort of song. In the row I saw a slightly tremulous head on a scraggy, forward-stretched neck—little more, in fact, than a nose and a huge, moist eye that, right at that moment, was somehow swimming in a crazy light: the rabbi. Soon I also picked out his words, particularly after others in the row had slowly taken them up from him—all the Finns, for instance, but many others as well. Indeed, though I don't know what the mechanism was, it somehow passed across to nearby groups, the other blocks, spreading and gaining ground as it were, because there too I observed a growing number of lips in motion and shoulders, necks, and heads cautiously, almost imperceptibly, yet distinctly rocking back and forth. Meanwhile the muttering was just about audible here, in the center of the row, with a continual "*Yitgaddal ve-yitkaddash*"[10] being sounded over and over again, like some murmur issuing from the ground below, and even I knew that this was the so-called "Kaddish," the Jews' prayer of mourning for the dead. It is quite possible that this too was sheer stubbornness, the final, sole, and perhaps, I could not help realizing, in some ways slightly forced, I might almost say prescribed and in a certain sense

---

[10]"Magnified and sanctified [be his great Name . . .]."

fixed, so to say imposed, and, at the same time, useless mode of stubbornness (for it altered nothing up at the front: apart from the last few twitches of the hanged men, nothing moved, nothing wavered at these words); yet all the same, I could not help somehow understanding the emotion in which the rabbi's expression seemed almost to dissolve, and even his nostrils quivered so strangely. As if it was only now that the long-awaited moment were here, that moment of victory of whose coming he had spoken, I recollected, back in the brickyard. Indeed, for the very first time, I too was now seized, I don't know why, by a certain sense of loss, even a touch of envy; for the first time, I now somewhat regretted that I was unable to pray, if only a few sentences, in the language of the Jews.

But neither stubbornness nor prayers nor any form of escape could have freed me from one thing: hunger. I had, naturally, felt—or at least supposed I felt—hunger before, back at home; I had felt hungry at the brickyard, on the train, at Auschwitz, even at Buchenwald, but I had never before had the sensation like this, protractedly, over a long haul, if I may put it that way. I was transformed into a hole, a void of some kind, and my every endeavor, every effort, was bent to stopping, filling, and silencing this bottomless, evermore clamorous void. I had eyes for that alone, my entire intellect could serve that alone, my every act was directed toward that; and if I did not gnaw on wood or iron or pebbles, it was only because those things could not be chewed and digested. But I did try with sand, for instance, and anytime I saw grass I would never hesitate; but then, sad to say, there was not much in the way of grass to be found, either in the factory or within the grounds of the camp. As much as two slices of bread was the asking price for just one small, pointy onion bulb, and the fortunate well-offs sold beets and turnips for the same price: I personally preferred the latter because they were juicier and usually larger in volume, though those in the know consider there is more of value, in terms of contents and nutrients, in sugar beets; but then who's going to be fussy, even though I find it harder to stomach their tough flesh and pungent taste. I would make do with, and even take a certain comfort from, the thought that at least others were eating. Our guards' lunch was always brought into the factory after them, and I would not take my eyes off them. I have to say, though, that I derived little joy from this as they ate quickly, without even chewing, just bolted it down; I could see they had no idea what they were doing, really. There was another time when I was in a workshop Kommando, and here the workmen unpacked whatever they had brought from home; I recollect watching for a long time—quite possibly, I would have to admit, not entirely without a smidgeon of obscure hope—a yellow hand covered in big warts as it fished long green beans, one after another, out of a tall jar. But that warty hand (by then I had thoroughly familiarized myself with every single one of its warts, every foreseeable grip it might make) just kept on moving, plying the passage between jar and mouth. After a while, though, his back concealed even that from my gaze, since he turned away, which naturally I understood as being out of a sense of decency, though I would have liked to tell him to just take his time, just carry on, as for my own part I set great store on the spectacle alone: that too was better than nothing, in a manner of speaking. The first time I purchased the previous day's potato peelings, a whole bowlful, it was from a Finn. He produced it very casually during the lunch break, and luckily Bandi Citrom was not with me in the Kommando to be able to raise any objections. He placed it in front of him, then dug out a tattered bit of paper, and from that some gritty salt, all very leisurely, at length, even picking up a pinch with the tips of his fingers and carrying that to his lips to taste, before calling over, just kind of casually: "For sale!" The price was normally two slices of bread or a dollop of margarine; he was asking for half of that evening's soup. I tried to haggle, appealing to all sorts of things, even equality. At this, he shook his head, the way Finns do: "*Di bist nist ki yid, d'bist a shaygets.* You no Jew." "So why am I here, then?" I asked. "How I know that?" he shrugged. "Lousy Jew!" I retorted. "That won't make me sell it any cheaper," he replied. In the end, I bought it for the price he had asked, but I have no idea from where he materialized that evening at precisely the moment my soup was being dished out, nor how he had managed to get wind in advance that it was going to be noodle milk pudding for supper that day.

I would maintain that there are certain concepts which can be fully comprehended only in a concentration camp. A recurrent figure in the dumb storybooks of my childhood, for instance, was that of a certain "itinerant journeyman" or "outlaw" who in order to win the princess's hand enters the king's service, and gladly so, because that amounts to only seven days altogether. "But seven days with me means seven years to you," the king tells him. Well, I can say exactly the

164

same about the concentration camps. I would never have believed, for instance, that I could become a decrepit old man so quickly. Back home that takes time, fifty or sixty years at least; here three months was enough for my body to leave me washed up. I can safely say there is nothing more painful, nothing more disheartening than to track day after day, to record day after day, yet again how much of one has wasted away. Back home, while paying no great attention to it, I was generally in harmony with my body; I was fond of this bit of machinery, so to say. I recollect reading some exciting novel in our shaded parlor one summer afternoon, the palm of my hand meanwhile caressing with pleasing absentmindedness the golden-downed, pliantly smooth skin of my tautly muscular sunburned thigh. Now that same skin was drooping in loose folds, jaundiced and desiccated, covered in all kinds of boils, brown rings, cracks, fissures, pocks, and scales that itched uncomfortably, especially between my fingers. "Scabies," Bandi Citrom diagnosed with a knowing nod of the head when I showed him. I could only wonder at the speed, the rampant pace, with which, day by day, the enveloping material, the elasticity, the flesh around my bones dwindled, atrophied, dissolved, and vanished somewhere. Every day there was something new to surprise me, some new blemish, some new unsightliness on this ever stranger, ever more foreign object that had once been my good friend: my body. I could no longer bear looking at it without a sense of being at war with myself, a species of abhorrence; for that reason alone, after a while, I no longer cared to strip off to have a wash, to say nothing of my antipathy to such superfluous exertions, to the cold, and then too, of course, to my footwear.

165

These devices, at least in my case, caused a great deal of vexation. In general I had little reason to be satisfied with the items of clothing with which I was equipped in the concentration camp; there was not much of the practicable, and a lot that was faulty about them, indeed they became direct sources of inconvenience; they failed to measure up at all, I can safely say. During spells of fine gray drizzle, for instance, which with the change of season were prolonged when they occurred, the burlap outfit was transformed into a stiff stovepipe, the clammy touch of which one's skin strove to avoid in any way possible—quite in vain, naturally. A prison overcoat (these were issued, it has to be said in all fairness) was quite worthless here, just another handicap, yet another damp layer, and in my view no satisfactory solution was provided even by the coarse paper from a cement sack that Bandi Citrom, like many others, had filched for himself and wore under his jacket, in spite of all the risks, since this sort of transgression soon comes to light: it only takes the whack of a stick on the back and another on the chest for the rustling to make the offense manifest. On the other hand, if it no longer crackles, I ask you, then what is the use of the fresh annoyance of this soaking-wet pulp, which again can only be discarded?

The wooden shoes, though, are the most irksome. It all started with the mud, in actual fact. Even in this respect, I can tell you, the notions I had formed hitherto turned out to be inadequate. Naturally, I had already seen, even trampled in, mud back home, yet I still had no clue that mud can at times be the arena for the bulk of one's cares, one's very life. What it means to sink up to one's calves in it, then put all one's efforts into freeing one leg from it with a single, loudly

166

squelching tug, only to plunge it in anew, no more than eight or twelve inches farther forward—in no way was I prepared, indeed it would have been pointless to be prepared, for all that. Now, one thing that has become clear about the clogs is that the heels wear down over time. When that happens, one has to go around on a thick sole that at a certain point suddenly thins and thus curves up in a gondola shape, requiring one to rock forward on the rounded sole like a sort of tumbler toy. On top of that, at the place where the former heel had been, a gap, widening day by day, opens up between the stiffer uppers and the extremely thin sole, so now cold mud, not to speak of tiny pebbles and sharp bits of debris of all kinds, can stream in unobstructedly at every step. Meanwhile those stiff uppers have long been chafing one's ankles and abraded countless sores on the softer tissues below them. Now, those sores by their very nature suppurate, and that pus is definitely sticky, with the result that it becomes impossible to free oneself from the clogs: they become stuck to the feet, veritably fused to them, rather like new body parts as it were. I wore them during the day and also wore them on turning in to sleep, if only so as not to waste time when I got up, or to be more precise, jumped down from my bunk two, three, sometimes even four times during the night. That's all very well at night: after a bit of bother, stumbling and slipping around in the mud outside, one somehow manages to find one's way to the goal by the glare of the searchlights. But what is one supposed to do by day, exactly what, if the urge to empty one's bowels seizes one—as it inevitably will—in the work detail? At a time like that, one plucks up every ounce of courage, bares one's head, and begs the guard's permission: "*Gehorsamst, zum Abort*"[11]—assuming, of course, there is a privy nearby, and specifically a privy that the prisoners may make use of. But let us suppose they do exist—suppose one's guard is well disposed and grants permission once, grants it a second time; but then—I ask you!—who is going to be so rash, so desperate, as to test that patience a third time? The only thing left at a time like that is mute turmoil, teeth clenched, bowels continually quaking, until the dice have rolled and either one's body or one's mind wins out.

As a final means, there are the beatings—whether expected or unexpected, sought or sedulously avoided—anywhere and at any time. I had my fair share of them too, naturally, no more but also no less than normal, the average, the ordinary, like anyone, any one of us—as many as are consistent with purely routine conditions in our camp rather than any particular personal accident. Inconsistent as it may be, I have to relate that I came in for these, not from an SS serviceman—someone who is in fact to some degree professionally called upon, authorized, even obliged in that respect—but from a yellow-overalled member of a more shadowy semimilitary "Todt" organization that, so I gather, has some sort of supervisory role over workplaces. He happened to be around and spotted it—Oh, what a yell! what a sprint!—when I dropped a bag of cement. Now, carrying cement must be welcomed by every Kommando—rightly so, in my opinion—with a peculiar joy that is accorded only on rare occasions and to which we would find it hard to admit,

---

[11]"Beg leave to go to the latrines."

168

even privately among ourselves. You bow your head, someone lays a bag over your shoulder, you amble over to a truck with it, and there someone else picks it up, after which you amble back, taking a nice wide detour, the bounds of which are determined by the vagaries of the moment, and if you are lucky they will be queuing up in front of you, so you can snatch another breather until it's your next turn. Then again, the bag itself weighs around twenty to thirty pounds altogether—child's play compared with back home, one could even safely play ball with it, I reckon; but here I was, stumbling and dropping it. Worse still, the bag's paper had burst and the contents spilled out, leaving a heap of the material, the treasure, the costly cement, powdering the ground. By then he was already on me, I had already felt his fist on my face, then, having been decked, his boot on my ribs and his grip on my neck as he pressed my face to the ground, in the cement, screaming insanely that I scrape it together, lick it up. He then hauled me to my feet, swearing he would teach me: *"Dir werd ich's zeigen, Arschloch, Scheisskerl, verfluchter Judehund,"*[12] so I would never drop a bag again in the future. From then on, he personally loaded a new bag onto my shoulders each time it was my turn, bothering himself with me alone; I was his sole concern, it was me exclusively whom he kept his eye on, following me all the way to the truck and back, and whom he picked to go first even if, by rights, there were others still ahead of me in the queue. In the end, there was almost an understanding between us, we had got the measure of one another, and I

---

[12]"I'll show you, asshole, shithead, goddam Jew-dog!"

noticed his face bore what was almost a smile of satisfaction, encouragement, even, dare I say, a pride of sorts, and from a certain perspective, I had to acknowledge, with good reason, for indeed, tottering, stooping though I might have been, my eyes seeing black spots, I did manage to hold out, coming and going, fetching and carrying, all without dropping a single further bag, and that, when it comes down to it, I would have to admit, proved him right. On the other hand, by the end of the day I felt that something within me had broken down irreparably; from then on, every morning I believed that would be the last morning I would get up; with every step I took, that I could not possibly take another; with every movement I made, that I would be incapable of making another; and yet for all that, for the time being, I still managed to accomplish it each and every time.

SEVEN

Cases may occur, situations present themselves, that no amount of ingenuity could possibly make worse, it would seem. I can report that, after so much striving, so many futile attempts and efforts, in time I too found peace, tranquillity, and relief. For instance, certain things to which I had previously attributed some vast, practically inconceivable significance, I can tell you, lost all importance in my eyes. Thus, if I grew tired while standing at *Appell*, for example, without so much as a look at whether it was muddy or there was a puddle, I would simply take a seat, plop down, and stay down, until my neighbors forcibly pulled me up. Cold, damp, wind, or rain were no longer able to bother me; they did not get through to me, I did not even sense them. Even my hunger passed; I continued to carry to my mouth anything edible I was able to lay my hands on, but more out of absentmindedness, mechanically, out of habit, so to say. As for work, I no longer even strove to give the appearance of it. If people did not like that, at most they would beat me, and even then they could not truly do much harm, since for me it just won some time: at the first blow I would promptly stretch out on the ground and would feel nothing after that, since I would meanwhile drop off to sleep.

Just one thing inside me grew stronger: my irritability. If anyone should encroach on my bodily comfort, even just touch my skin, or if I missed my step (as often happened) when the column was on the march, for example, and someone behind me trod on my heel, I would have been quite prepared instantly, without a moment's hesitation, without further ado, to kill them on the spot—had I been able to, of course, and had I not forgotten, by the time I raised my hand, what it was I had in fact wanted to do. I even had rows with Bandi Citrom: I was "letting myself go," I was a burden on the work squad, he would catch my scabies, he reproached me. But above all else, it was as if I somehow embarrassed or worried him in a certain respect. I became conscious of this one evening when he took me with him to the washroom. My flailing and protests were to no avail as he stripped me of my clothes with all the strength he could muster; my attempts to pummel his body and face with my fists to no avail as he scrubbed cold water over my shivering skin. I told him a hundred times over that his guardianship was a nuisance to me, he should leave me alone, just eff off. Did I want to croak right here, did I maybe not want to get back home, he asked, and I have no clue what answer he must have read from my face but, all at once, I saw some

172

form of consternation or alarm written all over his, in much the same way as people generally view irremediable trouble-makers, condemned men or, let's say, carriers of pestilence, which was when the opinion he had once expressed about Muslims crossed my mind. In any event, from then on, he tended to steer clear of me, I could see that, while I, for my part, was finally relieved of that particular bother.

There was no way I could shake off my knee, however, and an increasingly persistent pain in it. After a few days I inspected it, and for all my body's accommodation to many things by now, I nevertheless thought it advisable to promptly shield myself from the sight of this new surprise, the flaming red sac into which the area around my right knee had been transformed. I was well aware, naturally, that a *Revier*[1] was functioning in our camp as well, but then, for starters, the consulting hour coincided with supper time, and in the end I placed higher priority on that than on any treatment, and then too various incidents, this and that bit of knowledge of the place itself and of life, did not exactly boost one's confidence. For another, it was a long way off, two tents farther over, and unless forced by absolute neces-sity, I would not willingly have embarked on such a lengthy excursion, not least because my knee was by now extremely painful. Eventually, Bandi Citrom and one of our bunk-mates, forming a cradle with their hands, a bit like storks are said to carry their young to safety, took me over anyway, and after I had been set on a table I was given a warning, well in advance, that it was most likely going to hurt as immediate

---

[1] Sick bay or infirmary.

173

surgery was unavoidable, which for lack of any anesthetic would have to be done without that. As far as I could make out what was going on, a pair of crosswise incisions were made above the knee with a scalpel, and through that they expressed the mass of matter that was in my thigh, then bandaged the whole lot up with paper. Right afterward I even mentioned supper and was assured that this would be taken care of, as indeed I soon found to be the case. That day's soup was turnip and kohlrabi, which I am very partial to, and the portions doled out for the Revier had palpably been taken from the bottom of the vat, which was another reason to be satisfied. I also spent the night there, in the Revier tent, in a box on the uppermost tier that I had all to myself, the only unpleasant aspect being that when the usual time for a bout of diarrhea came around, I was no longer able to use my own legs, while my efforts to call for help, first whispering, then out loud, and finally yelling, were likewise fruitless. On the morning of the following day, mine and a number of other bodies were hoisted up onto the soaking-wet sheet-iron flooring of an open truck to be transported to a nearby place that, if I heard rightly, goes by the name of "Gleina," where our camp's actual hospital is situated. En route a soldier seated on a neat folding stool, a damply glistening rifle on his knees, kept an eye on us in the back, his face visibly surly, grudging, and at times, presumably in response to an occasional sudden stench or sight he could not avoid, grimacing in disgust—not entirely without due cause, I had to admit. Particularly upsetting to me, it was as if in his mind he had come to some opinion, deduced some general truth, and I would have liked to excuse myself: I was not entirely the only one at fault here, and in fact this was not the genuine me—but then that would have been hard for me to prove, naturally, I could see that. Once we had arrived, first of all I had to endure a jet of water from a rubber pipe, a sort of garden hose, that was unexpectedly unleashed on me and probed after me whichever way I turned, washing everything off me: the remaining tatters of clothing, dirt, and even the paper bandage. But then they took me into a room where I was given a shirt and the lower of a two-tier bed of boards, and on that was even able to lie on a straw mattress that, although obviously tamped and pressed down fairly flat and hard by my predecessor, and mottled here and there with suspicious stains, suspicious-smelling and suspiciously crackling discolorations, was at least unoccupied and on which it was finally left entirely up to me how I spent my time and, most of all, to have a decent sleep at long last.

It looks as though we always carry old habits along with us even to new places; in the hospital, I can tell you, I had to struggle at first with what even I myself found to be many inveterate and ingrained reflexes. Conscientiousness, for instance: to start with, it invariably awakened me at dawn on the dot. At other times I would start awake thinking I had slept through *Appell* and outside they were already hunting me; only after my racing heart had calmed down would I notice my error and accept what lay before my own eyes, the evidence of reality, that I was where I was, everything was all right, over this way someone was groaning, somewhat farther away people were chatting, and over there someone else had his pointed nose, stony gaze, and gaping mouth trained mutely on the ceiling, that only my wound was hurting, and besides that at most, as at all times, I was very thirsty, pre-sumably due to my fever, quite clearly. In short, I needed a bit of time until I had fully taken it in that there was no *Appell*, that I would not have to see soldiers, and, above all, did not have to go to work—advantages from which, for me at least, no inconsequential circumstance or illness, at bottom, could detract. From time to time, I too was taken up to a small room on the floor above, where the two doctors worked, a younger and an older one, with my being a patient of the latter, so to say. He was a lean, dark-haired, kindly looking man, in a clean uniform, with proper shoes, an armband, and a normal, recognizable face that put me in mind of an ami-able, aging fox. He asked where I was from and recounted that he himself came from Transylvania. In the meantime he had stripped off the peeling and by now caked, greenish yel-low wad of paper that had been rolled around the knee area, then, putting his weight behind both arms, squeezed from my thigh all the pus that had accumulated there in the interim, and finally, with some instrument resembling a cro-chet hook, poked a rolled-up length of gauze between skin and flesh—for purposes of "maintaining an open passage" and "the drainage process," as he explained, lest the wound heal prematurely. For my part, I was happy to hear this as, when you came right down to it, I had nothing to do on the outside; if I really thought things through, of course, my health was hardly of such pressing concern to me. Another comment he made, though, was less to my liking. He reck-oned the single perforation on my knee was not sufficient; in his opinion, a second opening ought to be made on the side and connected with the first by yet a third incision. He asked

176

if I was prepared to brace myself for that, and I was utterly amazed that he was looking at me as if he were actually awaiting an answer, my consent, not to mention authorization. I told him, "Whatever you wish," and he immediately said that in that case it would be best not to delay. He duly set to on the spot, but then I found myself obliged to act a little bit vocally, which, I could see, got on his nerves. He even commented several times: "I can't work like this," for which I tried to make excuses: "I can't help it." After making an inch or so of headway, he finally abandoned the attempt, without fully completing what he had planned to do; even so, he seemed tolerably well pleased, noting, "It's better than nothing," since now, he reckoned, he would at least be able to expel the pus from me at two sites. Time also went by in the hospital; if I happened not to be sleeping, then I would always be kept busy by hunger, thirst, the pain around the wound, the odd conversation, or the event of a treatment; but even without anything to occupy me, I can say that I got along splendidly merely by bearing this pleasantly tingling thought in mind, this privilege and the unbounded joy it always afforded. I would interrogate each new arrival for news from the camp: which block they were from, did they by any chance know of a guy called Bandi Citrom from *Block Fünf*, medium height, broken nose, front teeth missing, but no one could recall such a person. Most of the injuries I saw in the surgery room were similar to mine, likewise mainly on the thigh or lower leg, though some were higher up, on the hip, the backside, arm, even the neck and back, being what are known scientifically as "phlegmons," a term I heard a lot, the presence and particularly high incidence of which was neither odd nor amazing under normal concentration camp conditions, as I learned from the doctors. A little later on, there started to arrive cases who had to have a toe or two amputated, sometimes all of them, and they recounted that it was winter out there in the camp, so their feet, being in wooden shoes, had frozen. On another occasion, some manifestly high-ranking personage, in a tailored prison uniform, entered the bandaging station. I distinctly heard a quiet "*Bonjour!*" from which, along with the letter "F" on his red triangle, I immediately worked out he was French, then from the "*O. Arzt*" inscribed on his armband that he was clearly the chief medical officer in our hospital. I stared at him for a long time, because it was ages since I had seen anyone so elegant: he was not particularly tall, but his uniform was nicely filled out by appropriate bulges of flesh on the bones, his face similarly padded, every feature unmistakably his own, with expressible emotions, recognizable nuances, a rounded chin with a dimple in the middle, his olive skin gleaming softly in the light that fell on it, the way skin had generally done once, in the old days, among people back home. I assessed him as being not very old, maybe around thirty. I saw that the doctors too perked up a lot, striving to please him, explaining everything, but noticed this was not so much in the way that was customary within the camp as somehow in accordance with the old and, as it were, instantly nostalgic custom back home, with the sort of discrimination, delight, and social graces that one displays when given an opportunity to display how capitally one understands and speaks some cultured language like, as in this instance, French. On the other hand, though, I could not help noting that this cannot have signified much to the chief doctor, for he looked at everything, gave an occasional monosyllabic answer, or just nodded, but taking his time, quietly, gloomily, listlessly, with an immutable expression of some despondent, all but melancholic emotion in his hazel eyes from first to last. I was dumbfounded as I could not work out what might give rise to that in such a well-off, well-heeled Prominent, who had moreover risen to such a high rank. I tried to search his face, follow his gestures, and it only gradually dawned on me that, make no mistake, when it came down to it, even he was obliged to be here, of course; only gradually, and this time not entirely without an element of astonishment, a sort of serene awe, did the impression grow on me, and I reckoned I was on to something, that if I was right, then it must, it seemed, be this situation—in a word, captivity itself—that was troubling him. I would have told him to cheer up, since that was the least of it, but I was afraid that would be temerity on my part, and then it occurred to me that I didn't speak French anyway.

I slept through the transfer too, more or less. Prior to that, the news had reached me that in the meantime winter quarters, stone-walled barracks, had been constructed in place of the tents at Zeitz, and among those provision for a hospital had not been overlooked. Again I was tossed onto a truck—judging from the darkness, it must have been evening, and from the cold, sometime around midwinter—and the next thing I made out was a cold, well-illuminated anteroom to some immeasurably vast place, and in the anteroom a wooden tub smelling of chemicals. I was obliged to wash—all complaints, pleading, and protest being to absolutely no effect—to dip myself in it to the crown of my head, which, apart from the coldness of its contents, made me shudder even more since I could not help but notice that all the other sick people—wounds and all—had already immersed in that selfsame brown liquid before me. After which, here too time started to elapse, and in essentially the same manner as at the previous place, with only minor differences. In our new hospital, for instance, there were triple-decker bunks; we were also taken off to the doctor less frequently, and so it was more here that my wound cleared up, in its own way, as best it could. On top of that, not long afterward a pain started on my left hip followed by the now familiar flaming red sac. A few days after that, having waited in vain for it to subside, or maybe for something else to intervene, I was driven, like it or not, to mention it to the orderly, then after renewed urging, some further days of waiting, I finally took my place in the queue for the doctors in the anteroom to the barracks, as a result of which, to go with the incision on my right knee, another, roughly the length of my palm, was made on my left hip. More unpleasantness arose from where I was placed, on one of the lower bunks, since it happened to be directly opposite a tiny, unglazed window that was open to the invariably gray sky and on the iron bars of which the clouds of steaming exhalations in here had probably been responsible for forming permanent icicles with a perpetual coating of furry hoarfrost. All I had to wear, however, was what was issued to patients: a short, buttonless shirt and, with some regard to the winter season, the gift of a peculiar, green-colored woolly cap with circular flaps over the ears and a wedge-shaped protrusion over the brow that, although somewhat resembling the headgear of a speedskating champion or an actor doing Satan on stage, was nonetheless extremely useful. As a result, I was often freezing, especially after losing one of my two blankets, the tatters of which had, up till then, allowed me to make up quite tolerably for the shortcomings of the other: I should lend it for a short period, so said the orderly, he would bring it back later. Even using both hands, my attempts to hold fast to it were in vain, he proving the stronger; but what rather upset me, besides the loss itself, was the thought that, as best I knew, they generally had a habit of stripping the blankets most frequently off those for whom the end seemed predictable, not to say anticipated. On yet another occasion, a voice that had meantime grown familiar to me, from another lower bunk somewhere behind me, alerted me to the fact that an orderly must have made another appearance, once again with a new patient in his arms, and was in the middle of casting around to see which of our beds he might be deposited on. The gravity of the voice's case, we learned, and the doctor's approval entitled him to a bed of his own, and he roared and thundered "I protest!" invoked "I have a right to it! Just ask the doctor!" and again "I protest!" so stridently that the orderlies would indeed, eventually, keep carrying their load on to another bed—my own, for example; which is how I acquired another boy who looked to be roughly my own age as a bunk-mate. The sallow face and large, burning eyes seemed vaguely familiar to me, but then, equally, everyone here had a sallow face and large, burning eyes. His first words were to ask if I happened to have a glass of water, so I told him I wouldn't mind one myself, and that was followed immediately by: what about a cigarette? and of course he was no luckier on that score either. He offered bread for one, but I made it clear he should drop it, that had nothing to do with it, I simply didn't have any, at which he fell silent for a while. I suspect he must have had a fever as heat was pouring steadily from his persistently shivering body, from which I was able to take agreeable profit. I was less enchanted with all his tossing and turning during the night, which, to be sure, did not always pay adequate consideration to my wounds. I told him as well: Hey! Cut it out, ease up there, and in the end he heeded the advice. I only saw why the next morning, when my repeated attempts to rouse him for coffee were futile. All the same, I hastily passed his mess tin to the orderly along with my own since, just as I was about to report the case, he snappily asked me for it. I later also accepted his bread ration on his behalf, and likewise his soup that evening, and so on for a while, until one day he began to go really strange, which was when I felt obliged finally to say something, as I could not carry on stowing him in my bed, after all. I was somewhat apprehensive as the delay was by now rather obvious, though its reason—with a mite of acumen, on which I could still draw—seemed easy enough to deduce, but anyway he was taken away with the others and nothing was said, thank goodness, so for the time being I too was left without a companion.

One further thing that I truly made acquaintance of here was the vermin. I was quite unable to catch the fleas: they were nimbler than me, and for a very good reason too, after all, they were better nourished. Catching the lice was easy, only it made no sense. If I grew particularly exasperated with them, all I had to do was run a thumbnail at random over the canvas of the shirt stretched on my back to mete revenge, wreak devastation, in a series of clearly audible pops; yet within a minute I could have repeated it all over again, on the selfsame spot, with exactly the same result. They were everywhere, wriggling into every hidden crevice; my green cap was so infested as to turn gray and all but crawl with them. Still, the biggest surprise of all was the consternation, then horror, of feeling a sudden tickling sensation on my hip and then, on lifting the paper bandage, seeing they were now on my open flesh there, feeding on the wound. I tried to snatch them away, get rid of them, at least root and winkle them out, compel them to wait and be patient at least a little bit longer, but I have to admit that never before had I sensed a more hopeless struggle or a more stubborn, even, so to say, more brazen resistance than this. After a while, indeed, I gave up and just watched the gluttony, the teeming, the voracity, the appetite, the unconcealed happiness; in a manner of speaking, it was as though it were vaguely familiar to me from somewhere. Even so, I realized that, to some extent, and taking everything into account, I could see it their way. In the end, I almost felt relieved, even my sense of revulsion very nearly passed. I was still not pleased, still remained a little bit bitter about it, understandably enough I think, but now it was somehow more generalized, without acrimony, in acquiesing to a degree in nature's larger scheme, if I may put it that way; in any event, I quickly covered the wound up and subsequently no longer engaged in combat with them, no longer disturbed them.

I can affirm that there is no amount of experience, no tranquillity so perfect, nor any insight of such weight, it seems, as to lead us to abandon yet one more last chance in our favor—assuming there is a way, naturally. Thus, when I, along with all the others on whom it was clear not too much further hope can have been pinned of being set to work again here, in Zeitz, was returned to sender as it were—back to Buchenwald—I naturally shared the others' joy with every faculty that was left me, since I was promptly reminded of the good times there, most especially the morning soups. However, I gave no thought, I have to admit, to the fact that I would first have to get there, by rail at that, and under the conditions of travel that now implied; in any event, I can tell you there were things that I had never previously understood, indeed would have had trouble in crediting at all. A once so commonly heard expression as "his earthly remains," for instance, as far as I knew up till then, was applicable solely to someone deceased. For my own part, I could hardly have doubted it, I was alive: even if only guttering and, as it were, turned down to the very lowest mark, a flicker of life nevertheless still burned within me as they say, or to put it another way, my body was here, I had precise cognizance of everything about it, it was just that I myself somehow no longer inhabited it. I had no difficulty in perceiving that this entity, and other similar entities to its side and above it, was lying there, on the wagon's jolting flooring, on cold straw so dampened by all sorts of dubious fluids that my paper bandage had long since frayed, peeled, and become detached, while the shirt and prison trousers in which I had been dressed for the journey were pasted to my naked wounds—yet all this was of no immediate concern to me, of no interest, no longer had any impact, indeed I would maintain that it had been a long time since I had felt so easy, tranquil, almost lost in reverie—so comfortable, to be quite frank. For the first time in ages, I was freed of the torments of irritability: the bodies squeezed up against mine no longer bothered me, indeed I was somehow even glad that they were there with me, that they were so akin and so similar to mine, and it was now that an unwonted, anomalous, shy, I might even say clumsy feeling toward them came over me for the first time—I believe it may, perhaps, have been affection. I encountered the same on their part as well. True, they no longer held out much in the way of hope, as they once had. It could be that this—above and beyond all other difficulties, naturally—is what gave rise to other manifestations that could sometimes be heard alongside the general groaning, the hisses from between clenched teeth, the quiet plaints—a word of solace and reassurance—so hushed and yet, at the same time, so intimate. But I can say that those who still had any capacity at all were not remiss in actions either, and when I announced that I needed to urinate diligent hands were merciful to me too by passing on the brass can from who knows how far away. By the time ice-skimmed puddles on paved ground, instead of those on the train's floorboards, finally came to be under my back—how, when, and by dint of the hands of which person or persons, I have no idea—I can tell you it no longer meant all that much to me that I had arrived safely back at Buchenwald, and I had also long forgotten that this was the place, when all is said and done, that I had yearned so much to reach. I did not even have an inkling where I might be, whether still at the railway station or farther inside; I did not recognize the surroundings, nor did I see the road, the villas, and statue that I still clearly remembered.

In any case, it seemed I must have lain there in that way for some time, and I was getting on just fine, peacefully, placidly, incuriously, patiently, where they had set me down. I felt no cold or pain, and it was more my intellect than my skin which signaled that some stinging precipitation, half snow, half rain, was spattering my face. I mused on one thing and another, gazed at whatever happened to strike my eye without any superfluous movement or effort: the low, gray, impenetrable sky, for instance, or to be more precise the leaden, sluggishly moving wintry cloud-cover, which concealed it from view. Nevertheless, every now and again it would be parted by an unexpected rent, with a more brilliant gap arising in it here and there for a fleeting moment, and that was like a sudden intimation of a depth out of which a ray was seemingly being cast on me from up above, a rapid, searching gaze, an eye of indeterminate but unquestionably pale hue—somewhat similar to that of the doctor before whom I had once passed, back in Auschwitz. A shapeless object right next to me: a wooden shoe and on the other side a devil's cap similar to mine with, between two jutting appurtenances—a nose and chin—a hollow indentation: a face came into my field of vision. Beyond that were further heads, entities, bodies—what I understood to be the remnants or, if I may use the more precise term, debris of the freight consignment that had presumably been parked here for the time being. Some time later, and I don't know if it was an hour, a day, or a year, I finally picked out voices, noises, the sounds of work, and tidying up. All of a sudden, the head next to me rose, and lower down, by the shoulders, I saw arms in prison garb preparing to toss it onto the top of a heap of other bodies that had already been piled on some kind of handcart or barrow. At the same time, a snatch of speech that I was barely able to make out came to my attention, and in that hoarse whispering I recognized even less readily a voice that had once—I could not help recollecting—been so strident: "I p . . . pro . . . test," it muttered. For a moment, before swinging onward, he came to a halt in midair, in astonishment as it were, or so I thought, and I immediately heard another voice—obviously that of the person grasping him by the shoulders. It was a pleasant, masculine-sounding, friendly voice, slightly foreign, the Lager vernacular of the German attesting, so I sensed, more to a degree of surprise, a certain amazement, than any malice: "*Was? Du willst noch leben?*"[2] he asked, and right then I too found it odd, since it could not be warranted and, on the whole, was fairly irrational. I resolved then that I, for my part, was going to be more sensible. By then, however, they were already leaning over me, and I was forced to blink because a hand was fumbling near my eyes before I too was dumped into the middle of a load on a smaller handcart, which they then started to push somewhere, though as to where, I wasn't too inquisitive. Only one thing preoccupied me, one thought, one question that passed through my mind at this moment. It may well have been my fault for not knowing, but I had never had the foresight to inquire about the customs, rules, and procedures at Buchenwald—in short,

---

[2] "What? You still want to live?"

how they did it here: was it with gas, as at Auschwitz, or maybe by means of some medicine, which I had also heard about, or possibly a bullet or some other way, with one of a thousand other methods of which, having insufficient information, I was ignorant. At all events, I hoped it was not going to be painful; strange as it may seem, this too was just as genuine, and preoccupied me in just the same way, as other, more valid hopes that—in a manner of speaking—one pins on the future. Only then did I find out that vanity is an emotion that, it seems, attends a person right up to their very last moment, because truly, however much this uncertainty may have been nagging me, I did not address any question or request so much as a single word, nor even cast a fleeting glance behind me, to the person or persons who were pushing. The path, however, came to a high bend, and down below a broad panorama suddenly emerged beneath me. The dense landscape that populated the entire vast downward slope stood there, with its identical stone houses, the neat green barracks, and then, forming a separate group, a cluster of perhaps new, somewhat grimmer, as yet unpainted barracks, with the serpentine, yet visibly orderly tangle of inner barbed-wire fences separating the various zones, and farther off a trackless expanse of huge, now bare trees disappearing into the mist. I did not know what a crowd of naked Muslims were waiting for by a building over there, but I did indeed suddenly identify a few worthies who, judging by their stools and busy movements as they sauntered back and forth, were barbers, if I was not mistaken, which meant it must obviously be the day's intake for the bathhouse. Farther in, as well, the distant, cobblestoned streets of the

Lager were also inhabited by signs of movement, languid activity, pottering about, killing time: founder inmates, the ailing, prominent personages, storemen, and the fortunate elect of the in-camp work Kommandos were coming and going, carrying out their everyday duties. Here and there, more suspect plumes of smoke mingled with more benign vapors, while a familiar-sounding clatter drifted up faintly my way from somewhere, like bells in dreams, and as I gazed down across the scene, I caught sight of a procession of bearers, poles on shoulders, groaning under the weight of steaming cauldrons, and from far off I recognized, there could be no doubting it, a whiff of turnip soup in the acrid air. A pity, because it must have been that spectacle, that aroma, which cut through my numbness to trigger an emotion, the growing waves of which were able to squeeze, even from my dried-out eyes, a few warmer drops amid the dankness that was soaking my face. Despite all deliberation, sense, insight, and sober reason, I could not fail to recognize within myself the furtive and yet—ashamed as it might be, so to say, of its irrationality—increasingly insistent voice of some muffled craving of sorts: I would like to live a little bit longer in this beautiful concentration camp.

EIGHT

I must admit, there are certain things I would never be able to explain, not precisely, not if I were to consider them from the angle of my own expectations, of rule, or reason—from the angle of life, in sum, the order of things, at least insofar as I am acquainted with it. Thus, when they off-loaded me from the handcart onto the ground again, I was quite unable to grasp what I might still have to do with, for instance, hair-clippers and razors. The jammed space, look-ing at first glance uncannily like a shower room, with its slip-pery wooden laths onto which I too was deposited amid countless trampling, pressing soles, ankles, ulcerated shanks, and shins—that, by and large, conformed more to my rough expectations. It even fleetingly crossed my mind that, amaz-ing! it seems the Auschwitz custom must be in force here as well. My surprise was all the greater when, after a short wait

and a series of hissing, bubbling sounds, water, a copious jet
of unexpected hot water, started to gush from the nozzles up
above. I was not too pleased, however, because I would have
gladly warmed up a little more, but there was nothing I could
do about it when, all at once, an irresistible force whisked me
up into the air, out of the jostling forest of legs, and meanwhile some kind of big bedsheet and on top of that a blanket
were wrapped around me. Then I recollect a shoulder and
being draped over it, head to the rear, feet forward; a door,
the steep steps of a narrow staircase, another door, then
an indoor space, a chamber, a room so to say, where my
incredulous eyes were struck, over and above the spaciousness and light, by the well-nigh barrack-room luxury of the
furnishings; and finally the bed—manifestly a genuine, regular, single-berth bed, with a well-stuffed straw mattress and
even two gray blankets—onto which I rolled from the shoulder. In addition, two men, regular, handsome men, with faces
and hair, in white cotton pants and undershirts, clogs on their
feet; I gazed, marveled admiringly at them, while they scrutinized me. Only then did I notice their mouths and that some
singsong had been humming in my ears for quite some time.
I had a feeling they wished to get something out of me, but
all I could do was shake my head that, no, I didn't understand. On that, I heard coming from one of them, but with a
most peculiar German accent, "*Hast du Durchmarsch?*" or in
other words, did I have the runs, and somewhat to my surprise I heard my own voice give the answer, hard to know why,
"*Nein*"—I suppose as ever, even now, again no doubt merely
out of pride. Then, after a brief consultation and some hunting around, they pushed two objects into my hands. One was

a bowl of warm coffee, the other a hunk of bread, roughly one-sixth of a loaf, I estimated. I was allowed to take them and consume them without payment or barter. For a while after that, my insides, suddenly giving signs of life by starting to seethe and become unruly, occupied all my attention and, above all, my efforts, lest the pledge I had given shortly before should in some way be found to have been untrue. I later woke to see that one of the men was there again, this time in boots, a splendid dark blue cap, and a prison jacket with a red triangle.

So then it was up over the shoulder again and down the stairs, this time straight out into the open air. We soon stepped into a roomy, gray timber barracks block, a sort of infirmary or Revier, if I was not mistaken. There's no denying, I again found everything here, on the whole, to be roughly in line with what I had readied myself for, ultimately completely in order, not to say homely, only now I could not quite fathom the earlier treatment, the coffee and bread. En route, down the entire length of the barracks, I was greeted by the familiar triple tier of box bunks. Each was jam-packed, and a somewhat practiced eye of the kind that I too could lay claim to immediately recognized, on the basis of the indistinguishable tangle of onetime faces, skin surfaces with their blossoming scabies and sores, bones, rags, and scrawny limbs in them, that these must represent at least five and, in one or another, even six bodies per section. Apart from that, I vainly sought for a glimpse on the bare boards of the straw that had done duty as bedding even in Zeitz—but then, true, I had to admit, that was hardly a particularly important detail in view of the brief time that I obvi-

ously had to look forward to being there. Then a fresh surprise as we came to a halt, and words, some sort of negotia-
tion—evidently between the man carrying me and someone
else—struck my ear. To begin with, I did not know if I could
believe my own eyes (but then I couldn't be mistaken,
because the barracks were extremely well lit with strong
lamps). Over on the left I could see two rows of regular
boxes there too, except the planks were covered by a layer of
red, pink, green, and mauve quilts, above which was another
row of similar quilts, and between the two layers were poking, tightly packed together, the bald-cropped heads of children, some smaller, some larger, but mostly those of boys of
about my own age. No sooner had I spotted all that than they
deposited me on the floor, with someone propping me up so
that I wouldn't slump over, took the blanket from me, hurriedly bandaged my knee and hip with paper, pulled a shirt
on me, and then I was slipping between a row of quilting,
above and below, on the middle tier, with a boy on either side
hastily making room for me.

Then they left me there, again without any explanations,
so I was once more thrown back on my own wits. At all
events, I had to acknowledge that there I was, and this fact
undeniably kept renewing itself every second (again), con-
tinuing to sustain me anew. Later on I also became aware of
a number of necessary particulars. Where I was, for example, was most likely the front, rather than back, of the barracks, as indicated by a door opposite that opened to the
outside, as well as by the airiness of the well-lighted space
that was to be seen in front of me—an area in which dignitaries, clerks, and doctors moved and worked, and which was

even furnished, at its most conspicuous spot, with a sort of table covered with a white sheet. Those who had their shelter in the timber boxes behind mostly had dysentery or typhus, or if they did not have it, then at least they soon would in all certainty. The first symptom, as the unrelieved stench itself indicated, was *Durchfall*, or *Durchmarsch* by its other designation, as the men of the bathhouse Kommando had immediately inquired about, and according to which, I realized, my own place would in fact also have been back there, if I had told the truth. I found the daily food allowances and cuisine too, on the whole, similar to those at Zeitz: coffee at dawn, the soup arriving already early in the morning, one-third or one-quarter of a loaf for the bread ration, though if it was one-quarter then usually with a Zulage. The time of day, due to the constantly uniform lighting, unaltered in any way by the window's lightness or darkness, was more difficult to keep track of, being deducible solely from certain unequivocal signs—morning, from the coffee, the time to sleep, from the doctor's farewell every evening. I made his acquaintance on the very first evening. I became aware of a man who had stopped right in front of our box. He could not have been all that tall as his head was roughly on the same level as mine. His cheeks were not just rounded but positively plump, even flabby here and there in their abundance, and he not only had a moustache that was twirled in a circle and almost entirely grizzled, but also, to my great amazement—because in my time in concentration camps I had not previously encountered its like—similarly dove gray, a very carefully trimmed beard, a small one in the shape of a dapper spike on his chin. To go with that, he was wearing a large,

194

dignified cap, trousers of dark cloth, but a prison jacket, albeit of good material, with an armband on which was a red flash bearing the letter "F." He inspected me in the way that is customary with newcomers, and even spoke to me. I responded with the only sentence of French that I know: "*Dje ne kompran pa, mussiew.*" "*Ooee, Ooeee,*" he said, in an expansive, friendly, slightly hoarse voice, "*bon, bon, mo' fees,*" at which he placed a sugar lump before my nose on the coverlet, a real one, exactly the same as the kind I still remembered from home. He then made the round of all the other boys in both boxes, on all three tiers, with a single lump of sugar being dispensed from his pocket to each of them as well. With some he did no more than just place it in front of them, but with others he took longer, indeed a few were able to speak and he made a particular point of patting them on the cheek, tickling their neck, chattering and jabbering with them a bit the way someone chirrups to his favorite canaries at their regular hour. I also noticed that some favored boys, mainly those who spoke his language, also received an extra sugar lump. Only then did something that had always been preached back at home fall into place, and that was how useful an education can be, most particularly a knowledge of foreign tongues.

I grasped all this, as I say, took it on board, but only in the sense, on the proviso I might almost say, that I was continually waiting meanwhile, even if I could not know specifically for what, but for the denouement, the clue to the secret, the awakening, so to say. The next day, for example, when he must have had the time in the middle of his work with the others, the doctor pointed over to me too; I was pulled out of my place and set down on the table before him. He emitted a couple of friendly tones from his throat, examined me, percussed me, laid a cold ear and a prickly tip of his trim moustache against my chest and back, and gave me to understand, demonstrated, I should sigh then cough. Next he laid me on my back, got an assistant of some kind to take off the paper bandages, and then it was the turn for my wounds. He inspected them initially only from some distance away, then cautiously palpated around them, at which some matter immediately oozed out. At that he muttered something, shaking his head with a concerned air, as if that had somehow made him a little despondent or dampened his spirits, as I saw it. He quickly rebandaged them too, banished them from sight as it were, and I could not help feeling that they could scarcely have met with his approval, for there was certainly no way he could have been reconciled to or satisfied with them.

My examination turned out badly in one or two other respects too, I was obliged to conclude. No way could I make myself understood by the boys lying on either side of me. They, for their part, chatted blithely with one another across me, over or in front of my head, and in a way that made it seem I was merely some obstacle that happened to be in their way. Before that they had inquired as to who and what I might be. I told them: "*Ungar,*" and I could hear how that news was spread rapidly up and down the boxes: *Vengerski, Vengriya, Magyarski, Matyar, Ongroa,* and a great many other variations as well. One of them even called out "*Khenyir!*" the Hungarian for "bread," and the way he laughed out loud, to be joined straightaway by a chorus of others, could leave me in no doubt that he had already made acquaintance with my kind, and fairly thoroughly at that. That was unpleasant, and I would have liked somehow to inform them it was a mistake, since Hungarians did not consider me as one of them; that, broadly speaking, I too was able to share that same opinion of them, and I found it very odd, not to say unfair, that it should be me, of all people, who was being looked at askance on their account; but then I remembered the farcical barrier that, to be sure, I could only tell them that in Hungarian, or at best possibly German, which was even worse, I had to concede.

Then there was another shortcoming, a further transgression that, hard as I might try, I could not—for days on end—conceal any longer. I quickly picked up that on those occasions when needs must be attended to, it was customary to summon a boy, hardly older than ourselves, who seemed to be some kind of assistant orderly there. He would appear with a flat, suitably handled pan, which one would thrust under the quilt. Then one had to call out again for him: "*Bitte! Fertig! Bitte!*"[1] until he came along to collect it. Now, no one, not even he, could dispute the justification for such a need once or twice a day; only I was forced to put him to the trouble three and sometimes four times a day, and that, I could see, bugged him—perfectly understandably too, I couldn't deny it, there's no question. On one occasion he even took the pan over to the doctor, explained or argued something, showing him the contents, whereupon the latter

---

[1]"Here, please! I'm done!"

too mused for a short while over the exhibit, yet for all that, with a gesture of head and hand, unmistakably signaled a rebuff. Not even that evening's sugar lump was omitted, so everything was all right; I could safely nestle down again amid the undeniable, and so far—to the present day at least—still enduring, seemingly unshakable security of quilts and warming bodies.

The next day, sometime during the interval between coffee and soup, a man from the world outside entered, one of the distinctly rare Prominents, as I immediately realized. His artist's beret of black felt, his immaculate white smock, and under that trousers with razor-sharp creases, and his footwear of polished black shoes made me slightly alarmed, not merely by the somehow rough-hewn, somehow inordinately masculine, so to say chiseled features, but also by the conspicuously florid, purple, almost flayed impression given by the skin on his face, that seemed almost to expose the raw flesh beneath. Besides that, the tall, burly frame, the black hair with streaks of gray at the temples, the armband that, because he was clasping his hands behind his back, was indecipherable from where I was lying, but above all a red triangle that bore no lettering—all this marked the ominous fact of impeccable German blood. For the first time in my life, incidentally, I could now marvel at a person whose prisoner number did not run in the tens of thousands or even thousands, nor even in the hundreds, but consisted of just two digits. Our own doctor immediately scurried over to greet him and shake hands, give a little pat on the arm, in short win his goodwill, as with a long-awaited guest finally honoring the house with a visit, and to my great amazement, all at once, I could not help noticing, there could be no doubt about it, all the signs were that our doctor must be talking about me. He even pointed me out, with a sweep of his arm, and from his rapid talk, this time in German, the expression *"zu dir"* distinctly reached my ear. Then, amid explanatory gestures, he plugged away, averring, appealing to the other's better feelings, the way one proffers and sells an item of merchandise one wishes to dispose of as quickly as possible. The other, having first listened in silence, albeit somehow in the manner of the weightier party, what one might call a tough customer, in the end seemed to be fully convinced, or at least that is what I sensed from the quick, piercing, and already somehow proprietary look of the dark, beady eyes that he darted in my direction, his brisk nod, the handclasp, his entire manner, not to say the satisfied expression that brightened the face of our doctor as the other went his way.

I did not have too long to wait before the door opened again, and in a single glance I had sized up the prison garb, the red triangle containing the letter "P" (the distinguishing mark for a Pole, as was common knowledge), and the word *"Pfleger,"* which is to say the rank of a medical orderly, on the black armband of the man who entered. This one appeared to be young, maybe twenty or thereabouts. He too had a nice blue cap, though somewhat smaller, from beneath which chestnut hair spilled onto his ears and neck. Every feature on his long but rotund, fleshy face was as normal and pleasant as one could wish, the pink color of the skin, the expression on the perhaps slightly large, soft lips as engaging as you would like: in a word, he was handsome, and I would no doubt have been lost in admiration had he not immediately sought out the doctor and the latter immediately pointed me out to him, and had he not had a blanket over his arm into which, as soon as he had hauled me from my place, he wrapped me, and then, in what seemed to be the customary fashion here, draped me over his shoulder. He did not quite get his own way without let or hindrance, because I clung on with both hands to a strut separating the boxes which happened to be within reach—purely at random, instinctively so to say. I was even a little ashamed of doing so; nevertheless, I discovered the extent to which, it seems, one's reason can be deceived, how greatly one's affairs can be complicated by no more than a mere few days of life. Of course, he proved the stronger, and my flailing and pounding on his back and the area around his kidneys with both my fists was to no effect; all he did was laugh that off too, as I could feel from the heaving of his shoulder, so I gave up and let him carry me off to wherever he wanted.

There are some strange places in Buchenwald. It is possible to get to one of those neat, green barracks behind a barbed-wire fence that, to all intents and purposes, as a denizen of the Little Camp, you had hitherto only been able to admire from afar. Now, though, you find out that inside— that is to say, inside this one at least—is a corridor so suspiciously clean that it sparkles and glitters. Doors open off the corridor, real, proper, white-painted doors, behind one of which is a warm, bright room in which there is a bed already empty and made-up, as if it had been waiting for your personal arrival. On the bed is a crimson quilt. Your body sinks into a plumped-up straw mattress. Between these, a cool, white layer—no, you were not mistaken, as you may convince yourself: a layer of bedsheet, to be sure. Under the nape of your neck too you feel an unwonted, far from unpleasant pressure coming from a well-stuffed straw pillow, on it a white pillowcase. The Pfleger even double-folds the blanket in which he brought you and lays it by your feet, so it too, apparently, is at your disposal, in the event that you might possibly be dissatisfied with the room's temperature. Then he sits down on the edge of your bed, some sort of card and a pencil in his hands, and asks you your name. "*Vier-und-sechzig, neun, ein-und-zwanzig*," I told him. He writes that down but keeps on pushing, for it may take a while before you understand that he wants to know your name, "*Name*," and then a further while, as indeed happened in my case, before, after some rooting around among your memories, you hit upon it. He made me repeat it three or even four times until he finally seemed to understand. He then showed me what he had written, and at the top of some sort of ruled fever chart I read: "*Kevisztjerz*." He asked if that was "*dobro yesz?—Gut?*" I replied "*Gut*," at which he put the card on a table and left.

Well, since you clearly have time, you can take a look around you, inspect things, get your bearings a little. For example, you can establish—if it had not previously struck you—that there are others in the room. You only have to look at them to hazard the not particularly difficult guess that they too must all be sick. You may work out that this tint, this impression caressing your eyes, is actually the all-pervasive dark red color of some gleamingly lacquered material of the floorboards, and that even the quilts on each and every bed have been selected to be of that same shade.

Numerically, there are roughly a dozen of them. All of them are single beds, and the only tiered bunk is this one here, on the floor-level of which I myself am lying, with a partition wall of white-painted laths on my right, along with its twin in front of me, by the partition wall across the way. You may be mystified by all the unused space, the big, comfortable gaps, a good yard wide, in the even line of beds, and marvel at the luxury should you happen to notice that, here and there, the odd one is actually empty. You can discover a very neat window, split into lots of small squares, that provides the light, and on your pillowcase you may catch sight of a light brown seal in the form of a hook-beaked eagle, the "Waffen SS" lettering of which you will doubtless discern later on. Little point in trying to scan the faces, though, in search of a sign, some manifestation, of the event of your arrival, which after all, you might suppose, might surely count to some degree as a novelty, to see in them some interest, disappointment, jubilation, annoyance, anything at all, even a cursory flash of curiosity; yet the hush is unquestionably the strangest of all the impressions you will be able to experience, should you somehow chance to be washed up here, becoming all the more uncomfortable, all the more disconcerting, and in some respects, I would say, all the more puzzling the longer it lasts. Within the square of free space enclosed by the beds, you may also spy a smaller, white-covered table, then over by the wall opposite a larger one with a few backed chairs around it, and by the door a big, highly wrought, steadily crackling iron stove, with a glittering-black full coal scuttle beside it.

Then you may well begin to scratch your head as to what,

in fact, you are to make of all this, this room, this joke with the quilt, the beds, the stillness. One thing or another may cross your mind; you may attempt to remember, deduce, have recourse to your experience, pick and choose. It could be, you may meditate as I did, that this too may perhaps be one of those places that we heard about in Auschwitz where those being cared for are well looked after with milk and butter until finally, for instance, they have all their internal organs extracted, one by one, for instruction, for the benefit of science. But then, you have to concede, that is no more than one hypothesis of course, one among many other possibilities; besides which, anyway I had seen no trace of milk, let alone butter. Come to think of it, it occurred to me, over there it would long ago have been soup time by now, whereas here I had not detected any sign, sound, or smell at all of even that. Still, I was struck by a thought, a somewhat dubious thought perhaps, but then who would be in a position to judge what is possible and credible, who could exhaust, indeed even sift through, all the innumerable multitude of notions, escapades, games, tricks, and plausible considerations that, were you to summon up your entire knowledge, might be set in motion, implemented, effortlessly converted from a world of the imagination into reality in a concentration camp. Suppose, then, I deliberated, that one is brought into a room exactly like this one, for example. They lie you down, let's say, in a bed with an eiderdown exactly like this. They nurse you, take care of you, do everything to please you—all except for not giving you anything to eat, let's say. It could even be, if you prefer, that the manner in which you starve to death might be observed, for instance; after all, no doubt there is something of interest in that in its own right, maybe even a higher-minded benefit—why not? I had to concede. Whichever angle I viewed it from, the notion seemed all the more viable and useful, and therefore must plainly have already occurred to someone of greater competence than me, I reckoned. I turned my scrutiny to my neighbor, the patient about a yard or so away to the left. He was a trifle elderly, his pate rather bald, and he had managed to preserve some of the features of a former face, even a bit of flesh here and there. Despite that, I noticed his ears had suspiciously begun to take on something of the appearance of the waxy leaves of artificial flowers, and I was only too familiar with that jaundiced tint of the nose tip and the areas around the eyes. He was flat on his back, his quilt rising and falling feebly; he seemed to be asleep. Notwithstanding that, by way of a trial, I whispered over to ask whether he spoke any Hungarian. Nothing: he did not appear to understand or even hear anything. I had already turned away and was about to carry on spinning my thoughts when my ears suddenly caught a whispered but clearly comprehensible "*Igen* . . . yes." It was him, no doubt about that, although he had neither opened his eyes nor shifted position. For my part, I was so oddly cheered, I have no idea why, that for a few minutes I completely forgot what it was I had wanted from him. I asked, "Where are you from?"—to which he replied, after another seemingly endless pause: "Budapest." "When?" I inquired and, after further patience, learned "In November . . ." Only then did I finally ask, "Does one get anything to eat round here?" His answer to that, again only after the requisite period had elapsed that it seems he needed, for whatever reason, was, "No . . ." I was about to ask . . .

But at that very moment the Pfleger came in again, making a beeline for him. He folded up the coverlet, wrapped him in his blanket, and then I could only gape at how easily he shouldered and carried out through the door this, as I could see now, still quite bulky body, with a detached flap of paper bandaging somewhere on the belly waving good-bye as it were. Simultaneously, a brusque click, then an electrical crackling noise was audible. That was followed by a voice announcing: "*Friseure zum Bad, Friseure zum Bad*," or hairdressers to report to the bathhouse. Slightly rolling its "r's," the voice was very pleasant, suave, one could say ingratiatingly silky and melodic, the kind that makes you almost feel it was looking at you, and the first time it almost startled me out of the bed. But then I saw from the patients that this incident aroused about as much excitement as my arrival had done earlier, so I supposed that doubtless it too must obviously be something routine around here. In fact I spotted a brown case that looked like a sort of loudspeaker, above and to the right of the door, and guessed that the soldiers must make a practice of transmitting their orders from somewhere via this gadget. Not much later, the Pfleger returned again, and again went to the bed next to me. He folded the quilt and sheet back, reached through a slit into the palliasse, and from the way that he put the straw in it into order, then the sheet back on top, and finally the quilt as well, I gathered it was not very likely that I would see the previous man again. I could not help myself, then, from reverting to wondering whether it might, perhaps, have been in punishment for blurting out our secret, which might have been picked up and overheard—why not, after all?—via some sort of gadget, an appliance similar to the one up

205

there. However, my attention was again diverted by a voice—this time from a patient over toward the window, three beds away. He was a very emaciated, white-faced young patient, who even had hair on him, thick at that, blonde and wavy. He uttered, or rather groaned, the same word two or three times over, elongating, dragging out the vowels—a name, as I was gradually able to discern: "Pyetchka! . . . Pyetchka! . . ." To this the Pfleger said, in an equally drawn-out and, so I sensed, quite cordial tone, just one word: "*Tso?*" After that he also said something at greater length, and Pyetchka—for I had gathered that this must be what they call the Pfleger—went over to his bed. He whispered to him for a good while, somehow the way one does in appealing to someone's better feelings, urging him to be patient, to hold on just a while longer. As he was doing that, he reached behind the boy's back to raise him a little, plumped the pillow beneath him, set the eiderdown straight, and this was all done so cordially, with such alacrity, so affectionately—in such a manner, in short, as to utterly confound, all but belie, virtually all the suppositions I had been making. The expression on the face as it again sank back was such that I could only regard it as an expression of calmness, a measure of relief, while the feeble, sighing, and yet still distinctly audible "*Jinkooye . . . jinkooye bardzo . . .*" could only be words of thanks, unless I was mistaken. My sober deliberations were upended once and for all by an approaching rumble, then rattle, and, finally, unmistakable clatter that filtered in from the corridor, rousing my entire being, filling it with mounting, ever less suppressible anticipation, and in the end, as it were, obliterating any difference between myself and this state of readiness. Outside there was a clamor, much coming and going, a clopping of wooden soles, and then a gruff voice irritably crying, "*Zaal zecks! Essahola!*" which is to say "*Saal sechs! Essen holen!*" or "Room 6! Get your food!" The Pfleger went out then, assisted by an arm that was all I could see through the crack in the door, lugged in a heavy cauldron, and the room was immediately pervaded by the aroma of soup, and had it been no more than *dörrgemüze*, merely the familiar nettle soup, I would likewise have been mistaken on that score too.

I was to observe more later on, slowly becoming clear on many other matters as the hours, parts of the day, and eventually whole days passed. At all events, I could not help realizing after a while, however piecemeal, however reluctantly, however cautiously, that, so it seemed, this too was possible, this too was credible, merely more unaccustomed, not to say more pleasant of course, though essentially no odder, if I thought about it, than any of the other oddities that—this being a concentration camp, after all—are very naturally each possible and credible, this way or that. On the other hand, it was precisely this that troubled and disquieted me, somehow undermining my confidence, because after all, if I took a rational view of things, I could see no reason, I was incapable of finding any known and, to me, rationally acceptable cause for why, of all places, I happened to be here instead of somewhere else. Little by little, I discovered that all the patients here were bandaged, unlike in the previous barracks, and so in time I ventured the assumption that over there had been, possibly, a general medical ward, to say no more, whereas this here was perhaps—who knows?—the surgical ward; yet even so, naturally, I could not consider this in itself to be a sufficient reason and appropriate explanation for the work, the enterprise, the veritable coordinated concatenation of arms, shoulders, and considerations that had, in the end—if I seriously cast my mind back—brought me all the way from the handcart to here, this room and this bed. I also attempted to take stock of the patients, get some sense of how things were with them. In general, as best I could tell, most of them must have been older, long-established inmates. I would not have regarded any of them as functionaries, though somehow I would have been equally hesitant to put them in the same category as the prisoners at Zeitz, for example. It also struck me, as time went by, that the chests of the visitors, who popped in to exchange a few words for a minute, always at the same time in the evening, displayed nothing but red triangles; I did not see (not that I missed them in the slightest) a single green or black one, nor for that matter (and this was something more lacking to my eye) a yellow one. In short, by race, language, age, and somehow in other ways beyond that, they were different from myself, or indeed from anyone else, none of whom I had ever had any difficulty understanding up till now, and this bothered me somewhat. On the other hand, I could not help feeling that the explanation was perhaps to be found precisely here, in this. Here was Pyetchka, for instance: every night we fall asleep to his farewell *"dobra nots,"* every morning we awake to his greeting of *"dobre rano."* The always immaculate order in the room, the mopping of the floor with a wet rag fixed to a handle, the fetching of the coal each day and keeping the heating going, the distribution of rations and the cleaning of mess tins and spoons that went with it, the fetching and carrying of patients when necessary, and who knows how many other things in addition— each and every one of these was his handiwork. He may have wasted few words, but his smile and willingness were unvarying; in short, as if he did not hold what was, after all, the important post of the room's senior inmate but was merely a person standing primarily at the service of the patients, an orderly or Pfleger, as indeed is inscribed on his armband.

Or take the doctor, for as it has turned out, the raw-faced man is the doctor here, indeed the chief medical officer. His visit, or ward round as I could call it, was always a fixed and invariable ceremony each morning. No sooner had the room been made ready, no sooner had we drunk our coffee and the vessels been whisked off to where Pyetchka stows them, behind a curtain formed from a blanket, than the now familiar footsteps are heard clicking along the corridor. The next minute a vigorous hand throws the door wide open and then, with a greeting of what is presumably *"Guten Morgen,"* although all one can pick out is an extended guttural *"Moo'gn,"* in steps the doctor. For some unknown reason, it is not seen as appropriate for us to respond, and evidently he does not expect it either, except maybe from Pyetchka, who welcomes him with his smile, a bared head, and respectful bearing, but, as I was able to observe on many occasions over a long period of time, not so much with that already all-too-familiar respect that one is generally obliged to pay to authorities of higher rank than oneself, but rather as though he were somehow doing no more than simply paying him respect at his own discretion, of his own free will, if I may put it that way. One by one, the doctor picks up from the white table and, with an act of severe concentration, checks through the case-sheets that Pyetchka has set down by his hand—almost as if they had been, say, genuine case-sheets in, say, a genuine hospital where no issue is more cardinal, more self-evident than, say, a patient's well-being. Then, turning to Pyetchka, he attaches a comment to one or another, or to be more precise, only ever one of two types of comment. He may read "*Kevisch . . . Was? Kevischtjerz!*" for example, but as I soon learn it would be just as unseemly for one to respond to this, to offer any evidence of one's presence, as it would be to respond to his good-morning before. "*Der kommt heute raus!*" he may go on to say, by which in every case, as I notice over time, he always means that during the course of the afternoon the patient in question—on his own legs if he is able, or over Pyetchka's shoulder if not, but one way or the other in any case—must report to him, among the scalpels, scissors, and paper bandages of his surgery, some ten or fifteen yards away from the exit to our corridor. (He, by the way, unlike the doctor at Zeitz, does not seek my permission, and no loud protestations on my part seem to disconcert him in the least as, with an oddly shaped pair of scissors, he snips two new incisions into the flesh of my hip, but from the fact that, after doing that, he expresses the pus from the wounds, lines them with gauze and, as a final touch, smears them, albeit very sparingly, with some sort of ointment, I can only acknowledge his indisputable expertise.) The other observation he may make, "*Der geht heute nach Hause!*" means that he considers the person healed and therefore ready to return *nach Hause*, or home, or in other

210

words, naturally, to his block within the camp and to work, his Kommando. The next day it all happens exactly the same way, an exact replica of these same orderly arrangements, according to rules in which Pyetchka, we patients, and even the items of equipment themselves seem to participate, fulfill their role, and lend a hand, with uniform gravitas, in the daily recapitulation, enforcement, rehearsal, and, as it were, corroboration of this invariability—in brief, as if there were nothing more natural, nothing more incontestable, than that for him, as doctor, and for us, as patients, our manifest concern and worry, indeed our sole, not to say impatiently awaited aim, is the soonest possible treatment, then speedy recovery and return home.

Later on, I came to know a bit about him. For it might happen that the surgery would be very busy and others were present. At such times Pyetchka would set me down from his shoulder onto a bench at the side, and I would have to wait there until the doctor, with a breezily peremptory call of, for instance, "*Komm, komm, komm, komm!*" and with what is in fact a friendly yet, all the same, not exactly agreeable flourish grabs me by the ear, pulls me toward him, and hoists me in a single motion onto the operating table. On another occasion, I might happen to drop by in the midst of a veritable throng, with orderlies fetching and carrying away patients, the ambulant sick arriving, other doctors and orderlies also at work in the room, and it might happen on such occasions that another, lower-ranking doctor performs on me whatever treatment is scheduled, as it were modestly off to the side, away from the operating table in the center of the room. I made the acquaintance of, and might even say got on friendly terms with, one of them, a gray-haired man, on the short side, with a slightly aquiline nose, likewise bearing a red triangle with no letter and a number which, though maybe not of two or three digits, was still in the highly exclusive thousands. It was he who mentioned, and Pyetchka indeed subsequently confirmed, that our doctor had now spent twelve years in concentration camps. "*Zwölf Jahre im Lager,*" he said in hushed tones, nodding repeatedly, with a face that was, so to say, saluting some rare, not entirely plausible, and at least in his view, as best I could tell, plainly unattainable feat. I even asked, "*Und Sie?*" "*Oh, ich,*"[2] and his face changed immediately, "*seit sechs Jahren bloss,*" just six years, he disposed of it with a single dismissive wave of the hand as being nothing, a mere trifle, not worth mentioning. In truth it was more a matter of him interrogating me, asking how old I was, how I had ended up so far from home, which is how our conversation started. "*Hast du irgend etwas gemacht?*"—had I done anything, he asked, something bad perhaps, and I told him I had done nothing, "*nichts,*" absolutely nothing. So why was I there anyway? he inquired, and I told him that it was for the same simple reason as others of my race. Still, he persisted, why had I been arrested, "*verhaftet,*" so I recounted to him briefly, as best I could, what had happened that morning with the bus, the customs post, and later the gendarmerie. "*Ohne dass deine Eltern . . .*" or in other words, he wanted to know if, by any chance, that had been without my parents' knowledge, so naturally I said "*ohne.*" He looked utterly aghast, as if he had never heard of such a thing before, and it passed

---

[2]"What about you?" "Oh, me . . ."

through my mind too that he must have been well insulated from the world in here, then. What is more, he promptly passed on the information to the other doctor who was busy there, beside him, and he in turn on to other doctors, order-lies, and the smarter-looking patients. In the end, I found that people on all sides were looking at me, heads shaking, and with a most singular emotion on their faces, which was a little embarrassing because, as best I could tell, they were feeling sorry for me. I felt a strong urge to tell them there was no need for that after all, at least not right at that moment, but I ended up saying nothing, something held me back, somehow I couldn't find it in my heart to do so, because I noticed that the emotion gratified them, gave them some sort of pleasure, the way I saw it. Indeed—and I could have been mistaken of course, though I don't think so—but later on (for there were one or two other occasions on which I was similarly questioned and interrogated) I gained the impression that they expressly sought out, almost hunted for, an opportunity, a means or pretext for this emotion for some reason, out of some need, as a testimony to something as it were, to their method of dealing with things perhaps, or possibly, who knows, to their still being capable of it at all; and in that form it was somehow pleasing, for me at least. Afterward, though, they exchanged glances in such a man-ner that I looked around in alarm that some unauthorized eyes were watching, but all my gaze encountered were these similarly darkening brows, narrowing eyes, and pursing lips, as if all at once something had again occurred to them and, to their mind, been confirmed: maybe the reason why they were here, I could not help thinking.

Then there were the visitors, for example: I would look at

them too, trying to figure out, to fathom what wind, what business, might have brought them. What I noticed, first and foremost, was that they usually came toward the end of the day, generally always at the same time, from which I realized that here in Buchenwald too, in the Main Camp, it seemed there might well be an hour exactly like at Zeitz, here too, no doubt, likewise presumably between the time the work details returned to barracks and the evening *Appell.* Those in the greatest numbers, perhaps, were prisoners carrying "P" markings, but I also saw the occasional "J," "R," "T," "F," "N," and even "No" and heaven knows what else besides; in any event, I noticed many interesting things, and through them learned a lot that was new to me, indeed in that way gained a somewhat more precise insight into circumstances here, the conditions and social life, if I may put it that way. The original inmates at Buchenwald are almost all good-looking, their faces full-fleshed, their movements and step brisk; many are also permitted to keep their hair, and even the striped prison uniform tends to be put on only for daily wear at work, as I also observed with Pyetchka. If he were preparing to pay a visit, once our own bread ration had been distributed (the usual one-third or one-quarter loaf, along with the customarily dispensed or customarily withheld Zulage), then he too would select from his wardrobe a shirt or pullover and to go with that—while perhaps striving to pretend before the rest of us, and yet, for all that, with a pleasure that declared itself in the expression on his face and his gestures—a fashionable brown suit with a pale pinstripe, whose only imperfections were, on the jacket, a square cut out of the very middle of the back and mended with a patch of material from prison duds, and on the trousers, a long streak of indelible red oil paint down the legs on either side, not to forget the red triangle and prisoner's number on the chest and left trouser leg. A greater nuisance, or I might even call it an ordeal, arose for me when he was preparing to welcome a guest in the evening. The reason for this was an unfortunate aspect of the room's layout, for somehow or other the wall socket happened to be right by the foot of my bed. Now, however hard I might try to keep myself occupied at these times, staring at the immaculate whiteness of the ceiling and the enameled lampshade, immersing myself in my thoughts, when it came down to it I could not help but be aware of Pyetchka as he squatted down there with a mess tin and his own personal electric hot plate, hear the spitting of the margarine as it heated up, inhale the intrusive aroma of the onion rings frying on it, the slices of potato that were then added, and eventually, possibly, the wurst of the Zulage that was diced in or, on another occasion, notice the distinctive light clunk and sudden surge of sizzling caused (it was caught by my eyes just as I averted them again, though they long remained near-dazzled in total stupefaction) by a yellow-centered, white-fringed object—an egg. By the time everything was fried and ready, the supper guest himself would have come in. *"Dobre vecher!"* he says with a friendly nod, because he too is Polish; Zbishek by name, or Zbishkoo as it sounded at other times, perhaps in certain compounds or as a diminutive, and he likewise fulfills the office of Pfleger somewhere across the way, so I have been told, in another Saal. He too arrives all dressed up, in low ankle-boots of the kind suitable for sport or hunting, a dark blue serge jacket, though naturally this too has a patch on the back and a prisoner number on the chest, and under that a black turtleneck sweater. With his tall, burly frame, his head bald-shaven, either of necessity or maybe of his own free choice, and the cheerful, canny, and alert appearance of his plump face, I find him, all things considered, a pleasant, likable chap, even though I, for my part, would not willingly trade him for, say, Pyetchka. They sit down at the larger table at the back, eat their supper, and chat, with one or another of the Polish patients in the room occasionally dropping in a quiet word or comment, or crack jokes, or test their strength, elbows planted on the table and hands gripped, in the course of which—to the delight of everyone in the room, myself included naturally—though Zbishek's arm looks stronger, Pyetchka will generally manage to force it down; to put it succinctly, I realized that the two of them shared their blessings and disadvantages, joys and worries, all their concerns, but evidently also their wealth and rations, or in other words, they were friends, as they say. There were others too, besides Zbishek, who would drop in for a quick word with Pyetchka, occasionally with some object very hastily changing hands, and although I was never really able to see what it was, this too was always essentially obvious and easy to understand, naturally. Yet others would arrive to see one or another of the patients, hurriedly, scurryingly, furtively, all but surreptitiously. They would sit down on the bed for a minute, possibly set some little parcel wrapped in a scrap of cheap paper down on the blanket, humbly and, even more than that, somehow almost contritely. Then, although I could never make out what they

216

were whispering (and even if I had, would not have been able to understand), it was as though they were asking: How are you doing, then? What's new? and reporting that this or that was how things were going on the outside, passing on that so-and-so had said hello and had asked after him, assuring that greetings would be passed back, sure thing, then realizing that time was up, giving pats on arms and shoulders, as though to say never mind, they would come again very soon, and with that were already on their way, still scurryingly, hurriedly, usually visibly pleased with themselves, and yet otherwise, as far as I could make out, without any other upshot, advantage, or tangible profit, so I had to suppose that their sole reason for coming, it seemed, was for those few words, for nothing other than for them and the patient in question to be able to see one another. Apart from that, and even if I were unaware of it, the haste in itself would be indication enough that they were obviously doing something prohibited that presumably could only be accomplished by Pyetchka's turning a blind eye and, no doubt, on condition of its being brief. Indeed, I suspect, and on the basis of a fair bit of experience would venture to assert outright, that the risk in itself, that stubbornness, one could even say defiance, was to some extent part of the event, or at least that is what I gathered from their expressions, hard to read as they were but, so to say, lighting up with the successful completion of some piece of rule-breaking, as if (or so it seemed) they had thereby managed to change something after all, to punch a hole in or chip away at something, a particular order, the monotony of the daily routine, to a small extent at nature itself, at least the way I saw it. The oddest people of

217

all, however, were those whom I saw by the bed of one of the patients who was lying along the partition wall opposite me. He had been brought in during the morning on the shoulders of Pyetchka, who then spent a lot of time fussing over him. I realized it must be a serious case and also heard that the patient was Russian. That evening visitors half-filled the room. I saw a lot of "R's" but also plenty of other letters, fur caps, strange padded trousers. Men with hair on one half of the head, for example, but a completely shaved scalp from the center to the other ear; yet others with normal hair except for a long strip right down the middle, from the forehead to the nape of the neck, corresponding in width precisely to the ravages of a hair-clipping machine; jackets with the customary patch and also two crossed brushstrokes of red paint rather like when one deletes something unnecessary—a letter, a number, or a sign—from what one has written; on other backs a big red circle with a fat red point in the middle stood out from far away, invitingly, enticingly, signaling like a target as it were: this is where to shoot, if need be.

They stood there, hanging about, quietly conferring, one leaning over to adjust the pillow, another—as best I could see—possibly attempting to interpret what the patient was saying or a look he was giving, when all of a sudden I saw a glint of yellow, then a knife and, with Pyetchka's assistance, a metal mug materialized; a crunchy rasping—and even had I not believed my own eyes, my nose was now able to give irrefutable proof that the object I had just seen was, no two ways about it, truly a lemon. The door opened again, and I was utterly dumbfounded to see that this time the doctor hurried in, an occurrence that I had never previously witnessed at that uncustomary time of day. People immediately made way for him; he bent over the patient to examine and palpate something, only briefly, then vanished just as quickly and moreover with an extremely glum, stern, one could say snappish look on his face, without having addressed so much as a single word to anyone, even cast so much as a single look at anyone, indeed somehow rather trying to avoid the glances that were being directed at him—or at least that is how it seemed to me. Before long, I saw the visitors had fallen strangely silent. One or another separated from their midst to go over to the bed and bend down over the patient, after which they started to drift away in their ones and twos, just as they had come. Now, however, they were a bit more despondent, a bit more haggard, a bit more weary, and somehow even I myself felt sorry for them at that moment, because I could not help noticing that it was as if they had finally lost their hope, however irrationally it might have been sustained, or their faith, however secretly it may have been nourished. A while later, Pyetchka very circumspectly set the corpse on his shoulder and took it away somewhere.

Last of all, there was also my own guy, for example. I came across him in the washroom, seeing that, bit by bit, it no longer even occurred to me that I might be able to wash anywhere other than at the water tap over a washbasin in the bathroom at the end of the corridor, and even there not out of any compulsion, merely out of a sense of propriety, as I gradually came to find out; as time went by, indeed, I even noticed that I was almost starting to take exception to the fact that the place was unheated, the water cold, and there was no towel. Here too you could see one of those portable red contraptions resembling an open cupboard, the invariably spotless inner receptacle of which was maintained, changed, and kept clean by some mystery person. On one occasion, just as I was about to leave, a man walked in. He was good-looking, his brushed-back mop of silky black hair slipping back in unruly fashion over his brow on both sides, his complexion having that slightly olive shade sometimes seen with very dark-haired people, and from his being in the prime of manhood, his well-groomed external appearance and his snow-white smock, I would have taken him to be a doctor had the inscription on his armband not informed me he was merely a Pfleger, while the letter "T" in the red triangle told me he was Czech. He halted, seemingly surprised, even a little bit astonished perhaps, at my presence, from the way he looked at my face and the neck poking out from my shirt, my sternum, my legs. He immediately asked me something, and, using a phrase that had stuck with me from the Polish conversations in the ward, I said "*Nye rozumen.*" So he inquired in German who I was and where I came from. I told him *Ungar,* from here, *Saal sechs,* whereupon, bringing in an index finger to clarify his words, he said "*Du: warten hier. Ik: wek. Ein moment zurück. Verstehen?*"[3] He went off, then returned, and before I knew it I found that my hand was holding a quarter loaf of bread and a neat little can, the lid already opened and bent back, in which was an untouched filling of pinkish sausage meat. I looked up to thank him, only to see the door already swinging shut behind him. After I had returned to my room and tried to

---

[3]Broken German: "You, wait here. Me go. A moment back. Understand?"

recount this to Pyetchka, describing the man in a few words, he immediately recognized that it must be the Pfleger from the room next door, *Saal 7.* He even mentioned the name, which I understood to be Bausch, though on reflection I think it is more likely he said Bohoosh. That, at any rate, is what I heard later from my new neighbor, because in the meantime patients in our room had come and gone. Above me, for instance, having already taken a patient out the very first afternoon I was there, Pyetchka soon brought a new one, a boy of my own age and, as I later found out, also race, though Polish speaking, who was called Kuhalski or Kuharski, as I heard it from Pyetchka and Zbishek, with the stress always on the "harski"; at times they cracked jokes with him, and they must have annoyed him, maybe even pulled his leg, because he was often fuming, at least as far as one could tell from the irritated tone of his voluble chattering and thickening voice and the bits of straw that were sprinkled through the gaps between the wooden cross-boards onto my face by his tossing and turning on these occasions— to the great amusement of all the Polish speakers in the room, as I could see. Somebody also came in place of the Hungarian patient in the bed next to mine, another boy, though at first I had little luck in ascertaining where he was from. He and Pyetchka could make themselves understood, yet to my now steadily more practiced ear he did not sound entirely Polish. He did not respond to my Hungarian, but, what with the carroty hair he was now beginning to sprout, the freckles dotted over a fairly full-fleshed face that suggested a very tolerable manner, the blue eyes that seemed to quickly size up and soon get the measure of everything, I immediately found him a little suspect. While he was making himself comfortable, settling down, I spotted blue marks on the inner surface of his forearm: an Auschwitz numbering, in the millions. It was only one afternoon, when the door burst open and Bohoosh entered to set down on my blanket, as had become his regular practice once or twice a week, his gift—this time too, as usual—of bread and a tin of meat, and without leaving time for even a greeting, and with barely a nod to Pyetchka, before he was already off and away, that it turned out the boy spoke Hungarian, and what's more at least as well as I do, because he asked straight off: "Who was that?" I told him that, as far as I knew, it was the Pfleger from the next room, Bausch by name, and that was when he corrected me: "Bohoosh, perhaps," seeing as that was a very common name in Czechoslovakia, he declared, and that was where he himself was from, as it happened. I asked why he had not spoken Hungarian before now, to which he replied that it was because he did not like Hungarians. He was quite right, I had to admit; all things considered, I myself would find it hard to find much reason to like them. He then proposed that we speak Hebrew, but I had to confess I didn't understand that, so as a result we stayed with Hungarian. He told me his name too: Luiz, or maybe Loyiz, I didn't quite catch it. But I did note, "Ah! Lajos, in other words," however, he strongly objected to that; seeing as it is Hungarian whereas he was Czech and insisted on the distinction: Loiz. I asked him how he came to know so many languages, so he then told me that he actually came from Slovakia, but along with the great bulk of his family, relatives, and acquaintances had fled from the Hungarians, or "the Hungarian occupation" as he termed it, and that sparked off a memory of an event back home, long ago, when flags were flown, music played, and a day-long celebration had imparted the jubilation that was felt on Slovakia again being reannexed to Hungary. He had arrived in the concentration camp from a place that, as far as I could make out, was called "Terezin." He remarked, "You probably know it as Theresienstadt." I assured him that no, I didn't know it by either name, not at all, at which he was utterly amazed, though somehow in much the same way as I was used to being amazed at people who had never heard of the Csepel customs post, for example. He then explained: "It's the ghetto for Prague." He maintained that, apart from Hungarians and Czechs, and of course Jews and Germans, he was also able to converse with Slovaks, Poles, Ukrainians, and even, at a pinch, Russians. In the end, we got on quite famously; I told him, since he was curious, the story of how I had become acquainted with Bohoosh, then my initial experiences and impressions, what had passed through my mind the very first day in regard to the room, for instance, which he found interesting enough to translate for Pyetchka as well, who laughed uproariously at me; likewise my fright over the Hungarian patient and Pyetchka's response, which was that it had been expected for days, so it was pure coincidence that his death had come right then; and there were other things too, though I was now finding it irritating that he started every sentence with "*ten matyar*," or in other words, "this here Hungarian," before getting down, obviously, to he says such and such; but this turn of phrase, fortunately, somehow seemed to escape Pyetchka's attention, as far as I could see. I also noticed, though without thinking about it or drawing any inferences from it, how conspicuously often, and always for a prolonged period, he seemed to have things to attend to outside, but it was only when once he returned to the room with bread and a tin of food, obviously stuff that had come from Bohoosh, that I was somewhat surprised—quite unreasonably, no two ways about it, I had to acknowledge. He said that he too had met Bohoosh by chance in the washroom, just like me. He had been addressed just the same way as me, and the rest had happened just as it had with me. The difference was that he had also been able to speak with him, and it had turned out they were from the same country, and that had really delighted Bohoosh, which was natural enough after all, he maintained, and I had to agree that indeed it was. Looking at it rationally, I found all this, on the whole, entirely understandable, clear, and reasonable; I held the same view as he plainly did, at least insofar as it emerged from his final, brief remark: "Don't be mad at me for taking your guy," or in other words, from now on he would be getting what up till now I had been getting, and I could watch while he had a bite to eat, just as he had watched me before. I was all the more astonished when scarcely a minute later Bohoosh bustled in through the door, this time heading straight for me. From then on, his visits were meant for both of us. On one occasion he would bring a ration for each of us separately, on another just one in total, depending on what he could manage, I suppose, but in the latter case he never omitted a hand gesture to indicate that it was to be shared fraternally. He was still always in a hurry, wasting no time on words; his face was still always preoccupied, sometimes care-laden, indeed at times almost angry, all but furious, like someone who now had a doubled burden, a twofold obligation to carry on his shoulders but has no other option than to bear it, since it has landed on him; I could only suppose that this was merely because he apparently took pleasure in it; in a certain sense, he needed this, this was his method of dealing with things, if I may formulate it in such terms, because whichever way I looked at it, puzzled over, or pondered it, I was quite unable to hit on any other explanation, particularly in light of the price that could be commanded, and the great demand there was for such scarce commodities. Even so, I think I came to understand these people, at least by and large. In light of all my experiences, piecing together the entire chain, yes, there could be no doubt, I knew it all too well myself, even if it was in a different form: in the final analysis, this too was just the selfsame factor, stubbornness, albeit, I had to admit, a certain highly refined and, in my experience, so far the most fruitful and, above all, make no mistake, for me the most useful form of stubbornness, there was no disputing that.

I have to say that over time one can become accustomed even to miracles. Gradually, I even reached the point, if the doctor happened so to ordain in the morning, of making the trips to the surgery on foot, just as I was, barefoot, my blanket wrapped over my shirt, and among the many familiar odors in the crisp air I detected a new hint, no doubt that of spring, if I thought about the passage of time. On the way back, I caught a fleeting glimpse of a pair of men in prison uniforms just as they were dragging and hauling out of a gray barracks on the far side of our barbed-wire fence a large, rubber-wheeled trailer of the kind that can be hitched to a truck, from the full load of which I was able to pick out a few frozen yellow limbs and emaciated body parts. I drew the blanket more tightly around me, lest I by any chance catch a chill, and strove to hobble back to my warm room just as fast as I could, gave my feet a perfunctory rinse for cleanliness' sake, then popped swiftly under my quilt, and curled up in my bed. There I chatted with my neighbor, as long as he was there (because after a while he left to go "*nach Hause*," his place being taken by an older Polish man), looked at whatever there was to see, listened to the commands issuing from the loudspeaker, and I can tell you that from there in bed, with the aid of no more than these, plus a bit of imagination, I was able to gain a full conspectus and keep track of, conjure up for myself as it were, every color, taste, and smell, every coming and going, each episode and incident, great and small, from crack of dawn to late taps, sometimes even beyond. Thus, the "*Friseure zum Bad, Friseure zum Bad*" that would be sounded many times daily, with ever greater frequency, was clear: a new transport had arrived. Each and every time, that would be coupled with "*Leichenkommando zum Tor*," or "corpse-bearers to the gate"; and if there was a request for further contingents, then that would allow me to infer the material, the quality, of that transport. I would also learn that this was the time the "*Effekten*," which is to say the storeroom workers, were to hurry over—on some occasions, moreover, "*im Laufschritt*," or at the double—to the clothes depots. If, however, the call was, for example, for *zwei* or *vier Leichenträger* and, let's say, "*mit einem*" or "*zwei Tragbetten sofort zum Tor!*"[4] then

---

[4]"Two/four corpse-bearers with one/two stretchers to the gate at once!"

you could be sure that this time it was an isolated accident somewhere, at work, during an interrogation, in a cellar, in an attic, there was no knowing where. I found out that the "*Kartoffelschäler-Kommando,*" or potato-peeling squad, had not only a day shift but also a "*Nachtschicht*" and much else besides. But every afternoon, always at exactly the same hour, an enigmatic message was heard that was always exactly the same: "*El-ah zwo, El-ah zwo, aufmarschieren lassen!*" which prompted a lot of head-scratching on my part at first. It was actually simple, but it took a while before I worked out, from the commands "*Mützen ab!*" and "*Mützen auf!*" that would echo every single time from the ensuing solemn, endlessly vast, churchlike silence and the occasional thin, squeaky-sounding music, that across the way the camp was at *Appell*; that the "*aufmarschieren lassen*" accordingly meant that the camp inmates were to form up for *Appell*, while the "*zwo*" meant two, and the "*El-ah*" obviously LÄ, or Lagerältester, so therefore there must be a first and a second, or in other words, two senior camp inmates at Buchenwald, which, if I thought about it, was basically not so very surprising after all in a camp where they had already long ago started issuing numbers in the ninety thousands, so I have been informed. Gradually things would quiet down in our room too; Zbishek would have already gone by now, if it was his turn to receive guests, while Pyetchka would take one last look around before turning off the light with his usual "*dobra nots.*" I would then seek out the maximum comfort that the bed could supply and my wounds would permit, pull my blanket over my ears, and immediately be overtaken by an untroubled sleep: no, I could not ask more than this, I realized, I could not do better than this in a concentration camp.

Only two things bothered me a little. One was my two wounds: no one could deny them, with their surrounding areas still inflamed and the flesh still raw, but at the margins there was now a thin skin, with brownish scabs forming in places; the doctor was no longer padding the incisions with gauze, hardly ever summoning me for treatment, and the times that he did so, it would be over disturbingly quickly, while the expression on his face would be disturbingly satisfied. The other matter was actually at bottom, I can't deny it, an extremely gratifying event, no question about it. If Pyetchka and Zbishek, for example, should all of a sudden break off their conversation with faces alert to something in the distance, raising a finger to their lips to ask the rest of us to be quiet, my own ear does indeed pick up a dull rumble, and sometimes what sounds like broken snatches of a distant barking of dogs. Then, next door, beyond the partition wall where I suspect Bohoosh's room lies, it has been very lively of late, as I can make out from the voices that filter across from discussions that continue well after lights off. Repeated siren warnings are now a regular feature of the daily program, and I have now become accustomed to being awoken during the night to an instruction over the intercom: "*Krematorium ausmachen!*" followed a minute later, and now crackling with irritation: "*Khematohium! Sofoht ausmach'n!*" from which I am able to decipher that someone is rather anxious not to have inopportune light from the flames draw airplanes down on his head. I have no idea when the barbers get any sleep, for I am told that nowadays newcomers may have to stand around naked for two or three days in front of the bathhouse before being able to proceed farther, while the *Leichenkommando* too, as I can hear, is constantly at work on its rounds. There are no longer any empty beds in our room either, and only the other day, among the routine ulcers and gashes, I first heard from a Hungarian boy who is taking up one of the beds on the far side about wounds that had been caused by rifle bullets. He had acquired them during a forced march lasting several days, on the way from a camp in the countryside (which, if I heard right, went by the name of "Ohrdruf" and, as far as I could make out from his account, was by and large roughly like the one at Zeitz), constantly seeking to avoid the enemy, the American army, though actually the bullets had been intended for the man beside him, who was flagging and had just slumped out of the line, but in the process one had hit his own leg. He had been lucky it had not touched a bone, he added, and it even crossed my mind that, hell, now that could next happen with me. Wherever a bullet might hit my own leg, there was surely no place where it would *not* touch bone, there was no arguing otherwise. It soon emerged that he had only been in a concentration camp since the autumn, his number being in the eighty-something thousands—nothing to write home about in our room. In short, in recent days I have been picking up news and rumors at every hand of impending changes, inconveniences, disturbances, disorders, worries, and troubles. One time Pyetchka made a round of all the beds, a sheet of paper in his hand, and asked everyone, myself included, whether he was able to move on foot, to walk, "*laufen.*" I told him, *nye, nye*, not me, *ich kann nicht.*

"*Tak, tak*," he rejoined, "*du kannst*," and wrote my name down, just as he did that of everyone else in the room, by the way, even Kuharski's, even though both his swollen legs are covered, as I once saw in the treatment room, with thousands of parallel nicks that look like tiny, gaping mouths. Then, another evening, just as I was chewing on my bread, I heard coming from the radio: "*Alle Juden in Lager*"—all Jews in the camp—"*sofort*"—immediately—"*antreten!*"—to fall in, but in such a terrifying tone that I promptly sat up in bed. "*Tso to robish?*" Pyetchka asked curiously. I pointed to the device, but he just smiled in his usual manner and gestured with both hands to lie back down, take it easy, no need to get worked up, what's the hurry. But the loudspeaker was going the entire evening, crackling and speaking: "*Lagerschutz*," it says, summoning the club-wielding dignitaries of the camp's police force to instant action, and it seems it may not be entirely satisfied with them either as before long—and I found it hard not to listen without shuddering—it was asking the Lagerältester and the Kapo of the Lagerschutz—in other words, explicitly the two most powerful of the camp's prisoners that one could think of—to report to the gate, "*aber im Laufschritt!*" Another time, the continually badgering, summoning, ordering, popping, and crackling box was full of questions and reproaches: "*Lagerältester! Aufmarschieren lassen! Lagerältester! Wo sind die Juden?*"[5] and Pyetchka would just give an angrily dismissive wave or talk back to it: "*Kurva yego mat!*"[6] So I leave it up to him,

---

[5]"Senior camp inmate, get them on parade! Senior camp inmate, where are the Jews?"

[6]"Sonofabitch!"

he should know after all, and I just keep quietly lying there. But if the previous evening had not been to its liking, by the next day there were no exceptions: "*Lagerältester! Das ganze Lager: antreten!*"[7] then shortly afterward a roaring of motors, barking of dogs, cracking of rifles, thudding of clubs, pattering of running feet, and the heavier pounding of boots in pursuit shows that, if it comes down to it and some people would prefer it that way, then the soldiers themselves are quite capable of taking the matter into their own hands, and what comes of such failure to obey—until finally, goodness knows how, there is a sudden stillness. Not long after that, the doctor pops in unexpectedly, his customary ward round having already taken place that morning as if nothing out of the ordinary were happening outside. Now, though, he was not so cool nor so well-groomed as at other times: his face was worn, his not entirely immaculate white smock was stained with rusty flecks, and he hunted his grave-looking, bloodshot eyes around, obviously looking for an empty bed. "*Wo ist der . . . ,*" he asked Pyetchka, "*der, mit dieser kleinen Wunde hier?*"[8] making an indeterminate gesture around thighs and hips while letting his searching gaze rest on every face, mine as well for a moment, so I very much doubt that he failed to recognize me, even if he immediately snatched it away in order to rivet it again on Pyetchka, waiting, urging, demanding, obliging him, as it were, to answer. I said nothing, but I was already preparing myself to get up, don prison garb, and go out into the thick of the turmoil, but to my great surprise I noticed that

---

[7]"Camp senior inmates! The entire camp to fall in!"
[8]"Where's the one with the small wound here?"

Pyetchka, judging from his face at least, hadn't the slightest idea to whom the doctor was referring, then after a brief moment of perplexity, it suddenly dawned on him, as though the penny had dropped after all, and with an "*Ach ja*" and a sweep of the arm he pointed to the boy with the gunshot wound, a choice with which the doctor seemed straightaway to concur, he too like someone—yes, that's it— whose concern has been lighted upon and addressed in one go. "*Der geht sofort nach Hause!*" he ordered straightaway. And then a very peculiar, unusual, and, I might say, indeco- rous incident occurred, the like of which I had hitherto never seen once before in our room, and which I was barely able to witness without a certain discomfiture and embar- rassment. The boy with the gunshot wound, having got out of bed, first merely placed his hands together before the doctor, as if he were about to pray, then as the latter recoiled in astonishment, dropped to his knees in front of him and reached out with both hands to grasp, clutch, and enfold the doctor's legs; after which all I noticed was a swift flash of the doctor's hand and the ensuing loud smack, so I only under- stood he was angry and did not quite follow what he said when, having pushed the obstacle aside with his knee, he stormed off, his face drawn and even rawer red than usual. A new patient then arrived in the vacated bed, another boy, an all-too familiar stub of tight bandaging revealing to my eyes that his feet no longer had any toes at all. The next time Pyetchka came my way I said to him in a low, confiden- tial tone, "*Jinkooye, Pyetchka.*" But then, from his "*Was?*" his look of total incomprehension and complete blankness in response to my attempted explanation of "*Aber früher, vorher* . . ."—"just before, earlier on . . ."—and the bemused, baffled shaking of the head, I realized that it was now me, apparently, who might have been committing the faux pas, and thus, evidently, there are certain things that we are obliged to straighten out purely in our own minds. But then, to start with, it had all happened in due accord with justice (that was my opinion, at any rate), as I had been longer in the room, after all, and then he was fitter too, so there was no question (to my mind) that he would have a better chance on the outside, and above all, in the final analysis it seems I find it easier to reconcile myself to accidents that happen to someone else than to myself—that was the conclusion I had to draw, the lesson I had to learn, however I might view, ponder, or turn the matter over. But most of all, what do such concerns count for when there's shooting going on, because two days later the window in our room shattered and a stray bullet bored into the wall opposite. Another feature of that same day was a perpetual stream of suspicious-looking characters who dropped by for a quick word with Pyetchka, and he himself was often away, occasionally for prolonged intervals, only to turn up again that evening with a longish package or bundle under his arm. I took it to be a sheet—but no, it also had a handle, so a white flag then, and from the middle, well wrapped up in it, poked the tip or end of an implement I had never previously seen in a prisoner's hands, something at which the entire room bestirred itself, gave a sharp intake of breath, and was abuzz, an object that Pyetchka, before putting it under his bed, allowed all of us to see for a fleeting moment, but with such a broad smile, and hugging it to his chest in such a manner, that I too could almost imagine myself under the Christmas tree, clutching some precious gift that I had been looking forward to for ages: a brown wooden part and, sticking out of that, a short, bluishly glinting steel tube—a sawn-off shotgun (the word for it all at once came to mind), just like the ones I had read about in the old days in the novels about cops and robbers that I was so fond of.

The next day too promised to be another hectic one, but then who could keep tabs on each single day, and on every event of each day. What I can relate, in any event, is that the kitchens managed to keep working at their regular schedule throughout, and the doctor was likewise usually punctual. One morning, however, not long after coffee, there were hurried footsteps in the corridor, a strident call, a code word as it were, at which Pyetchka swiftly scrabbled his package out from its hiding-place and, gripping it under his arm, vanished. Not much later, somewhere around nine o'clock, I heard over the box an instruction that was not for prisoners but soldiers: "*An alle SS-Angehörigen*," then twice over, "*Das Lager sofort zu verlassen*," ordering the forces to leave the camp at once. I then heard the sounds of battle first approaching then receding, for a while almost whistling about my very ears but later gradually diminishing until finally there was a hush—altogether too great a hush, because for all my waiting, straining of ears, keeping eyes peeled and on the lookout, neither at the regular time nor later did I manage to pick out the by now long-overdue rattling and the attendant daily hollering of the soup-bearers. It was going on 4:00 p.m., perhaps, when the box at last gave a click and, after brief sputtering and blowing sounds, informed all of us that this was the Lagerältester, the camp senior inmate, speaking. "*Kameraden,*" he said, audibly struggling with some choking emotion which caused his voice first to falter, then to shrill to an almost high-pitched whine, "*wir sind frei!*"—we are free, and it crossed my mind that in that case the Lagerältester too, it seems, must have shared the same views as Pyetchka, Bohoosh, the doctor, and others like them, must have been in cahoots with them, so to say, if he was being allowed to announce the event, and with such evident joy at that. He proceeded to deliver a decent little speech, then after him it was the turn of others, in the most diverse languages: "*Attention, attention,*" in French, for example; "*Pozor, pozor!*" in Czech, as best I know; "*Nyemanye, nyemanye, russki tovarishchi nyemanye!*" and here the melodious intonation suddenly triggered a cherished memory, the language that, back at the time of my arrival here, the men of the bathhouse work detail had been speaking all around me; "*Uvaga, uvaga!*" upon which the Polish patient next to me immediately sat up in his bed in agitation and bawled out to all of us: "*Chiha bendzh! Teras polski kommunyiki,*" and then I recalled that he had been fretting, fidgeting, and squirming around throughout the entire day; then, to my utter amazement, all of a sudden: "*Figyelem, figyelem! A magyar lágerbizottság...*"— "Attention, this is the Hungarian camp committee ..."— amazing, I thought to myself, I never even suspected there was such a thing. However hard I listened, though, all I heard of from him, as from everyone before, was about freedom, but not a single word about or in reference to the missing soup. I was absolutely delighted, quite naturally, about our being free, but I couldn't help it if, from another angle, I fell to thinking that yesterday, for instance, such a thing could never have happened. The April evening outside was already dark, and Pyetchka too had arrived back, flushed, excited, talking thirteen to the dozen, when the Lagerältester finally came on again over the loudspeaker. This time he appealed to the former members of the Kartoffelschäler-Kommando, requesting them to resume their old duties in the kitchens, and all other inmates of the camp to stay awake, until the middle of the night if need be, because they were going to start cooking a strong goulash soup, and it was only at this point that I slumped back on my pillow in relief, only then that something loosened up inside me, and only then did I myself also think—probably for the first time in all seriousness—of freedom.

NINE

I reached home at roughly the same time of year as when I had left it. Certainly, the woods all around had already long turned green, grass had sprouted over the great pits of corpses, and the asphalt of the *Appellplatz*, derelict since the onset of the new age and strewn with the litter of cold campfires, all manner of rags, papers, and food cans, was already melting in the sweltering midsummer heat at Buchenwald when I too was asked whether I had any wish to undertake the journey. For the most part, the younger ones would be making the trip, led by a stocky, bespectacled man with graying hair, a functionary of the Hungarian camp committee, who is to take care of our travel arrangements. There is now a truck, and not least a willingness on the part of the American military, to transport us a stretch eastward, after which it will be up to us, he said, then encouraged us to call him "Uncle Miklós." We have to get on with our lives, he added, and indeed there was not much else we could do after all, I realized—provided of course one had been given the chance to do so at all. On the whole, I could by now call myself able-bodied, except for a few oddities and minor disabilities. If I dug a finger into the flesh at some points on my body, for example, its mark, the depression it left, would remain visible for a long time afterward, just as if I had buried it in some lifeless, inelastic material like, say, cheese or wax. My face also startled me a bit when I first inspected it in a mirror in one of the comfortable rooms of the former SS hospital, as my recollection from older days had been of another face. Its conspicuously low forehead, the pair of brand-new, amorphous swellings by the oddly broadening bases of its ears, and its loose bags and sacks elsewhere, all under a brush of hair now an inch or so long, were on the whole—at least if I could believe my onetime reading matter—more the wrinkles, creases, and features of people who had gained them in diverse sensual pleasures and delights and aged prematurely on that account, while the beady, shrunken eyes had been retained in my mind as having another, more friendly, not to say reassuring, look. Then again, I had a limp, dragging my right leg a little: never mind, so says Uncle Miklós, the air back home will sort that out. At home, he declared, we would be building a new land, and he promptly taught us a few songs as a start. When we were tramping through villages and small towns, as occurred from time to time during our journey, we were later to sing these as we marched three abreast, in good military order. I personally was very fond of one called "Standing on the barricades before Madrid," not that I could tell you why that one in particular. There was another too, though for different reasons, that I sang with pleasure, particularly for the sake of a passage that went: "We la-bor a-way all day long, / all but dying of star-va-tion. / But now our hands, hardened by travail, / clutch wea-pons that will pre-vail!" Again for different reasons, I liked the one with the line "The young guard of the pro-le-tar-i-at are we," after which we were supposed to interject a shout of "Red Front!" since each and every time it rang out I would catch the clatter of a window being shut or the slam of a door, and each and every time spot a figure, German, scurrying under or hastily ducking behind a doorway.

In other respects, I set off on the journey with light baggage: an exceedingly narrow yet also, by comparison, exceedingly long and therefore somewhat ungainly light blue canvas contraption, an American military kit bag. In it were my two thick blankets, a change of underwear, a well-knit gray pullover, with green bands decorating the cuffs and neck, that had come from the abandoned SS storehouse, and a few provisions for the road: cans and the like. I wore green American army twills and a pair of what looked like hard-wearing, rubber-soled shoes over which were leggings of impervious leather, with the buckles and straps that went with them. For my head I had procured an odd-looking and, as it proved, rather unseasonably heavy kepi which, judging from its steep peak and the edges and corners of its skewed-square crown—what in geometry they had called a rhombus, I remembered from long-past school days—must once have belonged to a Polish officer, so I was told. I might have picked out a decent jacket from the storehouse perhaps, but in the end I made do with the trusty old striped garment, unchanged except for lacking the number and triangle, that had done me good service up till then; indeed, I specifically opted for it, one could say insisted on it, for this way at least there would be no misunderstandings, I reckoned, apart from which I found it very comfortable, practical, and cool to wear, at least right then, during the summer. We traveled by truck and cart, on foot, and public transport—whatever the various armies could put at our disposal. We slept on the back of an ox-drawn wagon, on the benches and teacher's podium of a deserted schoolroom, or simply out under the star-studded summer night sky, on the flower beds and cushioned lawn of a park amid gingerbread houses. We even took a boat along a river—reminiscent, to my eyes at least, of the Danube, though smaller—that I learned was called the Elbe, and I also passed through a place that had clearly once been a city but was now no more than piles of stone with the occasional bare, blackened wall poking up here and there. The inhabitants were now living, residing, and sleeping at the foot of these walls, heaps of rubble, and also what was left of the bridges, and I tried to take pleasure at that sight, naturally, only I could not help being made to feel—by the self-same people—somewhat uneasy at doing so. I took a trip on a red streetcar, and traveled on a proper train that was pulling proper carriages in which there were proper compartments for people—even if, as it happened, the only place available was up on the roof. I alighted in a city where one could hear a lot of Hungarian being spoken as well as Czech, and a crowd of women, old people, men, all sorts, gathered around us near the station as we were waiting for the promised connecting train that evening. They inquired whether we had come from the concentration camps and interrogated a lot of us, me included, as to whether one had chanced to meet up with some relative, someone with such and such a name. I told them that in a concentration camp people generally did not have much use for names. Then they would endeavor to describe the external appearance, hair color, and distinctive features, so I tried to get them to see that it was pointless, since most people changed a lot in the camps. On that, those around me slowly dispersed, except for one man in very summery clothing of just shirt and trousers, his thumbs hooked behind the belt, just next to the straps of his suspenders on either side, and his fingers meanwhile drumming on the material; he was curious, and this made me smile a bit, as to whether I had seen the gas chambers. I said to him: "If I had, we wouldn't be standing around talking now." "Yes, of course," he rejoined, but had there actually been any gas chambers, so I said, sure, there were gas chambers too, naturally, among other things; it all depends, I added, what type of person was in which camp. In Auschwitz, for instance, you could bet on it. "But in my case," I noted, "I've come from Buchenwald." "From where?" he asked, so I had to repeat it: "Buchenwald." "So, from Buchenwald, then," he nodded, and I said, "That's right." "Let's get this straight, then," he said in response, with a stiff, austere, yet somehow almost preachy face. "You, sir," and I don't know why but I was almost stunned by this very formal and, I would say, somewhat punctilious mode of address, "you have heard about the existence of gas chambers," so I said, sure I had. "Nonetheless, sir," he carried on with that same austerity of one who is restoring things to order and clarity, "you personally, however, did not ascertain this with your own eyes," and I had to admit that I hadn't. To that he merely remarked, "I see," and after giving a curt nod strode away, stiffly, erectly, and as far as I could see, unless I was very much mistaken, satisfied in some manner. Soon after that the call came to get moving, the train was in, and I actually managed to grab quite a decent place on the broad wooden steps of the boarding platform. I awoke around dawn to find we were puffing along merrily. Later on, I became conscious that I was now able to read the names of all the places we were passing through in Hungarian. The body of water that was being pointed out and dazzling my eyes was the Danube; the land all around, baking and shimmering in the bright sunshine, was now Hungarian they said. A while later, we pulled up under a dilapidated roof with, at the far end, a concourse full of smashed windows: the Western Railway Terminal, people around me remarked, and so it was, I recognized by and large.

Outside, in front of the building, the sun was blazing down straight onto the sidewalk. The heat, noise, dust, and traffic were prodigious. The streetcars were yellow, with a No. 6 on them, so that had not changed either. There were vendors too, selling odd-looking pastries, newspapers, and other goods. The people were very good-looking, and palpably all of them had some errand, some important business; all were hurrying, rushing, running somewhere, jostling, in all directions. We too, I was informed, had to take ourselves straight off to the emergency bureau and get our names registered right away in order to receive as soon as possible the

money and documents that were now indispensable appurtenances of life. The place in question, I learned, was to be
found near the other main station, the Eastern Railway Terminal, so we boarded a streetcar at the very first intersection.
Though I found the streets rather shabby, with the terracing
of houses showing gaps here and there, while those still
standing were run-down or damaged, with holes in their
walls or without windows, I still could more or less recognize the route and thus the square too at which we got off.
We located the emergency bureau, just opposite what still
existed in my memory as—yes, that was it—a cinema, in one
of the bigger, ugly, gray public buildings, the courtyard,
vestibule, and corridors of which were already packed with
people. They were sitting, standing, bustling, shouting, chattering, or just silent. Lots of them were in miserable clothing, the cast-off gear and caps of concentration camps and
army stores, some—like me—in striped jackets, but now, as
touches of bourgeois tidiness, with white shirt and necktie,
hands clasped behind the back and immersed in dignified
deliberations about important matters, just as they had done
before they went to Auschwitz. In one place they were recalling and comparing conditions in different camps, in another
dissecting the likely prospects for the sum and extent of the
assistance, still others were considering what they saw as
fussy formalities and unlawful benefits, the advantages others were gaining at their expense, injustices in the procedures, but on one thing everyone was agreed: one had to
wait, and for a long time too. Except I found it all extremely
tiresome; so, slinging my kit bag over my back, I soon
traipsed back into the courtyard, then on outside the gate.

Spotting the cinema again, it occurred to me that if I were to turn right and go one or at most two blocks, that would bring me, if memory served me right, to Forget-me-not Road.

It was easy to find the house: it was intact, not a whit different from the other yellow or gray and somewhat ramshackle houses in the street—or so it seemed to me at least. From the dog-eared list of names in the cool gateway, I ascertained that the number also tallied and that I would need to go up to the second floor. At a leisurely pace, I climbed up the musty, slightly acrid-smelling stairwell, through the windows of which I was able to see the outside corridors and, down below, the woefully bare courtyard, a sparse patch of grass in the middle, then the usual disconsolate tree doing its best with its scrawny, dust-choked foliage. A woman with her hair in a net had just whisked out with a duster over on the other side; strains of music could be heard, and a child was bawling its head off somewhere. I was hugely surprised when a door opened in front of me, and after such a long time, all of a sudden, I again caught sight of Bandi Citrom's tiny, slanted eyes, only now in the face of a still fairly young, black-haired, slightly thickset, and not particularly tall woman. She took a slight step backward, no doubt, I supposed, because of my jacket, and to avoid having the door slammed in my face I immediately asked, "Is Bandi Citrom at home?" "No," she replied. I asked if he happened to be out just at the moment, to which she responded, with a little shake of the head and closing her eyes, "Not at all," and it was only when she opened them again that I noticed a glistening film of moisture on the lower lashes. Her lips were quivering a little as well, so I thought it best to make myself scarce as quickly as possible, but then all at once a slight elderly woman in a dark dress and headscarf emerged from the gloom of the hallway, which meant that before I could go I had to tell her too, "I'm looking for Bandi Citrom," to which she too said, "He's not home." She, though, took the line "Come back some other time; maybe in a few days," but I noticed that the younger woman responded to that by slightly averting her head, in an odd, defensive, and yet somehow feeble movement, meanwhile raising the back of a hand to her mouth, as if she were seeking, perhaps, to suppress, stifle as it were, some remark or sound she was anxious to make. I then felt bound to tell the old woman, "We were together," to explain, "at Zeitz," and to her somehow stern, almost reproachful question of "So why didn't you come home together?" almost apologize, "We got separated. I ended up somewhere else." She also wanted to know, "Are there still any Hungarians out there?" so I replied, "Sure, plenty of them." At that, in a tone of evident triumph, she remarked to the young woman "See!" then to me, "I'm always telling her that they are only now starting to return. But my daughter is impatient; she doesn't want to believe it anymore," and I was about to say, but then thought better of it and held my tongue, that in my view she had the clearer head, she knew Bandi Citrom better. She invited me in after that, but I told her I still had to get back home myself. "No doubt your parents are waiting," she said, to which I replied "Of course." "Well then," she remarked, "you'd better hurry; let them be happy," at which I left.

Since I was really starting to feel my leg by the time I got to the station, and since, among the many streetcars there, one with the number I knew from the old days just happened to be swinging in ahead of me, I got on. On the open platform of the streetcar, a gaunt old woman with a queer, old-fashioned lace trimming on her dress edged away a bit to the side. Soon a man in cap and uniform came along and asked me to show my ticket. I told him I didn't have one. He suggested I buy one, so I said I had just got back from abroad and didn't have any money. He inspected my jacket, me, then the old woman as well, before informing me that there were travel regulations, they weren't his rules but had been brought in by his superiors. "If you don't buy a ticket, you'll have to get off," he declared. I told him my leg was hurting, at which, I couldn't help noticing, the old woman abruptly turned away to face the outside scene, yet somehow, I had no idea why, with such an affronted air it was as if I had insulted her personally. However, at that moment, with a commotion already audible from some way off, a burly man with dark, matted hair burst through the doorway from the inside compartment. He was in an open-necked shirt and light linen suit, with a black box slung from a strap on his shoulder and an attaché case in his hand. What's all this, he was shouting, and then ordered, "Give him a ticket!" handing, or rather thrusting, a coin at the conductor. I tried to thank him but he cut me off and, casting a furious look around, said, "More to the point, some people ought to be ashamed of themselves," but the conductor was by then passing into the carriage while the old woman carried on gazing out into the street. His face calmer, he then turned toward me. "Have you come from Germany, son?" "Yes." "From the concentration camps?" "Naturally." "Which one?" "Buchenwald." Yes, he had heard of it; he knew it was "one of the pits of the Nazi hell," as he put it. "Where did they carry you off from?" "From Budapest." "How long were you there?" "A year in total." "You must have seen a lot, young fellow, a lot of terrible things," he rejoined, but I said nothing. "Still," he continued, "the main thing is that it's over, in the past," and, his face brightening, he gestured to the houses that we happened to be rumbling past and inquired what I was feeling now, back home again and seeing the city that I had left. "Hatred," I told him. He fell silent at that but soon volunteered that, sadly, he had to understand why I felt that way. In any case, "under the circumstances," he reckoned, hatred too had its place, its role, "even its uses," adding that he supposed we could agree on that, and he was well aware whom I must hate. "Everyone," I told him. He fell silent, this time for a longer period, before starting up again: "Did you have to endure many horrors?" to which I replied that it all depended what he considered to be a horror. No doubt, he declared, his expression now somewhat uneasy, I had undergone a lot of deprivation, hunger, and more than likely they had beaten me, to which I said: naturally. "Why, my dear boy," he exclaimed, though now, so it seemed to me, on the verge of losing his patience, "do you keep on saying 'naturally,' and always about things that are not at all natural?" I told him that in a concentration camp they *were* natural. "Yes, of course, of course," he says, "they were *there*, but . . . ," and he broke off, hesitating slightly, "but . . . I mean, a concentration camp in itself is *unnatural*," finally hitting on the right word as it were. I didn't even bother saying anything to this, as I was beginning slowly to realize that it seems there are some things you just can't argue about with strangers, the ignorant, with those who, in a certain sense, are mere children so to say. In any case, suddenly becoming aware that we had reached the square, still standing there, only a bit bleaker and less well tended, and that this was where I needed to get off, I told him as much. He stuck with me, however, and, pointing across to a shaded bench that had lost its backboard, suggested we sit down for a minute.

He seemed somewhat uncertain at first. The truth was, he remarked, only now were the "horrors really starting to come to light," and he added that "for the time being, the world stands uncomprehending before the question of how, how it could have happened at all." I said nothing, but at this point he turned around to face me fully and suddenly asked, "Would you care to give an account of your experiences, young fellow?" I was somewhat dumbfounded, and replied that there was not a whole lot I could tell him that would be of much interest. He smiled a little and said, "Not me—the whole world." Even more amazed, I asked, "But what about?" "The hell of the camps," he replied, to which I remarked that I had nothing at all to say about that as I was not acquainted with hell and couldn't even imagine what that was like. He assured me, however, that it was just a manner of speaking: "Can we imagine a concentration camp as anything but a hell?" he asked, and I replied, as I scratched a few circles with my heel in the dust under my feet, that everyone could think what they liked about it, but as far as I was concerned I could only imagine a concentration camp, since I was somewhat acquainted with what that was, but not hell. "All the same, say you could?" he pressed, and after a few more circles I replied, "Then I would imagine it as a place where it is impossible to become bored," seeing as how that had been possible in the concentration camp, even in Auschwitz—under certain conditions of course. He fell silent for a while before going on to ask, though rather as if it were now somehow against his better judgment: "And how do you account for that?" After brief reflection, I came up with "Time." "What do you mean, time?" "Time helps." "Helps? . . . With what?" "Everything," and I tried to explain how different it was, for example, to arrive in a not exactly opulent but still, on the whole, agreeable, neat, and clean station where everything becomes clear only gradually, sequentially over time, step-by-step. By the time one has passed a given step, put it behind one, the next one is already there. By the time one knows everything, one has already understood it all. And while one is coming to understand everything, a person does not remain idle: he is already attending to his new business, living, acting, moving, carrying out each new demand at each new stage. Were it not for that sequencing in time, and were the entire knowledge to crash in upon a person on the spot, at one fell swoop, it might well be that neither one's brain nor one's heart would cope with it, I tried to enlighten him somewhat, upon which, having meanwhile fished a tattered pack from his pocket, he offered me one of his crumpled cigarettes, which I declined, but then, having taken two deep drags, he set both elbows on his knees and leaned his upper body forward, not so much as looking at me, as he said in a somehow lackluster, flat tone, "I see." On the other hand, I continued, the flaw in that, the drawback you might say, is that the time has to be occupied somehow. For instance, I told him, I had seen prisoners who had already been—or to be more accurate were still—in concentration camps for four, six, even twelve years. Now, those people somehow had to fill each one of those four, six, or twelve years, which in the latter case means twelve times three hundred and sixty-five days, which is to say twelve times three hundred and sixty-five times twenty-four hours, and twelve times three hundred and sixty-five times twenty-four times . . . and so on back, every second, every minute, every hour, every day of it, in its entirety. From yet another angle, though, I added, this is exactly what can also help them, because if the whole twelve times three hundred and sixty-five times twenty-four times sixty times sixtyfold chunk of time had been dumped around their necks instantaneously, at a stroke, most likely they too would have been unable to stand it, either physically or mentally, in the way they actually did manage to stand it: "That, roughly, is the way you have imagined it." At this, still in the same position as earlier, only now instead of holding the cigarette, which he had meanwhile discarded, with his head between his hands and in an even duller, even more choking voice, he said: "No, it's impossible to imagine it." For my part, I could see that, and I even thought to myself: so, that must be why they prefer to talk about hell instead.

Soon after that, though, he straightened up, looked at his watch, and his expression changed. He informed me that he was a journalist, "for a democratic paper" moreover, as he added, and it was only at this point that it came to me which figure from the remote past, from this and that he had said, he reminded me of: Uncle Willie—albeit, I conceded, with about as much difference and indeed, I would say, authoritativeness as I could detect in, let's say, the rabbi's words and especially his actions, his degree of obstinacy, were I to compare them with those of Uncle Lajos. That thought suddenly reminded me, made me conscious, really for the first time in fact, of the no doubt shortly impending reunion, so I did not listen too closely to what the journalist said after that. He would like, he said, to turn our chance encounter into a "stroke of luck," proposing that we write an article, set the ball rolling on "a series of articles." He would write the articles, but basing them exclusively on my own words. That would allow me to make some money, the value of which I would no doubt appreciate at the threshold of my "new life"—"not that I can offer very much," he added with a somewhat apologetic smile, since the paper was a new title and "its financial resources are as yet meager." But anyway, the most important aspect right now, he considered, was not that so much as "the healing of still-bleeding wounds and punishment of the guilty." First and foremost, however, "public opinion has to be mobilized" and "apathy, indifference, even doubts" dissipated. Platitudes were of no use at all here; what was needed, according to him, was an uncovering of the causes, the truth, however "painful the ordeal" of facing up to it. He discerned "much originality" in my words, all in all a manifestation of the age, some sort of "sad symbol" of the times, if I understood him properly, which was "a new, individual color in the tiresome flood of brute facts," as he put it, after which he asked what I thought of that. I noted that before all else I needed to attend to my own

251

affairs, but he must have misunderstood me, it seems, because he said, "No, this is no longer just your own affair. It's all of ours, the world's." So I said, yes, that might well be, but now it was high time for me to get back home, at which he asked me to "excuse" him. We got to our feet, but he was evidently still hesitating, weighing something up. Might we not launch the articles, he wondered, with a picture of the moment of reunion? I said nothing, at which, with a little half smile, he remarked that "a journalist's craft sometimes forces one to be tactless," but if that was not to my liking, then he, for his part, had no wish "to push" the matter. He then sat down, opened a black notebook on his knee, speedily wrote something down, then tore the page out and, again rising to his feet, handed it to me. His name and the address of the editorial office were on it; after he had said farewell with a "hoping to see you soon," I felt the cordial grip of his hot, fleshy, slightly sweaty palm. I too had found the conversation pleasant and relaxing, the man likable and well meaning. Waiting only until his figure had disappeared into the swarm of passersby, I tossed the slip of paper away.

A few steps later I recognized our house. It was still there, intact, trim as ever. I was welcomed by the old smell in the entrance hall, the decrepit elevator in its grilled shaft and the old, yellow-worn stairs, and farther up the stairwell I was also able to greet the landing that was memorable for a certain singular, intimate moment. On reaching the second floor, I rang the bell at our door. It soon opened, but only as far as an inner lock, the chain of one of those safety bolts, allowed, which slightly surprised me as I had no recollection of any such device from before. The face peering at me from the chink in the door, the yellow, bony face of a roughly middle-aged woman, was also new to me. She asked who I was looking for, and I told her this was where I lived. "No," she said, "*we* live here," and would have shut the door at that, except that my foot was preventing her. I tried explaining that there must be a mistake, because this was where I had gone away from, and it was quite certain that we lived there, whereas she assured me, with an amiable, polite, but regretful shaking of the head, that it was me who was mistaken, since there was no question that this was where they lived, meanwhile striving to shut—and I to stop her from shutting—the door. During a moment when I looked up at the number to check whether I might possibly have confused the door, I must have released my foot, so her effort prevailed, and I heard the key being turned twice in the lock of the slammed door.

On my way back to the stairwell, a familiar door brought me to a stop. I rang, and before long a stout matronly figure came into view. She too, in a manner I was now getting accustomed to, was just about to close the door when from behind her back there was a glint of spectacles, and Uncle Fleischmann's gray face emerged dimly in the gloom. A paunch, slippers, a big, ruddy head, a boyish hair-parting, and a burned-out cigar stub separated themselves from beside him: old Steiner. Just the way I had last seen them, as if it were only yesterday, on the evening before the customs post. They stood there, mouths agape, then called out my name, and old Steiner even embraced me just as I was, sweaty, in my cap and striped jacket. They led me into the living room, while Aunt Fleischmann hurried off into the kitchen to see about "a bite to eat," as she put it. I had to answer the usual questions as to where, how, when, and what, then later I asked my questions and learned that other people really were now living in our apartment. "What else?" I inquired. Since they somehow didn't seem to get what I meant, I asked "My father?" At that they clammed up completely. After a short pause, a hand—maybe Uncle Steiner's, I suppose— slowly lifted and set off in the air before settling like a cautious, aging bat on my arm. From what they recounted after that, all I could make out, in essence, was that "unfortunately, there is no room for us to doubt the accuracy of the tragic news" since "it is based on the testimony of comrades in misfortune," according to whom my father "passed away after a brief period of suffering . . . in a German camp," which was actually located on Austrian soil, oh, what's the name of it, dear me . . . , so I said "Mauthausen"—"Mauthausen!" they enthused, before recovering their gravity: "Yes, that's it." I then asked if they happened by any chance to have news of my mother, to which they immediately said but of course, and good news at that: she was alive and well, she had come by the house only a couple of months ago, they had seen her with their own eyes, spoken to her, she had asked after me. What about my stepmother, I was curious to know, and I was told: "She has remarried since, to be sure." "To whom, I wonder?" I inquired, and they again became stuck on the name. One of them said "Some Kovács fellow, as best I know," while the other contradicted: "No, not Kovács, more like Futó." So I said "Sütő," at which they again nodded delightedly, affirming just as before: "Yes, of course, that's it: Sütő." I had much to thank her for, "everything, as a matter of fact," they went on to relate: she had "saved the family fortune," she "hid it during the hard times," was how they put it. "Perhaps," mused Uncle Fleischmann, "she jumped the gun a little," and old Steiner concurred in this. "In the final analysis, though," he added, "it's understandable," and that in turn was acknowledged by the other old boy.

After that, I sat between the two of them for a while, it having been a long time since I had sat on a comfortable settee with claret red velvet upholstery. Aunt Fleischmann appeared in the meantime, bringing in a decoratively bordered white china plate on which was a round of bread and dripping garnished with ground paprika and finely sliced onion rings, because her recollection was that I had been extremely fond of that in the past, as I promptly confirmed I still was. The two old men meanwhile recounted that "it wasn't a picnic back here either, to be sure." From what they related I gained an impression, the nebulous outlines of some tangled, confused, undecipherable event of which I could basically see and understand little. Instead, all I picked out from what they had to say was the continual, almost tiresomely recurrent reiteration of a phrase that was used to designate every new twist, turn, and episode: thus, for instance, the yellow-star houses "came about," October the fifteenth "came about," the Arrow-Cross regime "came about," the ghetto "came about," the Danube-bank shootings "came about," liberation "came about." Not to mention the usual fault: it was as if this entire blurred event, seemingly unimaginable in its reality and by now beyond reconstruction in its details even for them, as far as I could see, had not occurred in the regular rhythmic passage of seconds, minutes, hours, days, weeks, and months but so to say all at once, in a single swirl or giddy spell somehow, maybe at some strange afternoon gathering that unexpectedly descends into debauchery, for instance, when the many participants—not knowing why—all of a sudden lose their sanity and in the end, perhaps, are no longer aware of what they are doing. At some point they fell silent, then, after a pause, old Fleischmann suddenly asked: "And what are your plans for the future?" I was mildly astonished, telling him I had not given it much thought. At that, the other old boy stirred, bending toward me on his seat. The bat soared again, this time alighting on my knee rather than my arm. "Before all else," he declared, "you must put the horrors behind you." Increasingly amazed, I asked, "Why should I?" "In order," he replied, "to be able to live," at which Uncle Fleischmann nodded and added, "Live freely," at which the other old boy nodded and added, "One cannot start a new life under such a burden," and I had to admit he did have a point. Except I didn't quite understand how they could wish for something that was impossible, and indeed I made the comment that what had happened had happened, and anyway, when it came down to it, I could not give orders to my memory. I would only be able to start a new life, I ventured, if I were to be reborn or if some affliction, disease, or something of the sort were to affect my mind, which they surely didn't wish on me, I hoped. "In any case," I added, "I didn't notice any atrocities," at which, I could see, they were greatly astounded. What were they supposed to understand by that, they wished to know, by "I didn't notice"? To that, however, I asked them in turn what they had done during those "hard times." "Errm, . . . we lived," one of them deliberated. "We tried to survive," the other added. Precisely! They too had taken one step at a time, I noted. What did I mean by taking a "step," they floundered, so I related to them how it had gone in Auschwitz, by way of example. For each train—and I am not saying it was always necessarily this number, since I have no way of knowing—but at any rate in our case you have to reckon on around three thousand people. Take the men among them—a thousand, let's say. For the sake of the example, you can reckon on one or two seconds per case, more often one than two. Ignore the very first and very last, because they don't count; but in the middle, where I too was standing, you would therefore have to allow ten to twenty minutes before you reach the point where it is decided whether it will be gas immediately or a reprieve for the time being. Now, all this time the queue is constantly moving, progressing, and everyone is taking steps, bigger or smaller ones, depending on what the speed of the operation demands.

A brief hush ensued, broken only by a single sound: Aunt Fleischmann took the empty dish from in front of me and carried it away; nor did I see her return subsequently. The two old boys asked, "What has that got to do with it, and what do you mean by it?" Nothing in particular, I replied, but it was not quite true that the thing "came about"; we had gone along with it too. Only now, and thus after the event, looking back, in hindsight, does the way it all "came about" seem over, finished, unalterable, finite, so tremendously fast, and so terribly opaque. And if, in addition, one knows one's fate in advance, of course. Then indeed one can only register the passing of time. A senseless kiss, for example, is just as much a necessity as an idle day at the customs post, let's say, or the gas chambers. Except that whether one looks back or ahead, both are flawed perspectives, I suggested. After all, there are times when twenty minutes, in and of themselves, can be quite a lot of time. Each minute had started, endured, and then ended before the next one started. Now, I said, let's just consider: every one of those minutes might in fact have brought something new. In reality it didn't, naturally, but still, one must acknowledge that it might have; when it comes down to it, each and every minute something else might have happened other than what actually did happen, at Auschwitz just as much as, let's suppose, here at home, when we took leave of my father.

Those last words somehow roused old Steiner. "But what could we do?" he asked, his face part irate, part affronted. "Nothing, naturally," I said, "or rather, anything," I added, "which would have been just as senseless as doing nothing, yet again and just as naturally." "But it's not about that," I tried to carry on, to explain it to them. "So what is it about, then?" they asked, almost losing patience, to which I replied, with growing anger on my part as well, I sensed: "It's about the steps." Everyone took steps as long as he was able to take a step; I too took my own steps, and not just in the queue at Birkenau, but even before that, here, at home. I took steps with my father, and I took steps with my mother, I took steps with Annamarie, and I took steps—perhaps the most difficult ones of all—with the older sister. I would now be able to tell her what it means to be "Jewish": nothing, nothing to me at least, at the beginning, until those steps

258

start to be taken. None of it is true, there is no different blood, nothing else, only . . . and I faltered, but suddenly something the journalist had said came to mind: there are only given situations and the new givens inherent in them. I too had lived through a given fate. It had not been my own fate, but I had lived through it, and I simply couldn't understand why they couldn't get it into their heads that I now needed to start doing something with that fate, needed to connect it to somewhere or something; after all, I could no longer be satisfied with the notion that it had all been a mistake, blind fortune, some kind of blunder, let alone that it had not even happened. I could see, and only too well, that they did not really understand, that my words were not much to their liking, indeed it seemed as if one thing or another was actually irritating them. I saw that every now and then Uncle Steiner was about to interrupt or elsewhere about to jump to his feet, but I saw the other old man restraining him, heard him saying, "Leave him be! Can't you see he only wants to talk? Let him talk! Just leave him be!" and talk I did, albeit possibly to no avail and even a little incoherently. Even so, I made it clear to them that we can never start a new life, only ever carry on the old one. I took the steps, no one else, and I declared that I had been true to my given fate throughout. The sole blot, or one might say fly in the ointment, the sole accident with which they might reproach me was the fact that we should be sitting there talking now—but then I couldn't help that. Did they want this whole honesty and all the previous steps I had taken to lose all meaning? Why this sudden about-face, this refusal to accept? Why did they not wish to acknowledge that if there is such a thing as fate, then freedom is not possible? If, on the other hand—I swept on, more and more astonished myself, steadily warming to the task—if there is such a thing as freedom, then there is no fate; that is to say—and I paused, but only long enough to catch my breath—that is to say, then we ourselves are fate, I realized all at once, but with a flash of clarity I had never experienced before. I was even a little sorry that I was only facing them and not some more intelligent or, if I may put it this way, worthier counterparts; but then they were the ones there right now, they are—or so it appeared at that moment at least—everywhere, and in any case they had also been there when we had said farewell to my father. They too had taken their own steps. They too had known, foreseen, everything beforehand, they too had said farewell to my father as if we had already buried him, and even later on all they had squabbled about was whether I should take the suburban train or the bus to Auschwitz . . . At this point not only Uncle Steiner but old Fleischmann as well jumped to his feet. Even now he was still striving to restrain himself, but was no longer capable of doing so: "What!" he bawled, his face red as a beetroot and beating his chest with his fist: "So it's us who're the guilty ones, is it? Us, the victims!" I tried explaining that it wasn't a crime; all that was needed was to admit it, meekly, simply, merely as a matter of reason, a point of honor, if I might put it that way. It was impossible, they must try and understand, impossible to take everything away from me, impossible for me to be neither winner nor loser, for me not to be right and for me not to be mistaken that I was neither the cause nor the effect of anything; they should try to see, I almost pleaded, that I could not swallow that idiotic bitterness, that I should

260

merely be innocent. But I could see they did not wish to understand anything, and so, picking up my kit bag and cap, I departed in the midst of a few disjointed words and motions, one more unfinished gesture and incomplete utterance from each.

Down below I was greeted by the street. I needed to take a streetcar to my mother's place, but now it dawned on me that I had no money of course, so I decided to walk. In order to gather my strength, I paused for a minute in the square, by the aforementioned bench. Over ahead, in the direction that I would need to take, where the street appeared to lengthen, expand, and fade away into infinity, the fleecy clouds over the indigo hills were already turning purple and the sky, a shade of claret. Around me it was as if something had changed: the traffic had dwindled, people's steps had slowed, their voices become quieter, their features grown softer, and it was as if their faces were turning toward one another. It was that peculiar hour, I recognized even now, even here—my favorite hour in the camp, and I was seized by a sharp, painful, futile longing for it: nostalgia, homesickness. Suddenly, it sprang to life, it was all here and bubbling inside me, all its strange moods surprised me, its fragmentary memories set me trembling. Yes, in a certain sense, life there had been clearer and simpler. Everything came back to mind, and I considered everyone in turn, both those who were of no interest as well as those whose only recognition would come in this reckoning, the fact that I was here: Bandi Citrom, Pyetchka, Bohoosh, the doctor, and all the rest. Now, for the very first time, I thought about them with a touch of reproach, a kind of affectionate rancor.

But one shouldn't exaggerate, as this is precisely the crux

261

of it: I am here, and I am well aware that I shall accept any rationale as the price for being able to live. Yes, as I looked around this placid, twilit square, this street, weather-beaten yet full of a thousand promises, I was already feeling a growing and accumulating readiness to continue my uncontinuable life. My mother was waiting, and would no doubt greatly rejoice over me. I recollect that she had once conceived a plan that I should be an engineer, a doctor, or something like that. No doubt that is how it will be, just as she wished; there is nothing impossible that we do not live through naturally, and keeping a watch on me on my journey, like some inescapable trap, I already know there will be happiness. For even there, next to the chimneys, in the intervals between the torments, there was something that resembled happiness. Everyone asks only about the hardships and the "atrocities," whereas for me perhaps it is that experience which will remain the most memorable. Yes, the next time I am asked, I ought to speak about that, the happiness of the concentration camps.

If indeed I am asked. And provided I myself don't forget.

The End

www.randomhouse.co.uk/vintage